THIS WEEKEND DOESN'T
END WELL
FOR ANYONE

THIS WEEKEND DOESN'T
END WELL
FOR ANYONE

A NOVEL

CATHERINE MACK

MINOTAUR
BOOKS
NEW YORK

First published in the United States by Minotaur Books, an imprint of St. Martin's Publishing Group

EU Representative: Macmillan Publishers Ireland Ltd, 1st Floor, The Liffey Trust Centre, 117–126 Sheriff Street Upper, Dublin 1, DO1 YC43

www.minotaurbooks.com

Designed by Omar Chapa

Library of Congress Cataloging-in-Publication Data (TK)

ISBN 978-1-250-32616-4 (hardcover)
ISBN 978-1-250-32617-1 (ebook)

Our books may be purchased in bulk for promotional, educational, or business use. Please contact your local bookseller or the Macmillan Corporate and Premium Sales Department at 1-800-221-7945, extension 5442, or by email at MacmillanSpecialMarkets@macmillan.com.

First Edition: 2026

10 9 8 7 6 5 4 3 2 1

For the readers—this one's for you.
Okay, they're all for you, but this one especially.

You can't break a murder down into its constituent elements—it's not chemistry; it's alchemy. There's always a bit of the fantastical built in, that leap from rational thought to irrational solution. It's a kind of dark magic. But all magic leaves traces. You just have to know where to look.

—ELEANOR DASH, *WHEN IN ROME*

That was what murder was—as easy as that! But afterwards, you went on remembering.

—AGATHA CHRISTIE, *AND THEN THERE WERE NONE*

THIS WEEKEND
DOESN'T END WELL
FOR ANYONE

HOW TO WRITE A MURDER
by
Eleanor Dash

In this murder, we'll follow a three-act structure broken down into eight sequences.

Over the next three days, we'll discuss the following:

1. DAY ONE—ACT 1

A. Who's going to be sacrificed to become our inciting incident? (Killing someone no one likes is a good first step!)

B. Will our protagonist take up the challenge and try to solve the murder? (Yes, obviously, but *why?*)

2. DAY TWO—ACT 2

A. How are you going to raise the stakes for your protagonist? (And it can't *just* be killing someone else.)

B. What twist will you throw in at the midpoint to keep the reader guessing and turning the pages?

C. What subplots are you going to employ to keep your manuscript from sagging?

D. What is your protagonist's "all is lost" moment? (Someone else needs to die here.)

3. DAY THREE—ACT 3

A. How will your protagonist rise from the ashes and reach the climax of your story, where your NEXT brilliant twist will be revealed? (Yep, you need a lot of twists!)

B. Bringing it all back home—what is your *actual* big reveal/resolution? (Who dies, who survives, and who *really* did it??)

PROLOGUE

Are All Prologues Just the First Chapter?

My name is Eleanor Dash, and there are three things you should know about me:

1. I'm the bestselling author of the Vacation Mysteries series. It doesn't matter what that is right now. You just need to know that I plot murders for a living and I'm pretty good at it.

   You might think I'm being immodest, but I've learned enough about myself in the last thirty-five years to make an accurate list of what I'm good at and what I'm not. The good-at-it list is short: death plots. The bad-at-it list is longer: relationships, stopping at two glasses of wine, being self-sufficient, getting rid of toxic people in my life.

   I *could* use my one skill to take care of the last one. But if I did, I probably wouldn't get away with it—murders in real life aren't like murders in books—and I'm 100 percent sure I'd be terrible at prison. So, no murders then.

2. I like asking rhetorical questions, i.e., questions I know the answers to. Because I know how this is going to end, even if it won't seem like it sometimes. You'll have to trust me on that.[1] I also ask a lot of questions

---

[1] Here's a bonus thing about me: I love footnotes. So they're going to be in this.

I *don't* know the answer to. It's a writing technique that helps with the whole plotting murder thing. Like, I might ask myself, what else does the reader need to know right now? And I'll give myself an answer and write it down.

Which is how I decided to tell you the third thing about me:

I. I've been involved in *two* real-life murder plots. Involved, meaning I was the target or I was there when it was unfolding. Not as in I was the murderer, as I'm sure you'll be relieved to know, and as should be obvious if you're following along because I just told you I wasn't going to murder anyone.

But I should also confess that I *have* killed someone. And even though it wasn't on purpose but in self-defense, that changes a person. Being the reason someone's light goes out forever—you're never the same after that. You'll have to trust me on that, too. Not that you *should* trust me. I'm a professional liar, after all. Because that's what murder mystery writers are. We're like actors on a page. Which means I'm good at hiding things until I choose to reveal them. Don't say I didn't warn you.

So now that I've introduced myself, *why* are we meeting, exactly?

Oh, right. The dead body I've just discovered on the floor of my hotel room at an all-inclusive resort in the Bahamas.

Wait, *what?*

Yep.

Oh, you want to know more before you decide to read on?[2]

That wasn't enough to pique your interest?

If you don't like them, that's fine. Skip right over them. But then you'll always wonder: <u>What did I miss?</u>

[2] I'm a mind reader.

Fine. It's ten in the morning, and I arrived in the Bahamas about an hour ago. It's my first time in Nassau. I already love the light tan color of the beach, the turquoise water, and the lush greenery, all of which I could see from our early flight from Miami as we landed. The airport was typical hot-destination decor—white stucco and ads for Bahamian rum and sea turtle excursions on the hallway walls.

We didn't spend much time in the building after we went through a customs' line filled with sweating tourists because I'd insisted that my sister/assistant, Harper, and my boyfriend/co-writer, Oliver, each pack only a carry-on so we didn't have to wait for our luggage and could get to the resort as soon as possible.

We're only here for a weekend. I want us to get the most out of it.

But the universe doesn't work that way. Not *my* universe, anyway. So we didn't get to go to the resort immediately. Instead, we had to wait for Connor Smith, the protagonist of my novels and antagonist of my life, who packed *two* large suitcases, because of course he did, and Elizabeth Ben, the grande dame of detective fiction, who's one of the keynote speakers at the conference we're here for.

Elizabeth is in her late seventies, thinning out and frailer than the last time I saw her, and walks with a cane. But her dark brown eyes still shine with intelligence from her round, lined face. She's written *fifty* bestselling murder mysteries, and I've never figured out the ending of any of them. If you're imagining a slightly less fluffy Miss Marple, you wouldn't be far off.

I met Elizabeth shortly after my debut, *When in Rome*, was published ten years ago, at the first writer's conference I ever attended. I wouldn't quite call her a mentor, but she did take the time to sit with me and give me some career advice.[3]

---

[3] Maybe this doesn't seem like much, but authors get asked for advice <u>all the time</u>. If you say yes to every request, you'll never get any writing done. So if you ask me for advice and I say no, I'm not being an asshole; I'm just busy.

Connor is another creature entirely. I've described him before as Captain America with a smirk, and I stand by that description. Dark blond hair, piercing blue eyes, a strong jaw. He favors linen suits and fedoras and once worked as a private detective/consulting criminal. I met him ten years ago in Rome, where he swept me off my feet, got me involved in a real-life murder mystery, and then revealed he was married. But not before I wrote and sold a book where I made *him* the hero. Until recently, he's lived on his cut of my book royalties[4] and specialized in bedding up-and-coming authors. So yeah, he's hot. But also, there are many reasons besides the whole married to someone else thing why he's my ex.

Anyway, once Connor appeared with his light pink suitcases in tow (!), we all piled into the cornflower blue Footprints van, and I tried not to cringe while Connor attempted to get Elizabeth to read his recently released rom-com (*long* story), even though she rarely blurbs anyone and never blurbs books that don't have murders in them.[5]

The muscles in Oliver's jaw were working overtime. He hates Connor, and if we ever break up, I swear it's going to be because whatever charms I have don't outweigh the annoyance of having Connor Smith in his life forever. But Oliver's the best thing that ever happened to me, so I'm really hoping we don't break up. Again.

To ensure we didn't break up on the *van ride*, I ran my hand through his chocolate curls, then leaned my head against his shoulder as he undid the top button of his madras shirt, saying something about it being too hot for ten in the morning.

Harper watched the candy-colored houses roll by as we drove through light traffic. If you're wondering, she's a better-looking version of me— long dark brown hair that never seems to frizz, sky blue eyes that shift with her mood, and small teeth that never needed straightening. She's

---

[4] The result of a bit of blackmail.

[5] No, she's never blurbed me. It's FINE.

also had a lot of disappointment in her life, only some of which I'm the cause of.

The last three months have been particularly rough on her, and I don't know what to say to make it better.

That's right, this author is tongue-tied when it comes to fixing her sister's broken heart and broken dreams.

I only said I was good at plotting murder, not life.

I do have a plan to *try* to fix things, though.

If I'm brave enough to go through with it.

But more on that later.

For now, you should retain that we were all in our own little dramas in that van, as is so often the case. We didn't know we were driving over a bumpy road into something bigger than us.

Or maybe *someone* did. That remains to be seen.

I can't tell you everything up front.

What I can say is that by the time we got to the resort, I was counting down the seconds till my first gin and tonic.

Cue getting our room assignments and then following our luggage through the white stuccoed resort. It's not as lush as it looked in the brochure—the buildings need a new coat of paint, and the shrubbery hasn't been trimmed recently and is crowding into the cracked concrete paths. But I didn't pay to be here, so I can't be too picky.[6]

The porter ushered Harper, Oliver, and me past a large saltwater pool with a blue tile swim-up bar surrounded by (faded) teak deck chairs and sunburned people reading paperbacks,[7] then around one of the many à la carte restaurants, and finally to our private, two-room villa.

We're in suite 120, only the 2 is missing a screw at the bottom and hangs upside down on the battered door frame.

I'm not sure why my brain was cataloguing flaws, and it certainly

---

[6] But I'm going to be.

[7] On first glance, none of my books. Yes, I checked. You would, too.

didn't prepare me for what was about to happen. Because then the porter opened the door, and the body was there on the floor like someone wanted it to be the first thing we'd see.

So, mission accomplished, I guess.

Have I told you enough to keep you around?

I mean, *I* wouldn't stop reading if someone was about to be thrust into a real-life murder mystery where they were supposed to——wait for it——*teach* a seminar on how to write a murder.

But you do you.

Still here?

Good. You probably have some questions. Go ahead, ask me anything.

Oh, wait, ha! They haven't invented live books yet. Thank God. If you knew how many times I stopped to check the internet already, that would be embarrassing. Plus, you don't need to know how bad my spelling and grammar are before I use spell-check and professionals.[8]

Or should that be "how bad my spelling and grammar *is*"? Whatever. That'll get fixed in copyedits.

How about this? I'll answer the top three questions *I'd* be asking right now.

1. Is the fact that I keep speaking in threes important? Why, yes, it is. Remember that.
2. When I mentioned the Vacation Mysteries earlier, was that relevant? And on the cover, it says this is the third book in the series. Do you need to read the others before you read this one?
3. Nope, I'll provide enough backstory for you to understand this story on its own.[9] But it would be a richer experience for you (and for

---

[8] But not AI! I'm a *writer*. And, yep, I've used the —— (em dash) forever. You can check.
[9] I'll probably be doing that in the footnotes, though, so you've been warned.

me—hello, royalties) if you did. You can do it after, though. Don't stop reading now.

4. What was that whole thing with the steps for writing a murder back there? Were you supposed to be paying attention to that?

5. Yes, you were. But sorry, not to be all *Canadian* about it, I'm not going to tell you why right now. How come? Because I can't give away all my secrets. And also, it's only the prologue. I need to build tension and keep enough facts hidden so you keep turning the pages. All I *will* tell you is that if *you* always wanted to write a murder mystery, you can use the structure to help you plot one when you're done. Cool, right?

So, where was I?

Oh, right. The dead body on my villa floor.

He's lying on his back, his right hand arched toward his head like he's making one of those obnoxious finger guns Connor's always doing. The real gun—a black revolver—is lying a few feet away, just outside the edge of the pool of blood that's congealed around him like some macabre halo.

He's got dark brown hair and olive skin, and to be honest, the weirdest thing about him is that he's wearing the staff uniform—khaki shorts and a dark blue polo shirt with the Footprints logo on it. There's a name tag above the logo that reads BRIAN.

If you're taking notes—and you should be—this is a *clue*.

As we all process what we're looking at, Harper makes a sound like a cat dying and collapses onto a chair. She puts her head in her hands like she's hyperventilating, which she very well might be because *dead body*. But also, a few months ago, her girlfriend turned out to be working with a murderer and ended up dying in Harper's arms.

Right? I'd be hyperventilating, too.

Oliver isn't having trouble breathing, but he *is* shaking his head in a way I can read a little too easily. He has a lot of great qualities, but he's also the kind of person who sometimes says, "I told you so," which is what he's saying to me right now because I twisted his arm to come on this trip.

I'd done that even though he'd reminded me that, lately, every time I go on vacation, someone dies.

But this isn't a vacation, it's work, and I thought this would somehow protect me, which was stupid because, hello, *dead body*.

Did I mention the porter promptly fainted dead away the minute the death smell hit him?

I can't blame him for that.

If *you've* never smelled a dead body—and I'm going to assume you haven't because the opposite is a lot to assume about a person—it's overwhelming. Plus, the visuals. The blood is so much *redder* than you think it will be. I keep forgetting that, though I should know better by now.

Oliver's looking a little green around the gills, too, even though he's been to the morgue multiple times for book research, and he's been present for all the real dead bodies I have.[10]

But more importantly, it looks like someone attending this conference got the memo that you're supposed to drop the body in the first chapter.[11]

So, mission accomplished, I guess.

But also:

1. I'm feeling a bit faint, too;
2. No, I'm not pregnant; there's a dead body in front of me; and
3. I can't believe this is happening *again*.

That's enough to be getting on for now.

Oh, wait, one more thing. And yes, I know it's a *fourth* thing, but it's important if you're going to be solving this with me.

---

[10] Is that a coincidence? Pro tip: There are no coincidences in murder mysteries.

[11] Yeah, yeah, I know I dropped this body in the prologue. I like doing things quicker than you'd expect.

A murder mystery is never entirely self-contained in a book. There are the things that came before and the things that come after. Murder comes from somewhere, and murder leaves a trace.

You just have to know where to look.

Ready? Let's begin.

HAVE YOU EVER WANTED TO PLAN A MURDER?

IT'S **EASIER THAN YOU THINK!**
**JOIN US FOR A SUN-SOAKED WEEKEND IN THE BAHA-
MAS, AND YOU'LL COME AWAY WITH THE TOOLS YOU'LL
NEED TO PLAN THE PERFECT MURDER... AND WRITE IT.
WE'VE HANDPICKED OUR FACULTY SO YOU'LL BE EM-
BEDDED WITH THE BEST SCHEMERS AND PLOTTERS IN
THE BUSINESS.**

FEATURING
ELEANOR DASH
OLIVER FORREST
CONNOR SMITH
RAVI BOTHA

AND THE LEGENDARY ELIZABETH BEN
Along with Vicki Morgan (Editor) from Satyr Press,
and a *real* member of the police force!
**JOIN US AND YOU'LL BE DROPPING YOUR FIRST BODY
IN NO TIME!**
SPACE IS LIMITED!
ACT NOW TO GET OUR EARLY CONFERENCE PRICING

VISIT WWW.MURDERCONFERENCE.COM FOR MORE
DETAILS

DAY ONE
FRIDAY

Act I

The First Sequence

Central Question: Who's going to be sacrificed to become our inciting incident? (Killing someone no one likes is a good first step.)

- Act I will cover approximately 25 percent of your novel and will contain two sequences.

- The first sequence is where the audience meets the main characters and gets introduced to their current life, i.e., the status quo. Use this sequence to build up empathy for your protagonist.

- It's also where we typically meet the first murder victim and get an inkling of the tensions that will lead to their dying.

- The first sequence should also contain foreshadowing of the strains and conflicts to come.

- The sequence usually ends with the "inciting incident," i.e., the moment when everything changes and our protagonist is spun in a new direction, otherwise known as a "body drop."

- Pro tip: Do NOT write the first sequence (or even the prologue) from the perspective of the person who is going to die.

CHAPTER 1

Wait, Is This Already the Inciting Incident?

"What do you mean, it's a suicide?" I ask, my voice rising to a pitch I hope conveys precisely how incredulous I am.

"That is our preliminary determination, madam," says the officer from the Royal Bahamas Police Force. He's in his early forties, with a stern face and a black police cap with a red rim. He introduced himself as Officer Rolle, which I will learn later is the last name of over 13,000 in the Bahamas![12]

"Why would someone kill themselves in our villa? And how can you know so quickly that it's a suicide?"

Officer Rolle exchanges a glance with the hotel's manager, a man in his mid-twenties who looks too young to be managing a hotel. He's got a thick thatch of strawberry blond hair and what looks to be a permanent sunburn across his nose. His last name is Knowles, which is the fourth most popular last name in the Bahamas, for those who are counting.

Me, I mean. I'm counting.

You should be, too.

"I can't answer that now, madam," Officer Rolle says. He has a

---

[12] Almost certainly because of Denys Rolle, an American loyalist who came to Exuma and was at the forefront of the slave trade in the Bahamas.

traditional Bahamian accent—half British, half island lilt. "But I assure you it's nothing to worry about."

"Nothing to worry about? Seriously?"

"He means that it has nothing to do with you," Mr. Knowles says in a flat accent that almost sounds American, though I feel odd calling someone younger than me "mister."

He looks like a "Mark".

I'll be calling him that from now on until I learn differently.

"How can a dead body in my room have nothing to do with me?" I ask, though I know the answer. It's the difference between causation and correlation. The body might be connected to me by proximity, but that doesn't mean I'm the cause of it being here.

But who are we kidding?

This is the beginning of a *murder mystery*. This body's connected to me somehow.

"Is this part of the conference?" Harper asks. She's pulled herself together and is a bit less pale than she was a few minutes ago, but her voice is still shaky. "Like to get us in the mood?"

"The mood?" Officer Rolle asks.

"For murder," I say. "Like an interactive thing, maybe?"

We're both grasping at straws. Because even though we—unfortunately—have experience with this type of thing, it's not something either of us wants to repeat. So maybe, just maybe, this body isn't a *real* body and this is all part of some elaborate introduction to the conference and—

"This is not a game."

"Right, of course not, only . . ."

"Yes?"

"Nothing." I glance at Oliver, who's been shaking his head for the last five minutes.

Maybe I mentioned it before, but he didn't want to come to this conference. He believes in learning from experience, which is not something

I'm good at. But I told him I was going, knowing he'd follow along once he understood I was determined to attend.

Better to have me in his sights than to be worrying about me back in California.

Ditto for Harper. Only I'm her employer, so she had less choice in the matter.

So here we are.

Me, Oliver, Harper, and the *body*.

And I can't help but wonder—is this going to be a three-body problem? Because bad things come in threes, right, like celebrity deaths? Plus, that's what happened last time.[13] And the time before that, too.[14] Three bodies had to drop before I figured out what was going on.

And that's definitely *one* of the threes I was talking about in the prologue.

"Well, if you're sure this isn't connected to the conference—to us— then I guess that's that," I say, not believing a word of it, but there's this thing about speaking things into existence?

Like how Travis Kelce said he wanted to give Taylor his phone number on a friendship bracelet, and now he's dating her?

Does that work on dead bodies? Doubt it.

Anyway.

"We will remove the body shortly," Officer Rolle says. "We're waiting for the technicians to arrive to do our *in situ* assessment."

"Could we get another room in the meantime?" I ask Mark.

He turns toward me slowly. He has one of those blank stares I associate with deep trauma, but I'm not meeting him in the best of circumstances, and neither are you. "I'm sorry, but the entire resort is booked solid for the conference."

---

[13] *No One Was Supposed to Die at this Wedding.*
[14] *Every Time I Go on Vacation, Someone Dies.*

"So we have to stay *here?*" Harper says, gesturing vaguely to the room.

"We'll clean everything thoroughly."

"The room cannot be cleaned until all of the evidence has been collected and our investigation has been concluded," Officer Rolle contradicts.

"Is there any way to speed the process up?" Mark makes a rolling motion with his index finger like he's trying to move a meeting along.

"The investigation will take as long as it takes."

"Right, yes, but given that it's a suicide, as you just said, perhaps it could be expedited?"

Officer Rolle stares at Mark, blinking slowly, as I watch this exchange like a tennis match.

It has the same tension as a long exchange of baseline shots. You know someone will make a mistake eventually. Just not when. I don't have the patience to do that, though. When I play tennis, I rush the net, trying to end the point as soon as possible.

Are you surprised? You shouldn't be.

"I assume the answer to that question is no," I say. "There must be somewhere you can put us. We can pay, if it requires an upgrade."

Mark turns away from Officer Rolle and looks at me like he'd forgotten I'm here. Or maybe that's just his hotel-training face. I'm 100 percent sure hotel managers have to hide what they feel about their guests to keep their jobs.

"Let me see," he says after a beat. "There may be another suite . . ."

"We'll take anything," Harper says.

He gives us a polite smile. "I understand. In the meantime, you could wait in the lounge? Or I believe your welcome lunch is starting soon? We'll take care of moving your luggage."

"Yes, yes." Officer Rolle doesn't care about these details. "I'll need you to provide us with all of the camera footage, Knowles."

"Of course. Our head of security will be here soon. He's in charge of all of that."

"Where's the lunch taking place?" I ask.

"You can eat *now?*" Harper says.

"I'm supposed to be sitting at the head table. And I should talk to the organizers and let them know what happened so they can decide if they want to tell everyone."

"No," Officer Rolle says. "You will not be informing the other guests about this."

"Aren't they going to see when you take the body out?"

"We'll use the back entrance, through the staff quarters. That's how we arrived."

Um, *guys?*

Why do they seem to have a protocol for removing dead bodies from this resort? That's weird, right? Like it might've happened before. Or maybe I'm reading too much into it.

Ha ha. *No.*

"Have you had to remove a dead body from this resort before?" I ask just to make sure.

Officer Rolle and Mark exchange a glance, which is all I need to know.

It *has* happened before.

What. The. *Fuck?*

Who planned this conference? Because I want to speak to the manager.

Not the hotel manager—he seems useless—but the dark force that seems to be managing my life right now.

As Taylor would say: Who do I have to speak to? Because this prophecy sucks.[15][16]

---

[15] Okay, that's <u>two</u> Taylor references in one chapter. But don't worry, you don't need to like Taylor or her music to solve this case.

[16] It's great, though. If you've only ever heard her radio hits, start with "You're Losing Me," then "So Long, London," then "Peter."

I thought I took all the precautions I could before I came here. I even read the itinerary, which, if you know me, is something I *hate* doing. I thought I knew what was coming. But now it looks like I missed the boat. Because this conference was scheduled at a place where someone's died before.

And *I'm* here. Which is relevant because I tend to be the common denominator in bodies dropping. That's a fact. I'm not a narcissist or anything.

Not more than some people, anyway.

"So the answer to my question is yes?" I say.

"There *has* been another death on the premises," Mark says. "But it was many months ago, an older gentleman who died in his sleep. Nothing to worry about."

"Nothing to worry about, yet you took his body out the back way?"

"So as not to upset the guests."

"Right, sure. And *this* man, do you recognize him?"

Another exchange of glances. These two need to up their game.

"He used to work here," Mark says.

"Used to? He's still wearing the uniform."

"He was let go yesterday."

"*Yesterday?*"

"That's right.

"So you're saying this is some kind of postal situation?"

"Pardon me?"

"You know, when someone comes into work after they've been fired and shoots the place up? It's called going postal."

"Whyever?"

"Because it happened at several post offices . . ."

"El," Oliver warns.

"Sorry, but it's—"

Mark holds up a hand to stop me. "Brian did not 'shoot up the place,' as you say. He was distraught, but I had no idea this was how he'd react.

I'm very sorry for the inconvenience, and as I said, we will do our best to find you another room. In the meantime, let me accompany you to the lounge, where I'll have a bottle of our finest Champagne brought out. And then, of course, as I already mentioned, there is the welcome lunch."

I know a bribe when I hear one, and while Mark seems young and green, he's done his homework, because a bottle of Champagne is exactly what I need right now.

But what are the others going to drink?

"All right. We'll take you up on your offer."

He smiles in relief. I'm already a pain in his ass, which is never my intention but often the result of my personality.

I've tried to work on that, but it's hard to change who you are.

"Where's the lounge?"

"I'll take you there. Will you excuse me for a minute, Officer Rolle?"

"You should check on your head of security while you're at it," Officer Rolle says.

"I'm sure he'll be here any—"

"Someone asked for me?" a man says as he comes through the door. He's tall, has a thick neck, and he's wearing a black T-shirt that's straining against his muscles, and oh, shit—

"What the fuck are you doing here?" Oliver says.

You might not know this about him yet, but Oliver rarely swears. So when he does, it's something of significance.

Like the head of security being Guy Charles. As in Connor Smith's former business partner, who I immortalized in my books as Charles Guy.[17]

So, what the fuck is he doing here, indeed?

That's a question for the next chapter.

---

[17] Not my best work. But it _was_ enough to keep him from taking even more of my royalties than Connor did.

CONFERENCE SCHEDULE

FRIDAY
—Welcome Lunch—12:00–1:00 PM

—Craft Classes in Small Groups—1:30–3:30 PM

—Water Polo—4:30–5:30 PM

—Opening Cocktail—6:30–7:30 PM

—Dinner/Talk by Elizabeth Ben—Using Local Legends to Enrich
  Your Murders—7:30–10:00 PM

—Beach Party—10:00 PM–till dawn

SATURDAY
—Sunrise Yoga on the Beach—7:00–8:00 AM

—Breakfast—8:00–9:00 AM

—Craft Classes in Small Groups—9:30–11:30 AM

—Lunch—12:00–1:00 PM

—Excursions—1:30–3:30 PM

—Individual Sessions—4:00–5:30 PM

—Cocktail—6:00–7:00 PM

—Dinner/Talk by Connor Smith—Can Romance Bloom While
  Murder Is Afoot?—8:00–10:00 PM

SUNDAY
—Beach Walk—7:00–8:00 AM

—Breakfast—8:00–9:00 AM

—Editor's Talk—9:30–11:00 AM

—Farewell Lunch—12:00–1:00 PM

—Transport to Airport—2:00 PM

CHAPTER 2

Is Champagne Before Lunch Ever a Good Idea?[18]

"I think we should go home," Harper says once we've been deposited in the lounge, a once sumptuous room that overlooks the pool, with off-white marble on the floor and dark green velvet couches that have been matted down. The wallpaper is like something out of *Bridgerton*—heavy gold-leaf fleurs-de-lis on a thick teal background—and there's an ornate gold chandelier hanging slightly askew from the ceiling.

As promised, Mark instructed a waiter to bring us a bottle of Champagne. It's a brand I don't recognize, which makes me momentarily nervous. But then the cork is popped, and that sound always makes me happy, like a party beginning, and the first sip assures me that it's drinkable.

But who are we kidding? I'm not that picky where alcohol is concerned.

And yes, that first glass *did* go down quickly.

I'll drink this one more slowly, I promise.

"I don't think we can just leave," I say.

"Why not?" Oliver asks.

"Because I agreed to teach at the conference, and so did you, Oli."

---

[18] Remember when I said I like rhetorical questions?

Oliver's dark brown eyes are troubled, and his matching hair has curled in the heat, which just makes him hotter in my estimation. I actively try not to do this, but we ended up wearing matching pale green linen shirts and white shorts. Harper made a retching face when she saw us this morning in Miami, where we'd stopped overnight on the way here from LA.

"They should be canceling the conference given what happened," Harper says.

"That would be a logistical nightmare and probably bankrupt the conference."

"So, we'll just wait around for someone else to die, shall we?"

Wow, Oli's feeling salty today. I shouldn't be surprised, though. He's always on edge whenever he's about to spend some time in forced proximity to Connor.

"No, we'll be on our guard, obviously."

Oliver pushes back into the couch he's sitting on. I want to go and crawl onto his lap, but that's not before-lunch behavior.

"That sounds like it will work perfectly," Harper says.

"If you want to leave, you can."

"You know I won't leave if you don't."

I wish I could correct her. But Harper's right. I *do* know this. She's my sister and my assistant, and I know everything about her, just like she knows everything about me.

Well, almost everything. We can still surprise one another every so often.

The point is, it's not right that she feels obliged to stay in danger when she doesn't want to. It's one of the many reasons I'm going to be firing her at the end of this trip.

Did that take you by surprise? Me too.

"Why do you want to stay, El?" Oliver says. "The truth."

"What's all this talk of leaving?" my editor, Vicki, says as she walks into the room. She's wearing a colorful pool cover-up, a lemon-printed scarf over her dark blond hair, and large sunglasses, like a '50s movie star who doesn't want to be recognized.[19] "The conference hasn't even started yet."

Sidebar. Vicki's been my editor since my first novel. She's also Oliver's editor and, more recently, Connor's.

News I didn't take well. Oliver either.

"Vicki," Oliver says, "what are you doing here?"

"Didn't you read the conference materials?" I say with a glint in my eye.

Okay, I'm gloating.

"I helped organize it," Vicki says, ignoring our sparring. "With so many of my authors here, I couldn't resist attending."

I watch Oliver work through that Vicki is probably here for Connor—she's never come to any event like this for *us*—and then something weird happens. Instead of scowling or gnashing his teeth or any of the other gestures he's made since we got back together whenever Connor's mentioned, he looks . . . fine with it?

But no, that can't be.

Oliver loathes Connor more than I do.

"Plus, you're on the editor panel," I say, looking at Oliver with questions in my eyes.

"That's right." Vicki picks up the bottle of Champagne and pours herself a generous glass.

It was one of the things we'd bonded over when several editors were vying over the rights to *When in Rome* what feels like a million years ago. She got the book, she got *me*, and we'd polished off a bottle of something expensive over lunch.

I'm not saying I made a life-changing decision because of a good bottle of Champagne, but I'm not *not* saying that either.

"You're brave to come here," I say, and Oliver shoots me a look, then

---

[19] Her closest celebrity reference is Jean Smart in *Hacks*.

makes a slashing motion at his throat. "All those desperate people who'll be trying to slip you their manuscript in inappropriate places."

"I'm used to it," Vicki says. "I let people down gently."

Harper reaches for the bottle and pours herself another glass, and it's then that I remember. Harper's one of the people Vicki turned down. Not because she gave Vicki her manuscript at an inappropriate time, but because Vicki didn't think it was good enough to publish. Which is a massive disappointment in Harper's life that she says she's over, but do people ever get over that kind of thing?

I wouldn't know.

Which sounds *horrible* to say, I know.

It's not because terrible things haven't happened to me. Our parents died in a drunk driving accident when I was eighteen. I delayed college to look after Harper and gave up on my dream of going to drama school. But then, when I was twenty-five and finally free, I accidentally fell into a writing career that's been going strong ever since.

I've been lucky and I've worked hard, and not everything has worked out the way I wanted. But I know that's not the same as realizing you aren't going to get your lifelong dream.

And that reality lives between Harper and me, whether we like to admit it or not.

Which is 100 percent one of the reasons I'm firing her at the end of this trip.

Right after she helps me get through this conference alive.

"What was all the fuss when you were checking in?" Vicki asks. "There was chatter around the pool."

I can feel Oliver's eyes on me. "The room wasn't ready. They're moving us to another one."

She frowns, her Spidey sense tingling, I'm sure. "And the Champagne?"

"We're on vacation!"

"You owe me a copyedit."

"Oliver's doing it, right, Oli?" I point to him with my glass.

We wrote a book together that's a thinly veiled account of the last murder we were involved in, three months ago on Catalina Island. We agreed that we'd each do one of the boring after-draft tasks—the copy-edit, the proofread, and the second-pass queries, all things designed to make you hate your book because you've read it so many times by then you're convinced it's boring and terrible and obvious.

"I'm halfway through," Oliver says. "It'll be in your inbox by next Friday."

"Excellent," Vicki says. "So, leaving? Why? Give me."

Vicki tends to speak in abbreviated sentences like she's dictating texts.

"It wasn't a serious discussion," I say. "Just the usual grousing before we realize we're in paradise and we shouldn't be complaining about anything."

"Who's complaining?" Connor says as he enters. "And I wouldn't *quite* call this hotel paradise. It's seen better days. Not up to our usual standards."

Maybe Harper's right and we *should* leave.

I close my eyes and say a quick Serenity Prayer.

I have to accept the things I cannot change. But why?

"No one's complaining," I say. "Connor, did you know Guy's the head of security here?"

Connor shakes himself like he's heard an off note. "Guy *Charles?*"

"Do we know another Guy?"

"He's the head of security?"

"That's what I just said."

He cocks his head to the side. "How do you know this?"

Oops.

"Oh, um, there was a slight issue in our room and he came to resolve it."

"A slight issue?"

"Nothing serious."

"Serious enough to call in the head of security, but not that serious? Eleanor, please. You can do better than that."

"There was a dead body."

"Harper!"

"You started it."

"Are we ten?"

"Someone's dead?" Connor says. "And Guy's behind it?"

"No," I say. "We don't know who's behind it. The police say it's a suicide."

He touches the brim of his fedora. "That's not very likely, is it?"

I squint at him. Damn, he's still hot. "Why would you say that?"

"*You're* here, for one."

"That's enough of that, Connor," Oliver says lightly, but not with the usual bite of his speaking-to-Connor tone. "You were the one who was in business with Guy, not Eleanor."

"Right," I say. "And come to think of it, what are you even doing here? Your book isn't a mystery, it's a rom-com."

"I'm one of the keynote speakers."

"One of?" Harper says. "Isn't there usually just one?"

"My invitation clearly stated—"

"But why were you invited?" I say. "That's the question."

"You're just mad it wasn't you."

I mean, he's not wrong. When I saw he was giving a keynote and I wasn't, I *was* pissed.

Because this is a murder mystery conference, and there aren't any murders in his book.

Not that I read it. I just assume.

Okay, okay, I read it.

It was . . . *good?*

"Fine. FINE. Maybe we *should* go home."

"Seems like a good plan when the bodies start dropping," Harper says. "I've always wondered why people didn't do that in books. Like, if people are dying, why don't we all just scatter? Why wait around to see who's next?"

"Boring," Vicki says. "And not the point of the beginning of a book.

At all. Establish the tone and character of the people and environment. Set up a hint of mystery. Don't give the whole gambit away."

I smile at her. "Do you want to give my lecture?"

"Not a chance."

"Damn."

"Is someone going to fill us in on the details?" Connor says.

I give a big sigh and then do my best. Our arrival; the body; how the bellhop fainted, uh, *dead* away. The police arrival, the hotel manager, and then Guy.

"And he didn't explain what he was doing here?" Connor says.

"No, but you know Guy. He's not big on talking."

"He's up to something."

"You don't say."

"How did we end up *here*, Vicki?" Harper asks. "Is the conference here every year?"

"No," Vicki says. "It changes location. There's an executive committee that organizes it. Several locations were suggested, I believe. We chose this one." She finishes her glass of Champagne, then looks at it, like she's surprised she's holding it.

"Who's on the committee?"

"I am, along with a half dozen others."

"How did *we* get picked?" I ask.

"The publicity department pitches you for lots of conferences. The committee chooses who attends. You all had an in there." She winks.

A chill runs down my spine at the words "publicity department" because a woman named Marta, who used to work in the publicity department, was involved in a plot to kill me six months ago.

But there's zero chance there are two murderers in the same publicity department. Right?

I mean, publishing is broken, but not *that* broken?

"You'll see, Connor," I say. "You get invited to a lot of things like this, it's not sinister."

"Yes, thank you, Eleanor. I *have* been around publishing for ten years. I know *all about* what happens at book conferences." He leers at me and I turn away, praying Oliver didn't see.

I get a flash of the last time I slept with Connor.

It was at—*surprise!*—a book conference.

Why haven't they invented a delete button for our brains yet?

"Yes, fine. Well, maybe you'll have more luck than me getting Guy to tell you what he's doing here. And in the meantime, I think we have a lunch to get to?"

Harper stands, a bit unsteady on her feet. "Good idea, I'm—"

"My goodness, why are you all, how do you say, *gathered* in this room?"

I close my eyes and count to three.

Because maybe if I do that, this will all turn out to be an illusion.

But no, when I open them again, there he is. Inspector Tucci. The police officer from Italy who I can't seem to shake out of my life.

And maybe it's something I should've felt before, what with the dead body and all.

But now I . . . wait for it . . . have a bad feeling about this.

CHAPTER 3

Did I Really Read the Itinerary?

Let me, as they say, set the scene.

We're in a large open-air restaurant that's Italian-themed, because of course it is. I can't escape Italy even when I'm in the Bahamas. The off-white walls are painted in peeling frescoes of Pompeii, and there are dusty fake olive leaves wound around the wood beams in the ceiling. There's pizza and pasta on the menu, with a large salad bar covered in one of those Mylar sneeze guards they have in American chain restaurants. There are a dozen eight-tops along with a head table, which is where I'm sitting between Harper and Oliver.

It's just after noon. Some of the buzz from the Champagne has worn off, but I'm sure I can remedy that because there are large pitchers of what seems to be the conference's signature drink, a rum punch, on the table.[20] Even though Connor greeted its arrival by switching to talking in pirate (!), everyone else seemed happy enough to tuck in.

I recognize a few of the hundred or so participants—people I've seen at various conferences over the years who like going to exotic locations to learn how to improve their craft. The housewife who's been working on

---

[20] Light coconut rum, Campari, orange juice, and pineapple juice—surprisingly refreshing.

her debut semi-autobiographical novel for ten years. The retired army guy who's written five airport thrillers he's self-published. The eager twenty-five-year-old who's been writing novels since she was twelve, convinced she's going to take over the literary world any minute now.

Our little group is sitting to the left of Elizabeth, who's in the middle of the long head table, looking out over the participants with a small, welcoming smile.

I should learn how to look like that. She's always gracious, no matter the circumstance. Her now white hair also always looks the same; she has one of those haircuts that don't seem to exist anymore, feathered and chin-length. It's probably set at a salon once a week, but who has time for that?

As far as I can tell, everyone seems happy and excited to be here.

Except me.

Because something is amiss.

More than one thing.

Number one is Inspector Tucci, who was *not* on the invitation. It had only said that a "real member of the police force" would be attending, and it never occurred to me that it might be someone I'd know.

I should know by now not to make assumptions like that.

Maybe someday I'll learn.[21]

After his grand arrival in the lounge, Harper took Inspector Tucci aside to question him on his presence and so the event didn't start with a double homicide.

Not that *I'm* going to kill him.

If Inspector Tucci dies, Connor's the prime suspect.

Remember I said that.

Anyway, according to him, the officer who was scheduled to attend got assigned to an important case and had to prioritize justice over teaching a bunch of amateurs how to write a perfect murder.

Why that led to *Inspector Tucci* being here is still beyond me, but I'm

---

[21] I'm never going to learn this lesson.

sure it will be made clear to me in time. But having a police officer who once accused me of murder on the scene isn't enough from the universe. Nope. There are more surprises in store for me.

And you too, of course.

Though you're probably happy about the surprises.

I don't blame you. I would be, too, if it weren't for who it was.

"What's *she* doing here?" I ask Harper as I point at the culprit with my eyes.

"Which *she* are you referring to?"

"Her," I say, lifting my finger and pointing to a woman who's sitting at one of the other tables with some of the participants. Just shy of forty, she's of Haitian origin.[22] She grew up in Montreal but has lived in California for the last twenty years. She's an author, too, and I know this and a lot more about her because she used to be my author BFF, but now she hates me for reasons she's never explained.

I have my theories, though.

"Sandrine?" Harper says with a neutral tone. Harper has never said, but I always suspected she was jealous of Sandrine. For example, when I told her Sandrine and I weren't talking anymore, she'd shrugged and changed topics.

"Yes. She's not supposed to be here."

"She writes murder mysteries."

"I know."

"And this is a murder mystery conference."

"I know that, too. But you know we're not talking."

"I did know that, yes," Harper says and takes a deep sip of her drink. I'm not counting drinks, but she's had quite a lot for her small frame.

I shouldn't judge.[23]

---

[22] If we're describing in celebrities, she resembles Sydney Tamiia Poitier, Sydney Poitier's daughter.

[23] In case you're new here, judgment's kind of my thing.

"So why would she come to this conference, knowing I'm here?"

"She was invited?" Harper says.

"She wasn't on the itinerary."

Harper shrugs. "Plans change."

"You don't think it's weird?"

"We found a dead body in our room five minutes after getting here. It's *all* been weird."

"I meant what I said before, Harp. You can go. I've got Oli—right, Oli?"

He raises an eyebrow. "I'm not booking your travel."

"That's not what I meant, and you know it."

"It's fine," Harper says. "Let's just stop talking about it, okay?"

I agree, but my mind doesn't work like that. It *keeps* talking about it as I watch Sandrine being charming with her tablemates. She's deliberately not looking in my direction, but we can't avoid each other the whole time we're here.

And she knows that.

So why has she come?

The last time I saw her was two years ago. We were out for brunch at a spot on the Santa Monica toVenice boardwalk we loved to go to. I knew something was up from the way she was acting, but I didn't expect the text breakup she sent me a few days later.

Yep, she broke up with me in a text she sent at an odd time of day, full of vague accusations that made me wonder if she was having a breakdown.

But I was feeling pretty fragile at the time—it wasn't long after I'd humiliated myself by throwing myself at Oliver at yet another book event, only to be rejected—and I didn't want to feel like I had to fight for a friendship. I didn't have any fight left in me.

So I defended myself against what I thought she was insinuating and left it at that.

I miss her, though.

We used to spend hours talking about the book business, taking long walks on the beach, and stopping for cocktails at our favorite rooftop bar near my house in Venice. It's lonely being a writer sometimes, and Harper doesn't want to hear my grousing. And in the years when Oliver and I were apart, especially, Sandrine was a godsend.

But you can miss someone and not want to be trapped at a conference with them.

Sigh.

Remember when I told you bad things come in threes?

Well . . . the last person sitting at the head table is a man named Ravi Botha.

I knew he'd be here, but with all the other surprises, plus the dead body, it's making me reconsider.

Why?

Because he's the brother of someone I *did* know named Shek Botha. I met Shek at the same conference where I met Elizabeth and Sandrine ten years ago. He was murdered in front of me in Italy, and that's not something I can just erase from my brain.

Since then, Ravi has taken up writing Shek's detective series. His first book, coming out on the same day as the next in *my* series, is a thinly veiled account of the circumstances that led to Shek's death.

Our publisher is *diabolical*.

I mean this as a compliment.

If horrible things have to happen, why not capitalize on it with book sales?

Yeah, yeah, I know how that sounds, okay?

ANYWAY, as I watch Ravi cut through his pizza with a knife and fork (!), looking so much like Shek that it's disconcerting,[24] the fine hairs on the back of my neck start to prickle.

Is that it, universe?

_____

[24] Imagine Ben Kingsley and you're not far off.

A dead body and multiple surprise guests, including my ex–best friend?

Oh, and let's not forget Guy Charles is lurking around somewhere.

That seems like enough.

But I'm sure there'll be more.[25]

Which brings me to the look Elizabeth Ben is giving me when I catch her eye. She was a bit standoffish in the car on the way here, and now that I'm counting up bad things like my life depends on it, I start to wonder why.

When was the last time we spoke?

I search my memory, and oh! My! God!

The blurb! The blurb I was asked to give for Elizabeth's next book.

Did I send it?? Shit, shit, *shit*. Wait, no, I must have. Harper keeps a spreadsheet of the blurbs I've agreed to and reminds me to do them so I don't forget. But she's been distracted lately.

No. It's a blurb *for* Elizabeth Ben. She's never asked me for one before. I wouldn't just let that slip by. And neither would Harper.

Breathe, girl, breathe.

I must've done it. I just have to remember what the book was about, and I'll feel better.

Drawing a blank, though.

I pull my phone out and open my Kindle app. Her book is there—it's called *Sandoval's Revenge*[26]—but according to the app, I've only read 11 percent of it.

I am so screwed.

"Everything all right?" Oliver asks me.

"On a scale of one to ten, how bad would you rate forgetting to blurb someone?"

---

[25] Dude, there <u>is</u> going to be more. Count on it.

[26] Malik Sandoval is the long-time protagonist of her Sandoval series.

"Depends on who it is."

I lower my voice. "Elizabeth Ben."

His eyes go wide. "You didn't?"

"I might have?"

"How can you not remember?"

"It's been a crazy six months. You know that. Between almost getting murdered a bunch of times and turning in a couple of books—some things fell through the cracks."

He shakes his head in answer.

"I know. What should I do?"

"Maybe she doesn't care. Who did the request come from? Vicki?"

"I think she wrote to me directly."

"Yikes."

"That is *not* helping."

"What are you going on about?" Harper asks.

"She forgot to blurb Elizabeth," Oliver supplies.

Harper's eyes go even wider than Oliver's. "Uh-oh."

"Uh-oh, I'm screwed, or uh-oh, something else?"

"Uh-oh, I forgot to remind you."

I *knew* it.

Harper picks up her drink. "You can fire me if you want."

"Do you *want* me to fire you?"

There's a *tap-tap-tap* on a water glass like we're at a wedding, and Elizabeth rises from her seat into the burgeoning quiet. A hundred eyes turn to her.

A waiter tries to hand her a microphone, but she shakes her head and speaks in a surprisingly powerful voice for someone barely five feet tall.

"Welcome, everyone. I'll be giving my formal talk tomorrow night, but in the meantime, I've been asked to say a few words of welcome. This conference is in its twentieth year, and what a beautiful location for it to take place in. Thank you so much to the organizing committee for including me and making this wonderful weekend possible for all of you. It's an honor to be here."

The participants begin to applaud, starting with a few taps of rain, then crescendoing to a storm. Elizabeth takes in the attention for a moment, then *tap-tap-taps* her glass again.

"Now, to the *reason* we're all here. Through the next couple of days, you'll be immersing yourself in *murder*."

She says the word with relish, and a frisson goes through the room.

"That's what we're about here, ladies and gentlemen. Whether you're writing a cozy or the bloodiest of stories, they all have something in common." She pauses for dramatic effect. "*Bodies.*"

She steps back and smiles at the shocked silence. This is why she's the queen. She builds suspense and tension on every page without ever letting up. Like everyone in this business, I've studied how she does it, but I'll never be as good as her; that's just a fact.

"Now, there's much more to come, but for the moment, there's a surprise for all of you under your plates. A little personalized welcome so you'll know what you're facing." She waves her right hand, a large pink stone dazzling on her ring finger. "Come on now, don't be shy. Lift those plates."

The participants follow her instructions, lifting their plates and pulling out color-coded pieces of paper.

"Each of you has been sorted into a different group—just follow your symbol and you'll know where to go." Elizabeth turns to us. "You too, authors. Up, up, up."

I lift the plate in front of me. There's a black piece of stock board the size of an invitation. At the top, there's an illustration of a vial with the word POISON written on it in stylized script.

My name is embossed underneath it in pretty gold leaf, and the schedule's below it.

But that's not what's catching my eye at the moment.

Nope.

It's the phrase below my name that's got me—what do the kids say?—gagged.

Because this is what it says:

No one is getting out of here alive.

GROUP ASSIGNMENTS

GROUP 1—POISON—ELEANOR DASH

(noun) A substance that's capable of causing the illness or death of a living organism when introduced or absorbed.

Examples: strychnine, cyanide, arsenic. See: *The Mysterious Affair at Styles*.

GROUP 2—GUN—OLIVER FORREST

(noun) A weapon incorporating a metal tube from which bullets, shells, or other missiles are propelled by explosive force, typically making a characteristic loud, sharp noise.

Examples: Walther PPK. See: *Casino Royale*.

GROUP 3—KNIFE—RAVI BOTHA

(noun) An instrument composed of a blade fixed into a handle, used for cutting or as a weapon.

Examples: silver dagger. See: *The Murder of Roger Ackroyd*.

GROUP 4—ROPE—ELIZABETH BEN

(noun) A length of strong cord made by twisting together strands of natural fibers, such as hemp, or artificial fibers, such as polypropylene.

Examples: garrote, hangman's noose. See: *The Murders in the Rue Morgue*.

GROUP 5—HEAVY OBJECT—CONNOR SMITH

(noun) The solid mineral material forming part of the surface of the earth and other similar planets, exposed on the surface or underlying the soil or oceans.

Examples: shovel, rock. See: Murder in Mesopotamia.

Act I—Continued

THE SECOND SEQUENCE

<u>Central Question:</u> Will our protagonist take up the challenge and try to solve the murder? (Yes, obviously, but why?)

- This is the second half of Act I.

- Someone is dead, but your protagonist is not sure that they are/ should be involved.

- Similar to the "hero's journey," your characters will spend some time debating whether they can ignore the obvious issues in front of them and go on with their lives as they did before.

- Spoiler alert: They can't.

- Something—or many things—has to happen by the end of this sequence to convince your protagonist to change the course of their actions and begin to actively investigate.

- You must also introduce secondary plots and conflicts that will come to a head in the second act.

- The act should end with a twist/reveal/death that will set up the central question of the next sequence.

CHAPTER 4

Is This Murder Camp?

"Who's in charge here?"

I look up at the imperious voice demanding my attention from his front-row seat.

"I'm Eleanor," I say. "Are you in the Poison group?"

"Apparently," he says and rolls his eyes like a teenager. He's thirty-something, with close-cropped red hair the color of Ed Sheeran's. He has one of those mustaches that men seem to think make them look attractive these days,[27] and is wearing an oversized pair of wire-framed glasses I'm almost positive have clear glass in them because he's giving the try-hard, pick-me vibe of a millennial who wishes he were cool enough to be mistaken for Gen Z.[28]

We're in one of the conference rooms in the single-story white structure that sits next to one side of the pool. It's glinting at me through the windows under the strong sun like it's talking to me: *I'm here. You could be lazing in me with a nice drink, and instead, you're stuck in there, loser.*

That's what pools sound like, right?

It's the first session of the conference. When lunch ended, Elizabeth

---

[27] They don't.

[28] Whereas I'm a millennial who tries to project a Gen X vibe.

told us to break into our small groups, and the participants shuffled out of the restaurant with a buzz of excitement, while my heart beat with dread. And like the rule-follower that I (mostly) am, I shoved the threatening note into my pocket and followed instructions.

I wanted to tell Oli and Harper what I'd found under my plate, but I didn't. Instead, I told Oli I'd meet him after his session and watched as Harper ensconced herself on a chaise by the pool and pulled out a book.[29]

Why, I'm sure you're wondering, is this idiot ignoring basic clues that her life is in danger and just going along with it all?

I'm not sure, to be honest. All I can come up with is that I don't believe my life *is* in danger. I mean, how many murder plots can one person be involved in?

A few light threats, sure. Who doesn't get threats?

Oh, *you* don't? Fine. FINE. But when you're a public figure, it happens. I've had a stalker. I've made some enemies, real and imagined, and writing murder mysteries for a living draws in weirdos. Especially when you're a woman, because everyone always assumes you're writing about yourself. That you've done the things you imagined.

So those might be *some* of the reasons I'm ignoring the note.

But here's the truth. Because we're friends, right? I can confide in you? Cool.

I want to know who sent it, and if I leave, I'll never know.

Curiosity killed the cat, and all that.

Besides, if my life *is* in danger, I already have a list of suspects, and the woman who's staring at me from the other front-row seat with a mix of enmity and caution is at the top of it.

That's right. *Sandrine* is in this small group, because of course she is.

I'll get to her in a minute.

"What's your name?" I say to Ed Sheeran's taller brother.

---

[29] She's reading *Finlay Donovan Digs Her Own Grave*, the fifth book in the Finlay Donovan series, which is a hoot.

He holds his hand to his chest in mock shock. Or maybe it's real. I don't know this guy, though he looks vaguely familiar in a way that fills me with dread.

"I'm Stefano?"

"Okay."

"Dimitrov? From Booked4Life?" He says this like he can't believe he has to give me this much information to identify himself.

The problem is that it's not enough for me to know who he is. But he's left clues.

"Booked4Life. Is that your Instagram handle?"

"Tik. Tok."

Ugh. I've tried to do the whole TikTok thing, I have. But it's not for me. My videos get fifty views if I'm lucky, and I feel fake and stupid making them. I'm happier being a lurker. Let me watch my silly cat videos, home-improvement segments, and clowning for when Taylor's going to put out the *Reputation* vault tracks in peace.[30]

"Oh, right, of course."

"So convincing, El," Sandrine says in her slight French accent, and I try not to glare at her.

You already know I failed at this.

"I'm sorry, Stefano. Anyone will tell you I'm terrible with names. And social media is bad for my mental health, so I try to stay off of it. Especially review sites."

Did *that* sound convincing, Sandrine?

I think I'm a pretty good actress when I want to be.

Anyway, the truth is I read every review of every book I publish. Yep. Whether you tag me or not, I find them all.

Why? Well . . . I like to dull the knife so it won't hurt me. And so, yeah, I saw that "meh" review of my book, *Kirkus*. Bite me.[31]

---

[30] Please tell me she's released those by the time you read this!
[31] Please let me keep this, Vicki!

But back to the matter at hand. Do I know Stefano Dimitrov, Book-Toker?

I tried to block it out, but yes, it's all coming back to me now. He's even on my do-not-engage-with list. Which is *another* list Harper maintains for me when I send her the particularly egregious reviews of my books.

He does these videos where he judges books like fashion as they go by him on a carousel like they've been on the red carpet, designating books as "slay," or "prison," or "skip."

So, basically, he's like a Bond villain, but for books. And yes, I know that Bond started as a book character. You know what I mean. He twirls his little mustache and decides what *the* book of the season is.

And my book *was not it*.

He gave my last book "prison," even though he'd been flaunting the swag my publisher sent him for clout. The only saving grace was that Sandrine's last book got the same verdict.[32] But did that stop her from sucking up to him at every opportunity? Nope! She even sent him an early copy of her next book[33] to get his feedback on it.[34] And right now she looks like he's a trap I walked right into.

But joke's on *them*. I got them *both* banned from getting free review copies from my publisher because I'm petty like that.

"So, Stefano, you want to write a murder mystery?"

He raises a nonchalant shoulder. "Thought I'd give it a twirl. I read so many of them. Doesn't seem that hard."

"Ah. Well. Right. That is the purpose of this conference, so, let's get to it, shall we?"

I scan the participants. There are ten of them in total, including Sandrine, who I guess is taking this class?

---

[32] It's called *Murder Mystery* because titles have never been her strong suit.
[33] *Locked Room Mystery*. See what I mean?
[34] I hate-watch Sandrine's socials from a burner account because she blocked me!

Which is weird.

Anyway, what should I tell you about the others? They're all dressed in vacation clothes and have little branded notebooks next to their laptops. Their notebooks have the same motif that the note for me had: a tipped-over bottle of poison with a drop coming off the end.

There's a mix of men and women, and they range in age from middle thirties to mid-sixties.

And now I'm going to be honest with you for a second here. Just a second.

I'm not going to tell you the others' names.

Why?

I'll give you three reasons:

1. I've already introduced you to a lot of characters in the last couple of chapters.
2. They aren't crucial to the plot.
3. Do you know how hard it is to describe people in a memorable way?

Just remember that there are eight of them. But they're not the point of this chapter. They're the window dressing.

The important part was meeting Stefano. And Sandrine.

And okay, I know I haven't told you much about her yet, so I guess this is the time.

I met Sandrine at the first conference I went to.[35] We were both baby authors and got along like a house on fire. You know when you meet someone and there's that immediate *spark*? Sometimes it's romantic and sometimes it's friendship, but you always just kind of know. *This is my person.*

I felt it when I met Oliver. And when I met Sandrine. So when I learned she lived a couple of miles away from me, it felt like kismet. We

---

[35] Yes, the same one where I met Elizabeth and Shek. Is that important? Probably! That's why I'm burying it in a footnote.

became tight immediately, and we told each other everything. We celebrated each other's successes and were a shoulder to cry on when we failed. I'm not sure I would've made it through my breakup with Oliver without her, and a bunch of other things, too.

In between the highs and lows, we read each other's books and gave each other constructive feedback. We DMed each other Instagram posts by people who annoyed us and giggled over them. We buddy hate-read books by authors who'd been mean to us.

Maybe I'm telling you too much. We were human, okay?

I mean, I was. Sandrine, I'm not so sure. Because there was always something a bit . . . *off* about her. I could never put my finger on it, but I know I ignored the warning clang at the back of my mind like I often do because that thing goes off *a lot*.

Here are three red flags I knew about but ignored:

1. She speaks almost unaccented English because she's been in the States for so long, but when she wants to get her way with a stranger, she puts on this charming French Canadian accent.
2. Her husband travels a lot for work, and she's been conducting an affair with someone who lives in her building for *years*.
3. She's like Sally in *When Harry Met Sally*: high-maintenance, but she thinks she's easygoing.

There were other things I let go because when you make a friend as an adult, that's what you do. We all have flaws. I have tons. I figure if you're spending time with me, it's because you've decided my good parts outweigh the bad, and vice versa.

So I pushed hers aside.

I thought we were on the same page.

Then she needed a new agent and wanted to query my agent, Stephanie. I introduced them, and Stephanie turned her down. It happens. It wasn't my fault.

She didn't get an agent for the longest time. And when she did, it wasn't someone she was excited about. Her book sold after being on submission for months, but only to a small press when she was hoping to get a major deal. Her career was going one way, and mine was going another. I knew she was jealous, and I got it. I'd be jealous, too. But I'd also be happy for her. That's what friendship is.

Not Sandrine, though.

She pulled away slowly, and I let her do it because I thought she'd take a bit of time and then things would go back to normal. Instead, I got a text one afternoon that said she was done with me. A friendship-breakup text!

And *then* she'd accused me of stealing her book idea. Which was ridiculous. I have flaws, but book-plot theft is not one of them. But people accuse you of the things they'd do, I've noticed.

So, that happened.

And now here she is, sitting with her notebook open, looking like I'm going to teach her something about how to write a murder mystery.

Will she take notes? Is she here as a spy? Will the reasons she ended our friendship eventually be declassified?[36]

Anyway, enough of that. I need to start this class, or I'll never finish on time.

"Hi, everyone, thanks for coming to the conference and being part of the Poison group." My voice is high and squeaky. I clear my throat. "This morning we'll be covering the opening sequence. You should have all received the handout?"

Stefano puts up his hand.

Is that really his name? Were his parents big *Days of Our Lives* fans?

"Yes?"

"Are we going to be able to plot a murder by the end of this?"

"That's the idea."

---

[36] Great song, Taylor. IYKYK.

He holds the schedule in his hands. "I don't see anything about picking your victim."

"Pardon?"

"How do you decide who to kill first? Because that's how it has to start, right? With a murder?"

"With a death, yes."

"Right, so, who dies first?"

"That's kind of getting ahead of ourselves."

"How can it be getting ahead of ourselves when it's the first chapter?" Sandrine says, batting her black eyelashes like an innocent.

"Did you want to teach the class, or . . . ?"

A small gasp escapes one of the older women, and I sink in my shoes.

I shouldn't let Sandrine provoke me. I'd promised myself that if (when) I ran into her, I'd be nonchalant. But what the actual fuck is she doing here?

"Sorry about that, folks. That rum punch at lunch must've been stronger than I thought."

I pause for a laugh I do not get.

"Ahem, so, sure, we can start there, good idea. It fits in with the prompt for today, which is to write your three opening paragraphs from a sentence I'll give you.

"So, there are three theories about who to murder first. You can do what I call the P. D. James method, which is to spend the first third of your book showing all the ways the other characters want the same person to die and then kill them. Or you can do what I call the decoy death, which is to start by killing off a minor character, who it turns out was killed by mistake or because they knew too much. And then the third way is to kill off the main target in the first chapter, and then have the book be about solving that murder, and we learn why people might want them dead after the fact."

"Which one do you recommend?" one of the nameless participants asks.

I flash to the body I found in my room this morning. A suicide, Officer Rolle had called it.

But now this conference is full of people who don't seem to like me—or my books—very much, and a threatening note was left under my plate.

And it's right about now that something occurs to me.

Is this fucking play about *us?*[37][38]

---

[37] Yep, I got that from TikTok. See I <u>don't</u> steal ideas. I give them credit.
[38] And right. TikTok got it from <u>Euphoria</u>, the TV show. All credit where credit is due.

First Writing Assignment—Poison

Prompt: It was a bright, sunny day.

It was a bright, sunny day, but that didn't change how black she felt inside. It was like tar; it stuck to everything she thought and touched and breathed. She'd tried everything she could think of to get rid of it, but she never managed. It was all she could do to concentrate on other things because the truth of it was, she wanted to kill someone. Not someone. *Her.*

And there she was, sitting so close to her she could smell her scent. Not her perfume, but what lay underneath it. That *you* smell that clings to your skin no matter what. If you get close enough. And that's what she wanted. To get close enough to smell it brighten right before the life seeped out of her. Did that make her a bad person? She didn't think so. Whatever people might think, everyone has someone like that in their life. A justifiable homicide. The one the jury would let you off of if they could.

Jury nullification. That's what it's called when a jury overlooks the law and acquits. And that was what *this* person was like in her life. Her free pass. *Her get-out-of-jail-murder.* The one she was going to get away with so long as she could keep the tar from sticking to her, too.

CHAPTER 5

Is the Enemy of My Enemy Really My Friend?[39]

"Maybe we *should* go," I say to Harper when I meet her back at our (new) villa after my lecture's over.

The police didn't release our original room, so Mark hemmed and hawed and eventually told us there was *one* room free after all. It's much fancier than the last one we were in, likely the honeymoon or presidential suite. It looks recently renovated, and the furniture is so crisp and white, I'm worried about sitting on it. The Georgian blue walls have white stenciling on them along with a series of portraits of the former colonizers who ran this place, including Edward VIII.[40]

"Oh, *now* she wants to go," Harper says. She got a bit of color around the pool, which I'm glad about. She's been too much of a shut-in lately, holing up in her room and following a weird sleep schedule.

---

[39] The rhetorical answer to this question is: no.

[40] Yep. The guy who abdicated the throne of England. They parked him and Wallis Simpson here during World War II, which went about as well as you'd imagine. The public story was that he was sent here to be the governor-general, but really, it was because he was a secret Nazi sympathizer!

Maybe this trip will be a good thing for her, even *if* my life is in danger.

But not if I die. She'd be upset about that.

"Yeah, I *do.*"

"Why?"

"Someone left a threatening note under my plate at lunch."

"What?" Oliver says from the doorway. His shirt is open at the collar, and I can't help it. Even in the worst of times, I want to jump into bed with him. "Why didn't you tell me?"

"I was in shock."

He gives me a look. "What did it say?"

I take it out of my bag and show it to both of them.

"I think someone wants to hurt me."

"Why?" Harper asks.

"The note's not enough to draw that conclusion?"

"That could be part of the conference. We all had notes under our plates, right? With our group assignments?"

"What did yours say?"

"Something about keeping your friends close and your enemies closer."

"Hmmm. Oli?"

"'The truth, however ugly in itself, is always curious and beautiful to seekers after it.'"

An alarm bell goes off in my brain. "That's from *The Murder of Roger Ackroyd.*"

"Interesting. Who says it?"

"Can't remember. But it's not a threat. Mine was a threat."

"Well," Harper says, "actually . . ."

"Yes?"

She taps at her phone and nods. "Thought so. The full quote is 'None of us are getting out of here alive, so please stop treating yourself like an afterthought. Eat the delicious food. Walk in the sunshine. Jump in the ocean. Say the truth you're carrying in your heart like hidden treasure. Be silly. Be kind. Be weird. There's no time for anything else.' I thought I recognized it. It's from Nanea Hoffman."

"So, it's not a threat but an admonition to live life to the fullest?"

"Yep."

"Why would they be using a self-help quote at a murder conference?" I ask.

"How should I know? It sounds good?"

"That's not . . . You seriously don't want to go? What about everyone who's here who shouldn't be?"

"Like who?"

"Inspector Tucci. Guy. *Sandrine.*"

There's a knock at the door. I turn to open it. A maid is standing there with a large pile of towels in front of her face.

"I'm sorry, ma'am. They told me to bring these."

"It's fine. I'll take them." I reach my arms forward and take them out of her arms. She's in her mid-twenties and has what I'd call California coloring—blond hair, blue eyes, a natural tan.

"Do you need anything else?"

"No, thank you." She gives me a flustered smile, then turns away.

"You need help there, El?" Oliver asks.

"I got it." I put the towels down on the dining table as the door clicks shut. I can feel Harper's eyes on me.

"What?"

"This is about Sandrine being here."

"No, she's just one of the symptoms. It's about all of it. The note, the dead body in our room this morning. You can't ignore that."

"That *was* a shock," Harper says. "But it doesn't have anything to do with us."

"Come on. I was *just* teaching this in my lecture. The first body that drops is *always* part of the story."

"In books."

"Yes, but . . ." I stop. What am I missing?

I was sure that the minute I mentioned leaving, Harper would announce she'd already packed our bags and that our flight was leaving in two hours. But now she's trying to talk me out of it.

Why?

"Three hours ago, you would've both been happy to get out of here. What's going on?"

She and Oliver exchange a glance.

"Yes?"

"There are at least three reasons why you can't leave," Harper says.

"Give."

"There are no flights today, and maybe not tomorrow either."

"Why?"

"If I said the weather, would you believe me?"

"Not *another* hurricane."

"No, it's something to do with a solar storm. All flights have been canceled for the next two days as a precaution."

"Like an actual storm on the sun?" I ask.

"Yes."

"Sounds made-up. What's the second reason?"

"I mentioned the possibility to Vicki, and she said something about a breach of contract."

"Meaning?"

"Everyone's paid quite a bit to be here and you're a star attraction."

"Don't try to stoke my ego. I'm not even one of the keynote speakers."

Harper rolls her eyes. "They've had problems with people leaving in the past, and it causes a cascade of refund requests. The org is on shaky ground as it is, so they'd rather you not."

"And if someone kills me, what then?"

"Don't be melodramatic, El. Who here wants to kill you? And don't say Sandrine."

"I wasn't going to."

I mean, I was, but so what? I'm not wrong to suspect her. She already murdered our friendship without provocation.

"Maybe she's here to make it up with you?" Oliver says.

"Doubt it."

"She doesn't want you dead," Harper says.

"She just wants my book career dead."

"What does *that* mean?" Oliver says.

I look away. Talking about Sandrine makes me feel emotional, and I've never gone into much detail about what happened between us with Oliver. It was before we got back together, so I didn't feel the need to download the entire saga.

Besides, what does it say about me that I either let a psycho into my life *or* was such a bad friend I got dumped?

"Just a theory I have."

"What?"

I look at my shoes because what I'm about to admit is quite embarrassing. "Well, you know how *Amalfi Made Me Do It* has the lowest rating of all my books?"

"It's not even out yet," Harper says.

"I mean in pre-ratings. Like on NetGalley. It all started with one review."

"Explain," Oliver says.

"It's the way it works on there. People read the other reviews before they post theirs. People are always like 'I agree with the other reviews' or 'I don't agree and here's why.' Anyway, one of the first reviewers complained about Cecilia thinking about the calories of something she ate and made it the whole focus of her review, and then the others started agreeing with her, and it wasn't quite review-bombing, but it kind of was."

"What's all this got to do with Sandrine?" Oliver asks.

"She wrote that review."

"How? You didn't send her the book, did you?"

I'd wanted to. To show her that her fears were completely unfounded and our books had nothing to do with one another. But I'd chickened out. It seemed too needy.

"It's not hard to get approved on NetGalley," I say. "Especially if you're an author. I know she has an account."

"But that doesn't mean it's her."

"And the username. It's a bunch of numbers, but I know what they mean."

"Like an easter egg?" Harper says like she might be laughing at me. "Like Taylor does?"

"It's a date that's significant to her. To something private she told me about herself."[41]

"That could be a coincidence," Oliver says.

Only there are no coincidences. Not in my life. And definitely not in books that start with a death.

"Then there's the way it's written. I can hear her voice. I know it's her. I've read everything she ever wrote. I could even write like her if I tried hard enough."

"So, she gave your book a bad review," Oliver says. "That doesn't mean she wants you dead."

"No, but it does mean she's messing with me. And that's what this feels like. Someone is messing with me. The body, the surprise guests, the threat, even that TikToker who's here who *also* gave my book a bad review. Both of them are in my small group. Something feels off." My voice rises to a pitch that a certain type of man would call hysterical.

But Oliver isn't that guy.

Instead, he walks to me and envelops me in his arms, and this is why I love him. Because he knows what I need and he isn't afraid to give it to me.

"You okay?" he asks against my ear.

"Am I tempting fate if I say I'll live?"

---

[41] It's her lover's birthday.

He pulls back and smiles. "We're stuck here for now."

I feel suddenly like I might start to cry, which is not a rational response to what's happening, but it's not *not* a rational response.

I kiss him on the cheek and walk out of his arms.

"You said there were three things," I say to Harper. "What's the third?"

They glance at one another again.

"If you guys do that one more time, I'm going to lose it."

"It's a surprise," Oliver says.

"So you're not going to tell me."

The side of his mouth curls up. "That would be ruining the surprise, wouldn't it?"

There's something about Oliver's tone that stops me from asking more. Because now my *heart* has quickened, but in a good way. I think I know what the surprise is, and even though I'm a *feminist*, thank you very much, I can't help but swoon a little at the thought.

The last time we talked about getting married was at my friend Emma's wedding on Catalina Island. We'd decided—I mean *he'd* decided—that proposing at someone else's wedding was tacky, and then, with everything that happened, it hadn't come up again.

But the furor over two massive movie stars being involved in a murder has started to die down, so maybe that's what's going to happen here?

That I'm not going to get murdered, but I *am* going to get proposed to?

And he told Harper about it. Does that track? I mean, it might.

But it also might mean that he's going to do it in a public way, which, you might be surprised to learn, is not my thing.

Oh God, stop it.

Don't ask too many questions, El. You want to be surprised. You want it to be romantic. Not something you've forced out of Oliver.

So I'm deciding to let this go, right now.

The surprise, I mean.

Not the other stuff.

"Okay, I'll let you have your surprise, but if we're going to stay here, then we have to at least look into the guy who died in our room."

"Why?"

"It felt like the start of something. And if it is, I want to know. We need to know."

Oliver sighs in resignation. "Where do you suggest we start?"

I take a beat, but I know the answer. "I know just the person."

CHAPTER 6

Who's Afraid of Little Old Me?

"What are you doing here?" I ask Guy in his small office near the staff quarters.

It's got a wooden desk, shutters on the windows, a sleek laptop, and not much else. It's also neat as a pin, nothing else on the desk other than an old-fashioned desk calendar.

I'm not sure what I expected. I've never been to the staff quarters in a resort before, and maybe they're all different, but this one feels like a microcosm of the summer camp Harper and I went to when we were kids: a tight cluster of small white buildings built into the overgrown greenery with communal showers and rooms.

If there was somewhere I thought of finding Guy Charles, it wasn't this.

We first met ten years ago when he was working with/for Connor. Since then, he's been in and out of my life like a bad tide.

"I don't have to tell you anything," Guy says in his gruff voice.

And for the first time since I met him, I try to place his accent.

Will it surprise you to learn that I have no idea where Guy is from or what he did before he met Connor? Or even *when* he met Connor?

All I know about him is that he and Connor worked in Europe for a decade until Connor met *me* and I wrote about *them* and they got too famous to do their nefarious deeds out in the sunlight. Maybe I'd know more if I'd read Guy's book—*The Guy Behind the Man in Rome*—but, alas, I don't even own a copy.

Does this make me a bad person?

You don't have to answer that one.

"There was a dead body in our room when we got here. We want to know what happened."

Guy looks past me to Harper and Oliver. But we're a united front on this one.

"You heard Officer Rolle," Guy says. "It was a suicide."

"You don't believe that."

He meets my eyes and I know he doesn't. Guy and I have never been close, but we've spent enough time together to know some essentials about one another.

Like Guy is a very good liar. But he does have a tell.

Silence.

"Did you know him?" Oliver says. "The victim?"

"I'd met him a few times. And I was there when he was fired."

"Why?" I ask.

"Standard operating procedure."

"At a resort?"

Guy takes a moment to deliberate before he speaks. "There are a lot of big names that stay here. You'd be surprised. They want to make sure no one leaves with passwords or other confidential information."

Given the current state of this resort, I highly doubt that, but I could be wrong.

Others could have been lured here by the brochure's false promise of five-star luxury and been shocked to find that the mini fridge didn't even have Diet Coke in it.[42]

"What did he do here?" I ask.

---

[42] Only Pepsi products which <u>are not it</u>!

"He worked in customer relations."

"What does that mean?"

"He dealt with high-profile clients. Getting them whatever they needed."

"And why was he fired?"

Guy's eyes shift around the room as he takes another beat. "There have been some thefts on property."

"He was the *thief*?"

"He was seen on camera entering a guest room he had no business being in, and then something went missing. So yes, he was the thief."

"Did you find the missing things on him?" Oliver asks.

"No, but that doesn't mean anything. He could've fenced it or hidden it."

I bite the end of my thumb. "So a thief gets fired, then he kills himself in our room? Why?"

"That was the room he stole from."

I shudder. "He was sending a message."

"Looks like."

"How was he able to get into the room?" Oliver asks.

"It's not that hard if you have access to the key card changer."

"Which is kept where?"

"At the front desk," Guy says. "You need a key to operate it, but it's an easy enough access point, which I've told Mark more than once."

"Who's Mark?" Harper asks.

"Mark Knowles, the manager. You met him this morning."

"So his name *is* Mark!" I say.

"Pardon?"

"It was just what I guessed, it doesn't matter." I think it over. "How long was Brian in the room? Do we know when he died?"

"That will have to wait for the path report."

"When was the room cleaned? Did someone check out of it this morning?"

"No. You'd reserved an early check-in. The room was vacated and cleaned yesterday."

"So he could've been there all night?"

"By the looks of the blood, yes."

I flash back to the sight and scent of the body. Guy's right. I don't know as much about the drying times of blood as you might think I would, but it had to have been several hours at least.

"So he could've been killed yesterday?" I ask.

"Yes," Guy says.

"Are there cameras on the doors?" Oliver asks. "Can we see who got in the room?"

"There's only a camera on the front entrance."

"There are two entrances?"

"There are French doors leading to the cuddle puddles in every room."

"I'm sorry," Oliver says, almost choking on his laughter. "Did you say 'cuddle puddles'?"

Guy makes a growling sound in his throat. "It's the little personal pool on the balcony. That's what they call them."

"So, if someone breaks into a room the back way, then there's no way to tell how or who it is?"

"That's right."

"But those doors are kept locked from the inside, right?" I say. "They don't have a key?"

"That's right."

"The victim could've left it unlocked."

"Yes," Guy says. "But why?"

"Maybe he opened it to get some air . . . have a think." I click my teeth together. "Was there anyone on the front-door cameras?"

"Not after Brian went in."

"Which was when?"

Guy sighs, then answers: "Last night. After dinner."

"And the back door, was it locked?"

"Yes."

"That doesn't mean it was locked originally . . . ," Harper says. "The murderer could've locked it behind himself when he left."

"Or it was always locked," I say.

"A locked-room murder, El?" Harper says. "That seems unlikely."

"You do have a point there." I've always wanted to write a locked-room murder, but that shit is *hard*.[43]

"What about the other person that died a few months ago?" I ask.

"He died in his sleep from natural causes," Guy says.

"Nothing suspicious?"

"No. I checked the file. It was cut-and-dried."

"Which brings us back to our original question: How did *you* get here exactly?" Oliver asks.

"I applied for the job."

"Obviously," I say. "But why?"

"Needed a change of scene."

"A resort in the Bahamas? Doesn't seem like your thing."

"I agree entirely," Connor says, entering the room behind us.

My sigh is loud enough for Connor to hear, but I don't care what Connor thinks of me.

Honestly, the less thinking he does about me, the better.

Was that convincing?

No, right?

"There's no need for that," Connor says in a hurt tone. "I'm sure we're all here for the same reason."

"What's that?"

"To find out what Guy is up to."

"He says he's just working here."

Connor scowls. "I don't believe that for a minute."

---

[43] Doesn't mean that's not what I'm doing here, though.

"Why not?"

"He just happens to be at the *same* resort as us?"

Good point. Damn it. I meant to make that point at the beginning of this conversation.

I might need to stop drinking. It's dulling my senses.

My life is going to be so boring!

"He makes a good point," Oliver says. "When exactly *did* you arrive here, Guy?"

"Six weeks ago."

"And why did you apply to *this* resort?" I ask. "Did you know we'd be here?"

Guy shifts from foot to foot. "I may have seen an advertisement."

"What kind of advertisement?"

"In a newsletter."

I feel the start of dread. "Whose newsletter?"

"His." He points to Connor.

"What?" Connor says when I scowl at him. "I was advertising the event like Vicki told me to."

I turn back to Guy. "So you saw this, and what then?"

"I checked it out, didn't I?"

"Yes, and?"

"I was on the website and I saw they were looking for a head of security."

"And you applied for it because . . . ?"

"Like I said, I needed a change of scene."

"In the Bahamas. At a resort you knew Connor, Oliver, and I were coming to?"

"Hey, what about me?"

"And Harper. And Sandrine."

He gives me a cold stare. "What about it?"

"Did you know Sandrine was going to be here?"

"She may have mentioned it, yes."

"You're in touch with Sandrine?" Oliver says as Harper starts to cough.

"What of it?"

Harper's coughing increases.

"Are you all right, Harper?"

"Just peachy." She makes a motion with her hand to tell me to move on.

I make a mental note to come back to this later.

Remind me if I forget, okay?

"Did *you* suggest that Sandrine come to the conference?" I ask Guy.

He doesn't say anything, just looks at me with his sad, dark eyes.

Which is his way of saying yes.

Fantastic.

What was that under Harper's plate? "Keep your friends close and your enemies closer"? I've always preferred "The enemy of my enemy is my friend."

But what is the friend of your enemy? An enemy, that's who.

"Is that all?" I ask Guy. "Anything more to tell us?"

"I didn't have anything to tell you in the first place."

"What I want to know is," Harper says, "are the police going to investigate the death? Or have they just washed their hands of it?"

"Harper. Don't speak-ay on the death-kay in front of Onnor-Cay."

"That's *not* pig Latin."

"Whatever."

"And you're the one who spilled the beans earlier. In the lounge?"

Shit, she's right.

Goodbye, alcohol, my old friend. It's been nice knowing you.

Mostly, I mean.

"Answer the question, Guy," Oliver says with a hint of a threat.

Guy takes a moment to consider, then relents. "There will be a post-mortem as I mentioned earlier. That's standard operating procedure. We'll likely have the results in a few days."

"And in the meantime, are you doing anything to increase security?"

"I'm keeping an eye out."

"From in here?" Connor scoffs. "Who did you put down as your references when you applied for this job? Because no one spoke to me."

Guy goes silent again, and I don't know whether to be worried or annoyed.

I don't feel like he's telling the whole truth, but I do feel a bit calmer.

I mean, I still have an unlikely suicide/potential murder to solve, but some of the panic has started to recede. There's an explanation for why everyone who's surprised me is here. And maybe the note wasn't a threat. Maybe I've been worried because I'm self-involved and have had some bad experiences lately when I left my house.

I expel a slow breath, feeling my shoulders come down to a reasonable level.

Sometimes the simple explanation is the right one. Not everyone is out to get me all the time. And just because someone dying is the way you start most murder mysteries doesn't mean that I'm living in one rather than teaching it.

Wow.

I'm almost convincing myself.

As long as nothing else happens, maybe I'll be okay.

"Eleanor! *There* you are. I've been looking *everywhere* for you."

And then again, maybe not.

CHAPTER 7

If My Stalker's Here, Is Something Bad Going to Happen?

"Cathy, what are you doing here?" I ask, working hard not to call her "crazy."

Because that's who she is. Crazy Cathy, my stalker, who always seems to show up just when the shit is about to hit the fan.

So. Stand back.

"What do you mean?" Cathy says in a hurt tone, which is her default setting. "You were advertising this event for *months*. I wanted to make sure you weren't going to be embarrassed."

"Embarrassed?"

"You know, if it didn't sell out." Cathy puts her hands on her ample hips. She's dyed her frizzy hair a bad red shade that will require a lot of maintenance and is wearing a kaftan made of colorful silk that looks complicated to put on.[44]

"What are you even talking about?"

"She means she saw it in *your* newsletter," Harper says. "Ticket sales were a bit slow, so I sent out a couple of extra issues. Vicki asked, like Connor mentioned before."

I pull Harper aside. "I thought we were unsubscribing Cathy from the newsletter?"

---

[44] She gives major Kathy Bates–in–*Misery* vibes. Is it intentional? Probably.

"I did. She must've signed up with a new email address."

"I'm allowed to! You should've asked for my consent to remove me!"

Serenity now. "Cathy, we've talked about listening in on conversations."

She bats her wide eyes at me slowly.

Do all crazy people blink oddly, or is it the slow blinking that makes you nuts in the first place?

"You're talking about me right in front of me!"

Deep breaths, Eleanor. Deep breaths. "Why were you looking for me?"

"Someone was asking for you at the reception. I overheard and thought I'd come to find you."

"Who?"

"I don't know. He looked kind of official. A police officer maybe? Are you in trouble?"

Only if I commit the homicide I want to right now.

"Thanks for the tip."

"Maybe he'll be at the water polo?"

"You should get to that," Guy says, flicking his hand at us in a *go, go* gesture.

"I could use a beverage by the pool," Connor says.

"Hard day?"

He squints at me. "I was teaching. And I'm on *deadline*."

"For what?"

"Book two in the series."

"Wait. It's a series?" I look at Harper. "Did you know this?"

She gives me a half smile, clearly enjoying herself. I learned recently that Harper's been working as Connor's beta reader/editor, which I took as well as you'd imagine.

No, worse.

"*You* knew this, El," Harper says. "He got a multi-book deal, remember?"

"I must've blocked out that information."

"We should make an appearance at the water polo," Oliver says gently.

"You're kidding."

He gives me a small smile. "It's a conference tradition, apparently. Staff against participants."

"I have to get *in* the pool?"

"That is where water polo takes place, traditionally."

"Shut it, Connor." I close my eyes and count to five. I can do this. I open them again and give Guy a hard stare. "We're not done here."

Guy could not care less about my vague threat, so we shuffle out of Guy's office, Harper, Connor, and Cathy trailing behind us.

"What do you think of all that?" Oliver asks once we're a little down the path toward our villa.

"Which part? Crazy Cathy being here or Guy's explanations?"

"Either."

I glance back at Connor and Cathy. "I guess there's an innocent explanation for all of it."

"I hope so."

Turns out that Oliver wasn't joking about the mandatory water polo. So, here I am, thirty minutes later, in a pool that's *just* warm enough to stand, treading water in a bathing suit that's a bit too tight around the chest and doesn't hide my pooch as well as my regular clothes do. I know Oliver doesn't care about things like that, and I hope there's eventually a day when I don't either, but today is not that day!

Harper's wearing a cute striped suit that has one shoulder strap, and she slips easily into the water on the participants' side. She's joined by Sandrine, wearing a suit that can only be described as *European*, with high slits on the sides and a deep V between her breasts. She's got her hair in an elegant swimming cap and a determined look on her face. Next to her, Stefano looks ridiculous in his 1920s-inspired one-piece—it's half wet suit and half statement piece and entirely out of place. But he high-fives with Cathy, who's in a black swimming dress, and one of the other members of the Poison group, an older man who's already got a ridge of sunburn across his nose and his shoulders.

The rest of the participants are lazing around the pool on the loungers, watching us with notebooks in hand as if they'll get tips on writing murder mysteries from watching a bunch of writers toss a ball around for thirty minutes.

That's how long a water polo match lasts, right?

It's not *longer* than that.

Fine, fine, I don't want to know.

The faculty team is made up of me, Ravi, Oliver, Connor, and Vicki. Elizabeth's here, too—she's going to be acting as the ref and is trying to explain the rules to us because who knows the rules to water polo?

"There's supposed to be seven people a side," Connor says as he slips a red cap on his head that has ear flaps. "Six players and a goalie."

"Where did you learn that?" I ask.

He lifts his chin. "I know things."

"Have you . . . *played* water polo?"

"As a boy, yes."

I start to laugh.

"What?"

"That is so . . . geeky . . . Wait . . . It's that what that helmet you're wearing is?"

"It's called a *cap*. It protects your ears from getting injured."

I try to hold in my snort. I fail. "What position did you play?"

"Hole set."

"What now?"

"Hole set. It's the focal point of the offense." He holds up a hand. "Don't say it. I don't want to hear it."

I'm full on laughing now. "Oh my God, you're embarrassed!"

"I am *not*."

I glance at Oliver. "Connor was a *nerd*. Like an athletic nerd, which I didn't think was possible."

The corner of Oliver's mouth twists. Did I mention he looks great in a bathing suit? No? Not the time. "What school did Connor go to that it had a *water polo* team is what I want to know."

"Smart." I turn back to Connor. "Care to enlighten us?"

"I do not."

"Fine. Elizabeth, what are the rules here?"

Elizabeth taps her cane against the concrete. She has an inscrutable expression on her face and is wearing a wide-brimmed sun hat that shades her eyes. "Pretty simple. Each team tries to score a goal by tossing it into the opposing team's net." She points to the ends of the pool. There's a small net set up on each side.

"How many goals do we need to win?" I ask.

"There's no set amount. Whoever has the most when the time is up wins. Like hockey. I'll start the game by throwing the ball in."

"So, there's no serve?"

"That's volleyball, El, *franchement*," Sandrine says.

And then Harper giggles. Actually *giggles*.

It's the first time I've seen her laugh freely in a while. And Sandrine did it.

Ugh.

"Whose team are you on?" I ask Harper.

"Um, this one?" She motions around her. "I'm not on the faculty."

"Fine, good point. Shall we go?"

Elizabeth nods and holds up what looks to *me* like a volleyball above her head, but what do I know? "Someone needs to go in net on each side."

"I'll do it," Stefano says like he's making a grand gesture. "Good luck getting it past me!" He splashes off to the other end of the pool and sets himself into the goal, moving back and forth with vigor. "Just try me!"

"How Ron Weasley of him," Oliver drawls.

"Yes! Exactly. I knew he reminded me of someone! Now, who's in net for us?"

"You'll need *me* for goal scoring," Connor says. "It's my specialty."

"Mm-kay. Oliver?"

He looks to the net and back to me. "What about Ravi?"

Ravi has been completely quiet since we got in the pool, just staring at me in a way that makes me uncomfortable. And not just because of the male gaze. He looks so much like his dead brother, and it's disconcerting to be this close to him. Especially since he's clearly feeling some kind of way about being around me, which is something I didn't think about before this very moment because, hello! Have you met me? I do not disasterize in advance!

I leave that to Harper.

"Can you be goalie, Ravi?" I ask him gently. "It's probably like wet soccer."

"You mean football," he corrects me. "Only Americans call it soccer."

"Aren't you American?"

"We were born in Mumbai," he says, his chin lifted as if it's an affront that I don't know this. It's also not an answer to my question.

Why is everyone so sketchy with their personal details?

That might be a clue.

Or maybe not. Not sure yet.

"What's with all the genealogy questions?" Connor says. "Let's play." He touches Ravi on the shoulder. Ravi jumps back as if he's been electrocuted. "Take it easy, Ravi. Go in goal. I'll defend you."

Ravi looks like he wants to say something, but he doesn't. Which is different from his brother, for sure. Shek never held back.

But back to the matter at hand. This sports game that I'm definitely winning. Because I'm intensely competitive, particularly at sports. I was the captain of the tennis team in high school and a walk-on in college, and while I always knew I wasn't good enough to go pro, that doesn't mean I didn't take it seriously. Especially with Sandrine on the other side.

I'm beating *her* for sure.

"Everyone ready?" Elizabeth says, holding the ball above her head.

"Ready!"

She bounces the ball on her hand and then pops it into the pool. Four of us rush for it—me, Connor, Sandrine, and Harper—and we're soon in a four-way tangle trying to get a handle on a very slippery ball. Connor comes up the winner and holds it above his head. Since he's taller than all of us, it's an easy game of keep-away.

But my God, does he look ridiculous in that helmet. I mean cap.

"Swim up to the net, El!" he shouts.

I follow instructions, swimming past Sandrine and Harper, trying to get open for Connor's pass. I watch as he launches the ball, and I try to jump up to catch it.

But I can't.

Someone's got ahold of my leg and they're pulling me down.

Pulling me under.

I open my mouth to scream as I'm dragged beneath the surface, and all I get is a strangled squeal as I fight for breath.

No.

I'm fighting for my life.

CHAPTER 8

Is Drowning the Worst Way to Die?

I've been close to death before. I almost choked on a fish bone once. I nearly fell down a flight of stairs. In both cases, someone saved me before it faded to black.

Oliver.

He was the hero.

And as I fight to reach the surface as my lungs scream for air, his name is forefront in my mind.

Oliver. Oliver will save me.

And yeah, I know I'm supposed to be a feminist about this. I *know* I'm supposed to save myself. Find a way to kick whoever has a firm grip around my ankle in the face and twist out of their grasp. That's the way I'd write it because that's what the audience expects.

But that's not what happens.

Instead, two firm, strong, *male* hands grab my shoulders and haul me out of the grip that's trying to drown me, and the next thing I know, I'm on the side of the pool, the rough pebble of the concrete rubbing against my thighs as I cough out the water that's accumulated in my lungs.

I look up. The person standing over me is partially blocked by the sun. But I'd know that outline anywhere.

It's Connor.

Connor. Not Oliver.

Fuck.

"You all right?"

"Looks like I'll live."

His mouth curls into a smile as Oliver arrives next to me. "What happened?"

I look away from Connor. "Someone tried to kill me."

I look down at my ankle. It's rubbed red from whoever was gripping me, and there's a small crescent moon from a nail.

"It was you," I say to Sandrine. "You did it."

"It's a game, Eleanor. I was trying to win."

"By drowning me?"

"I did nothing of the kind."

I look over to Elizabeth. It's hard to read her expression under her large hat. "What did you see, Elizabeth? Is dragging someone under allowed?"

"All's fair in water polo," Ravi says.

"Well, actually," Connor says, "there are strict rules against what kinds of holds are permitted."

I roll my eyes at Oliver and he smiles back. My breathing has returned to normal, and it's hard to feel under threat soaking wet, under the bright sun, with a hundred people watching as they sip on their cocktails.

Would Sandrine try to kill me here, in front of everyone, and use *water polo* for an excuse?

No, right?

That seems silly.

Though I do know some of her deepest, darkest secrets. Some I *might* have threatened to spill when I texted her a couple of times when I couldn't sleep after our breakup.

I'm not proud of it, okay?

Anyway, I've blocked her now, so I can't do things like that anymore. And it was a while ago. She can't know about me stalking her socials every couple of months to find out if she has a new book coming out. It's not like LinkedIn, where people can see who looked at their profile.

Please tell me I'm right.

"Don't be so dramatic, El," Sandrine says.

"What are you talking about? I'm sitting here recovering from you trying to drown me."

"See, that's *précisement* what I'm talking about. Next thing I know, you're going to do some Storytime about it on your TikTok."

Stefano frowns. "I thought you said you don't have TikTok?"

"I don't," I say. "She's . . . It's just a jab at me." I hold out my hand to Oliver. He pulls himself onto the deck and helps me up.

"Hey," Connor says. "We have a match to play."

"Match over," I say.

"Who wins, then?"

"What does that matter?"

"There is a cup," Elizabeth says. "A trophy of sorts."

"Give it to Sandrine. She wants it bad enough."

"I say," Connor says. "Can we simply continue *without* Eleanor?"

"Go right ahead."

Elizabeth looks around, a bit flustered, which is not something I'm used to seeing from her. "No, no, of course we will postpone the match. We can try again tomorrow."

I close my eyes and breathe in.

Tomorrow. Someone can try again to kill me tomorrow.

Can't wait.

An hour later, Oliver and I walk arm in arm through the complex to the British pub where the welcome cocktail is taking place with a sense of trepidation.

It's been a hard launch into this conference. A body, unexpected guests, arguments, a near drowning. My *stalker*. This resort isn't what I expected it to be, and I don't just mean the peeling paint and mediocre food.

But the show, as they say, must go on, so I got changed into a light pink summer dress that—once again, sorry, Harper!—matches the coral linen shirt and chinos Oliver's wearing.

I wish I didn't have to go to this party or the dinner after it. But since I do, I wish it was at the beach bar instead of inside. The air tonight is soft in that way you only get in the tropics, and I love being near the water. The ocean here is the blue of postcards and Instagram you-wish-you-were-here ads. The sand is white and looks pillowy soft.

Tomorrow, after I teach my class, I'm plunking myself in a deck chair and burying myself in a book.

Or not *burying myself* . . . That seems like tempting fate.

You get what I mean. Do something to help me find my inner peace.

Maybe I'll go to that sunrise yoga I saw on the schedule.

Ha ha ha.

For now, there's this. Music is spilling out of the pub along with the clatter of party voices. There's a sign on an easel outside welcoming us:

GRAB A GLASS, SOLVE A MURDER!

Okeydokey, then.

A British pub is an odd thing to find in this warm clime, but I guess it's in keeping with the colonial theme. It certainly mimics the inside of a real British pub—wood on the walls, beer signs, triangular plastic flags hanging from the ceilings, and a mahogany bar with a brass railing. There's a bunch of British beers on tap, and the menu is classic pub food—fish and chips, ploughman's platters, and cottage pie. Not the kind of food I want to eat when it's this hot, but the gin and tonic the nice Bahamian man behind the bar makes me hits the spot.

I rest my back against the railing and take in the crowd as Oliver spots someone he knows and goes to join them.

All of the main characters are here, along with the members of the various small groups. It's noisy and everyone seems happy.

Except for me.

Okay, there are probably other people who aren't that happy.

They're probably doing a better job of hiding it.

"Having fun?" Vicki asks as she approaches with a glass of Prosecco in hand. Her English-rose skin already glows with too much sun. She's wearing a pretty light blue wrap dress and looks happy and relaxed, a nice change from her perpetual half frown as she frets over her roster of authors.

"I was just thinking I wasn't. But I should be."

"What happened?"

"The usual." I take a sip of my drink as I scan the room again. Elizabeth is sitting in a corner booth with Sandrine and Harper. She's drinking a cocktail filled with citrus while Sandrine monopolizes the conversation.

Not that I can hear them from here. It's just what Sandrine always does.

Which reminds me.

"Has Elizabeth said anything to you about a blurb I was supposed to give her?"

Vicki's hand lowers slowly. "You forgot to blurb Elizabeth?"

"No. I mean, maybe?"

"Which is it?"

"Harper forgot to remind me."

"Good Lord."

"I'm sorry."

"Has she said anything?" Vicki asks.

"No. Is it too late?"

She nods slowly. "We went to press last week."

My heart thumps in relief. "It's not like my blurb is important. I mean, she's *Elizabeth Ben*! She doesn't need me to sell her book."

"Her sales have been soft lately."

I almost choke on my drink. "What?"

"Her last two only sold ten thousand copies."

"How can that be?"

"Tastes change. She's not big on TikTok. Maybe marketing fumbled the bag. Take your pick." She finishes her glass. "What did *you* think of the book?"

To be honest or not to be honest?

"I didn't finish it."

"Where did you stop?"

"About 20 percent in?" Okay, it was 11 percent. Yes, I remember looking at my Kindle earlier. Still can't remember anything about the book, though.

"Can you be more specific?" Vicki says.

"Is this a test?"

"Humor me."

"Honestly? I can't remember anything about it."

Vicki sighs. "That's the problem."

"What? It's not just me?"

She leans closer. "I think it's the end."

"She's dying?"

"Of her career. She just turned in *Sandoval's Last Case* and it's a mess."

"She's ending the series? That should make waves."

"Not if no one cares."

Ouch. Does that happen? Do people read book after book in a series and then stop caring about what happens to the characters?

Yes, yes. I know it does. But *I* write a series. Yep, making it about me again.

"There must be a way to save it."

Vicki shakes her head. "I've tried to talk to her, but it's delicate."

"What about what Patterson does? Have her come up with the outline and have someone else write it."

"I've tried that. I even hired someone to work with her. A nice young man with a fresh MFA looking to break in. Full of enthusiasm. But it didn't make a difference."

"So, what's going to happen?"

"There's an extremely uncomfortable conversation in my future."

"I'm sorry, Vic."

She drains her glass. "Comes with the territory. But I wouldn't count on her blurbing you."

"She never has. It's fine."

"She said she would this time. I sent her the book."

I sink in my seat. "Oh, that makes me feel extra bad."

She pats my hand. "You ready for your release?"

I give her a bright smile. "Of course. All I have to do is get out of here alive."

"Do not joke about that."

I bite my lip. "What about Oli?"

"What about him?"

"I know I shouldn't ask, but are you going to make an offer on his manuscript?"

Her eyes darken. "No, you shouldn't ask." She motions to the bartender behind me for a refill. "El, I love you, but please don't put me between you."

"I'm sorry."

"It's all right. I know it must be . . . complicated for you."

"He's very supportive. He wants me to succeed."

"You're a very nice girlfriend."

"What do you mean?"

"*Something Borrowed, Blue or Murdered*? The one you owe me copyedits on?"

"That wasn't a favor to Oli."

She winks at me as she picks up her glass of Champagne. "Between us."

I feel a bit sick, searching around for Oli to make sure he hasn't overheard anything Vicki just said. He's still talking to the man who must be from his small group and blissfully unaware.

Not so for Connor, who, it turns out, is disturbingly close to where I'm standing and is smiling at me like he overheard our entire conversation.

He should come with a warning bell.

Or a klaxon.

"I should mingle," I say to Vicki.

"Course."

I walk away from her feeling seasick. Is Vicki right? Did I suggest to Oliver that we write a book together to help his career?

Okay, okay, yes, I did. But he's an amazing writer who deserves more recognition. And I'm not just saying that because he can do things with his mouth that make me blush even now. He has better reviews than I do, even if his sales are lackluster. It's hard being in the same business as your lover, and I should've kept my mouth shut because I didn't want to know what I asked Vicki.

So why did you ask, then, El?

I should probably tell him. Secrets between us are never a good idea. But I'll do that later. Right now I need to put things right with Elizabeth without blurting out that I know *her* career might be over. So, this is going to be tricky.

I gulp my drink to steady my nerves.

Oh, wait, wasn't I supposed to stop drinking? I guess that's a tomorrow problem.

I make my way through the crowd to her table. Harper and Sandrine are still there, even though Elizabeth looks bored AF about whatever they're talking about.

I stand there, waiting for her to notice me as a sense of betrayal works its way through me. What's Harper doing hanging around with Sandrine? They've known each other almost as long as I've known Sandrine, of course, but she's supposed to be on my side in all things, including broken friendships.

"El," Sandrine says. "Whatever are you doing standing there like that? *Lurking*."

Something in me snaps. "*Laissez-faire*, Sandrine."

She reacts the way I hoped she would. She knows that when I speak to her in French, it's the equivalent of a parent using a middle name.

But will she play along?

She appraises me for a minute, then gives me a slight nod of the head. "*D'accord.*"

Sandrine doesn't want to mess with me right now. Not if she doesn't want me spilling some of her deep, dark secrets to her spouse.

Yeah, I *would* go there. If pushed.

Sandrine stands, and Harper follows suit. It's my turn to give her a confused look as she shrugs and follows Sandrine.

I'll deal with that later.

"Do you mind if I sit?" I ask Elizabeth.

"Be my guest."

Was that sarcastic? Hard to tell over the din of the party. Elizabeth speaks in one of those voices that easily gets lost in ambient noise.

But in for a penny.

I sit next to her. "I wanted to apologize."

"Whatever for, my dear?"

"I owe you a blurb. I don't know how I forgot, but—"

"You've been very busy these last six months."

God, she knows about that? I shouldn't be surprised, though. Feels like everyone does.

"It's been a lot. But it's no excuse. You did me the honor of asking me to blurb your wonderful book, and I spaced. But I'm going to make it up to you. I'm going to blab about it all over the internet."

She pats me on the hand. "Thank you, dear, but that's not necessary."

"It's the least I could do. I still remember how nice you were to me at the beginning of my career."

"Was I?"

"You were. You took the time to tell me all about the business, and you must get asked to do that all the time. I don't think I've ever thanked you for that properly either. So thank you. Thank you so much."

"This business," Elizabeth says with a glint in her eye. "It makes liars of us all."

"Oh, I . . . I was telling the truth."

"I know you were, my dear, and it is very endearing." She stares off into the middle distance for a moment, then returns. "Tell me . . . Did Abishek suffer?"

"Pardon?"

"When he died . . . You were there, weren't you?"

My throat goes dry remembering. "Yes, I was. You knew him?"

"I did."

"Of course. I knew that. We even all met at the same conference." She gives me a tight smile. "So long ago, when I still felt young."

"You *are* still—"

"No." She stops me, then pats my hand again like I'm a puppy. "Time comes for us all. Now run off and find that extremely attractive man of yours."

"Oliver can take care of himself."

"I meant Connor." She suggestively raises her eyebrows.

"We're not together."

She pats my hand again. And she doesn't have to say it.

Whatever you say, my dear.

I pick up my drink. "Can I get you anything?"

"A time machine perhaps."

"Whatever for?"

"You'll understand when your best days are behind you."

Tears spring to my eyes, and there's nothing I can say to that. So, instead, I kiss her on the cheek. Her skin feels papery, dried out. She smells like the same perfume my grandmother wore.

"What was that for?" She touches her cheek.

"You can do whatever you want. Still. You're the best there ever was."

"Don't flatter me, girl."

"I'm not. If you know me at all, you know I'm bad at dissembling. I wouldn't be here if it wasn't for you. None of us would."

"Thank you for saying that. And now do run along. You wouldn't want to miss the next part."

I'm not quite sure what she means, but I leave anyway.

As I weave my way back through the crowd toward a drink I shouldn't have, it occurs to me that I haven't found whoever it was Cathy said was looking for me. My eyes travel the room again. Officer Rolle isn't here. Neither is Inspector Tucci. I still need to talk to him. Just to dot the i's and cross the t's about how he got here.

Not that I think Inspector Tucci would leave me threatening notes.

Not grammatically correct ones, anyway.

But before all of that, it looks like I have to have a little meetup with Ravi Botha. He approaches me like a shark moving through a flat body of water.

"I'd watch your back," he says as he grazes past me without stopping.

And despite the heat in this room, I shiver.

Shit like this is why I'm still drinking.

CHAPTER 9

Shouldn't You Have Just Said If You Wanted Me Dead?

I grab Ravi's arm just before he's out of reach.

"Did you just threaten me?"

He pulls back. "I did nothing of the sort. Sandrine was right about you."

"Sandrine is a snake. I'd be careful."

"She told me you'd say that."

"Isn't that nice? I'm sure someone who turned on one of her best friends is super trustworthy."

Ravi's eyes narrow. "You stole her book idea."

"Did I?"

"She said."

"I know what she said, but what do *you* think? Does that seem like something *I'd* do?"

"I believe you are capable of anything."

I shake my head slowly. I think I know where this is coming from. "I'm sorry for your loss, Ravi. Truly. Shek was very nice to me at the beginning of my career, and there's a big hole in the mystery community since his death. I'm sure he'd be touched that you've stepped in to take his place."

"He died because of *you*."

I hold my ground. "No, he died because he got involved in something he shouldn't have. I was almost killed, too. More than once."

"You would say that."

I put my hand on his arm. He starts to recoil, but I hold on. "I *am* saying that. Is this what Shek would've wanted? Us squabbling? Can't we be friends?"

"Friends?"

"Yes, you know, book friends. I'll repost your releases on Instagram and blurb your next book."

"I don't think so."

"I don't know what else to say."

"What's all this?" Sandrine says, coming up behind me. "Are you in danger, Ravi?"

I turn on her. Harper's standing next to her, her cheeks red, her face glowing from the heat or the alcohol or the thrill of hanging out with someone I despise, maybe all three.

"Why would Ravi be in any danger from me?"

She shares a glance with Harper.

Have I mentioned that I *hate it* when people do that?

"Has she read the book?" Sandrine asks Harper.

"Don't think so."

"*What* book?"

Harper's eyes meet mine, and I think there's an apology in them, but honestly? Who knows. "Ravi's continuation of Shek's series."

I get a nervous feeling in the pit of my stomach. Ravi seems entirely unconcerned, but I wish I hadn't cast aside the copy of his book Vicki sent me. In my defense (am I on trial?—feels like it), I get sent so many books I never asked for I can't read all of them.

"Why do you want to know if I've read it?"

"It's about a bunch of authors who go on a book tour and then one of them ends up dead," Harper says.

"Okay, I knew that."

"A character named Leonora Bash did it. She writes pulpy mysteries."

"Seriously?"

"Deadly."

I turn to Ravi. "So you wrote a book based on something that happened to your brother and made *me* the murderer?"

How come no one told me? How come no one *warned* me?

"Is that all of it?" I ask Harper when Ravi says nothing.

"She's also involved with a sketchy detective who wears stupid hats."

"Awesome."

"My book has nothing to do with you."

"Tell yourself whatever you need to." I think it over, wondering if I can do anything about it, but I know I can't. If he changed enough details to make the fictional me not me, I'm shit out of luck.

Not that I would sue him even if I could.

I don't need to call attention to whatever he's written about me.

But, wait. Did Vicki send me a copy of the book so she didn't have to tell me I was the murderer?

What did she say before? She already had one uncomfortable conversation coming up. Maybe two if you counted her turning down Oliver's manuscript. So, a little light parody of one of her other authors probably wasn't high on her list of priorities.

"Is this why you came to the conference?" I say to Ravi. "To tell me off? To gloat?"

"I received an invitation to a prestigious mystery conventions, and you want to make it about *you*?"

"She does that."

"Shut it, Sandrine."

"Mature as always."

I've had enough of this conversation. I search around the room for some escape hatch, by which I mean Oliver, but he's been swallowed up by the crowd.

But I don't have to stay. I can leave.

Run away. Whatever you want to call it. I don't even have to say goodbye.

I turn around and start walking, passing snippets of conversation as I make for the exit.

"—*Yellowface* had a brilliant opening, but there wasn't any twist in the third act."

"But that was the *point*. You missed the whole thing—"

"—I heard that this resort is owned by the Mafia. Do you think the organizers knew that?"

"Don't be ridiculous, Maureen. There's no *Mafia* in the Bahamas."

"—Have you seen the resort next door? Chef's kiss."

"I *will* be complaining on my comment card. There weren't even fresh towels in my room!"

"—Nothing's been as good as *When in Rome*. I know they broke up, but Connor brought out something in Eleanor that's been missing ever since."

"100 percent."

I almost stop because, for God's sake, is everyone a literary critic now?

I mean, yes, of course they are, but it's one thing to graze past a negative review online, and quite another to hear it in person.

But if I've learned one thing in this business, it's this: never engage with a bad review.

You can write that down, too.

I burst through the doors and suck in the night air. It's humid out, my hair frizzing instantly in the heat as I grab the porch railing for support.

I feel like I've escaped a room where everyone hates me. Oh, wait, that was high school.

Ha.

I'm being melodramatic, but it's been a day. I can feel the bad thoughts pressing in all around me. Bad intentions, too.

I should've listened to Oliver when he said it was a bad idea to leave Los Angeles.

But there's a reason every one of my books is set on vacation. It's not just because it's fun to write about incredible vistas and sand between your toes.

I need it. The travel. Leaving behind whatever version of myself is driving me crazy for long enough to feel renewed and then returning to my life of yoga pants and daily word counts.

But Oliver was right. And now we're stuck here because of some solar storm. I can feel the danger. Like a charge in the air that could cause a spark at any moment.

I'm pulled to the water. There's a lighted path leading down to it, the lights on even though it's not dark yet. The sun is sinking through the horizon quickly, the way it always does at the end of the day in the tropics. Draining like it can't wait to go to sleep.

I get to the edge of the path and take off my sandals. I let my feet sink into the soft sand and walk slowly toward the water. When I get to the end of the beach, I stand there, letting the waves crash against my toes, covering my feet. There's nothing better than this feeling.

It calms me. Makes me see reason when my brain is a riot of thoughts.

It also drowns out the external noise, which is why I don't hear anyone approaching until the hand on my shoulder makes me jump right out of my skin.

I turn around, clutching at my chest like I might have to start my heart up again.

"Inspector Tucci!"

"I am sorry to have frightened you."

"What are you doing here?"

He gestures vaguely. "I am, how do you say, investigating."

"On the beach?"

"On the property."

"Why?"

"A dead body was found, was it not? In *your* room, I believe?"

"Wait. How did you hear about that?"

"I am a *detective*, Ms. Dash. Nothing gets by me."

Hmmm.

So much to say.

No point in saying any of it.

"The official word is that it was a suicide."

"I heard that."

I take a slow breath. My heart is racing like a race car. Galloping like a horse. No, that's not a good analogy.

You get it. My heart is beating fast.

"I still don't get what you're doing other than scaring people on the beach."

He smiles at me. I can't tell if it's friendly or not. "Tell me, how did you come to this conference?"

"I was invited."

"Yes, but why?"

"I get invited to a lot of conferences. And my editor's on the selection panel. Why?"

"And myself. Why was *I* invited?"

"That's a good question. Why were you invited?"

"I was told by my *capitano* to come here."

"What does that mean?"

"The invitation was extended. My boss, as you would call him, advised me that I would be attending."

"You keep saying this as if it's significant, but I'm not getting it."

He nods his head in a way that indicates that he's not surprised that I'm puzzled.

I sigh internally. This is the way that Inspector Tucci works. In riddles and puzzles. Also with lots of mistakes and missteps.

"I was told to keep my attendance quiet," Inspector Tucci says.

"Why?"

"Perhaps they thought *you* would not attend if you knew I would be here."

"Why would anyone care if I was coming to this conference? I mean, I was already coming. It's been on my agenda for months."

"You could have changed your mind."

"I . . . Why?"

"Tragedy seems to follow you."

I try to smile. "I've noticed."

"You have not caught my meaning?"

"No."

"You are missing one crucial fact, of course."

"Naturally." I pause to wait. Why am I constantly surrounded by drama queens?[45] "Are you going to tell me, or was that simply a statement of fact?"

"What have you discovered about the man who died?"

"He was fired yesterday."

"Yes, but why?"

"Guy told us that he'd been found in a guest's room. That he was stealing things."

"And did you believe that?"

"Why wouldn't I?"

He cocks his head to the side. "It is a convenient story, no?"

"That's not what happened?"

"What do you think?"

It's wrong that I want to kill this man, yes?

"Just spit it out, Tucci, for fuck's sake."

"I am not familiar with this term."

"Pretty sure you can figure it out from context." The waves crash into my feet as the sun dips lower on the horizon. I can't believe I'm pushing Inspector Tucci to tell me something I doubt I want to know.

But when has acting reasonably ever been my course of action?

---

[45] Yes, I'm including myself in that.

"He did not steal anything from someone's room. He stole, how do you say, *information*."

"Information about who?"

"Among others . . . *you*."

Sigh.

I should've seen this coming.

You did, right?

I'm losing my touch. Maybe with reality.

It feels like the time for a dramatic pause.

So, see you on the flip side.

CHAPTER 10

If Your World Tilts Sideways, Do You Fall Off?

"What information about me?" I ask Inspector Tucci.

"I do not know yet. My source did not want to say too much."

"Your source."

"Yes."

"Who is it?"

"That does not matter."

This man is infuriating. "Of course it matters. How can I know if what you're saying is trustworthy if I don't know where it's coming from?"

He stands up straighter. "It is coming from *me*."

"You can understand why that doesn't give me much comfort."

"You have always misunderstood me, Ms. Dash. I am not your enemy."

"You did want to put me in jail."

"And yet here you are." He raises his hand to his chin. "I am not the one who took up with criminals. Who continues to cavort with them."

"'Cavort'? Seriously?" I take in a deep breath. There's no point in arguing with Inspector Tucci. And it's distracting me from the point of this conversation. "Why would the dead man want information about me?"

"His name was Brian."

I see a flash of his face. He looked young, innocent, and very dead. "Why would Brian want information about me?".

"I believe that he was looking for information to blackmail guests with."

"Based on?"

"He would not have been killed for some petty thefts."

"He was *killed*?"

Even though I was sure this was the case, it still has the capacity to take me by surprise.

Murder is like that. You never expect it.[46]

"I am fairly certain," Inspector Tucci says. "For instance . . . the resort—it did not even inform the police of the thefts."

"That's interesting, though there could've been other reasons for that."

"Such as?"

"Maybe they didn't want to destroy his life."

Inspector Tucci scratches his chin. "That is possible, I suppose. But it does not change the fact that he was searching for information."

I think it through, but it doesn't add up. "What information could he find out about me in the computer system? I hadn't even registered yet. And Harper made the room reservation, or the conference did. It was public information that I was coming to the resort."

"Your room assignment, for one."

That stops me for a second. "But that wouldn't be hard to figure out once I got here. All he'd have to do was ask around or follow me, if it came to that."

"What if he wanted access to your room *before* you arrived?"

"Why?"

"To plant a listening device."

---

[46] Just like the Spanish Inquisition.

My blood runs cold. Is there anything more violating than knowing someone's listening when you think you're alone? Safe?

Okay, sure, there are worse things, but you get what I mean.

"Is this all speculation, or did your source tell you this, too, Tucci?"

"It is basic deductive reasoning."

"So this man, Brian, was trying to get information on me to blackmail me? About what?"

"You tell me."

"That can't be it. Maybe some of the other guests, the ones before me. But if he wanted access to my room, it was for some other reason."

Inspector Tucci purses his lips. "To keep tabs on you, perhaps. To know your comings and goings."

"But if that's the case, then why kill him? I'm assuming you're saying he was working with someone else."

"Yes, that must be true."

"Someone who killed him *in my room* to keep him from revealing something."

"Yes."

"Before I even got here."

"Yes."

"Are you hearing yourself?" I say. "That doesn't track at all."

"If you will just consider . . ."

I put up my hand to stop him. "No, Tucci. I know the impulse to make it seem like there's something nefarious going on when weird things happen. Believe me. But sometimes people do things we can't understand. It doesn't mean they're trying to harm someone else. Whatever he was doing, he was caught. Maybe he felt trapped. Maybe he didn't believe they wouldn't go to the police. So, he took the only way out he could think of. Perhaps he wanted to cause embarrassment or damage to the hotel. But it doesn't have anything to do with me."

Inspector Tucci considers me calmly. "Are you so sure of that, Ms. Dash?"

I'm not. I'm not sure at all. But expressing opinions with extreme confidence has worked for men for centuries, so I'm giving it a try.

How'm I doing?

I turn to walk away.

"Where are you going?"

"It's dinnertime. I'm hungry."

"I will accompany you."

"I'm fine.

I start to leave again, but his voice catches up to me.

"There is one more thing, Ms. Dash. His gun."

I stop, my toes digging into the sand. "What about it?"

"Where did he get it?"

"People have guns."

"No, Ms. Dash. Not in the Bahamas, they don't. It is against the law to own any kind of firearm here."

I turn around slowly. "But there must still be guns."

"I'm sure there are. But this is not America, where you can buy a gun at a—how do you call it?—a Wal-*Mart*. That fact alone should have you questioning what you think you know."

"I . . ."

"And it is not the first time that someone has had an unaccounted-for gun in your life."

"What are you talking about?"

"Mr. Charles, in Italy. Do you remember? Where did it come from?"

I stare at him, wishing I could see inside the cogs of his brain. Is he playing with me or trying to help me? I can't tell the difference.

"Didn't Guy tell you?"

"I was prevented from interrogating him."

This is news to me. "Why is this the first I'm hearing about this?"

"I cannot answer that, Ms. Dash. But I would warn you. He has some level of protection that I only see in certain circles. Do you know what I mean?"

"You mean the Mafia."

"Precisely."

"But there's no Mafia in the Bahamas."

He blinks at me with a slow smile that makes that tingle start at the back of my brain again. "Are you so certain of that, too?"

I stumble away from Tucci and back to the resort.

It seems deserted, the lights inside the pool highlighting the tranquil water, a bartender wiping down the counter without any customers. The pink snack truck is boarded up, and it occurs to me that this entire place has been rented out for the conference.

So I know where everyone is. Or at least, where they should be.

And yet still, I hesitate. Because I've felt this way before.

Standing outside a door I know will change my life if I walk through. That's how I feel right now. Like I'm in a *Sliding Doors* version of my life.

I could turn and leave and then I'd have one version. Or I can go where I'm expected and another will unfold. That's true for everyone's life. It's not predetermined. Every step is a choice. Only some choices are harder to make than others.

And if I walk away, where am I going to go?

"What are you doing outside here all by yourself?"

I jump scare for the second time tonight. When I get home, I'm having a thorough cardiac assessment.

A man with a dark face and a crisp blue shirt steps out of the shadows.

"Officer Rolle! I wasn't expecting you."

"While I have been looking for you."

"You have? Why?"

"We have the results of the pathology reports and I wanted to let you know the results."

"So soon? Guy said it would be forty-eight hours."

"I'm afraid Mr. Charles doesn't know our local procedures."

"Yes, of course."

"Are you not curious about the results?"

"It wasn't suicide?"

He looks grim. "It was not."

"How do they know?"

"The angle of the wound, for one. It would be extremely unlikely for someone to shoot themselves at that angle. And then there is the fact that he is left-handed and the shot is to his right temple."

"No *way*."

"Why are you so surprised?"

"Sorry, it's just . . . isn't that how fake suicides get discovered all the time in movies?"

"I wouldn't know."

"Seems like a basic thing to get right."

His mouth turns grim. "Criminals often make mistakes, I've found. Which is how we catch them."

"Not through detective work?"

"That is important. But usually, the perpetrator of a crime is obvious."

"Do you have a lot of experience in murder?"

"We have over a hundred murders each year. And we are a small island, a small population. So I have a lot of experience, yes."

And yet you were willing to immediately believe it was suicide.

"What was that?"

Oh, was that out loud? I do that sometimes.

Are you thinking I'm an idiot at this point? I *am* mostly an idiot. But I have my moments.

"I'm just puzzled by why you seemed to believe it was a suicide in the first place?"

"It fit the facts as I knew them at the time."

"But not now."

"No, Ms. Dash. Not now. There was also a subdural hematoma on the back of his head. He was hit with something to knock him out, then shot, and the body was staged."

"So it was planned."

"Yes."

"Someone lured him to that room and then killed him."

"That is what fits the facts."

"Why?"

"We will discover the reason."

We stare at one another, and it feels like a contest of wills. "Why did you want to tell me this?"

"It's a matter of courtesy."

"Because it was my room?"

"Precisely."

No, my brain says. That's not it.

"There must be something more than that. It's Oliver and Harper's room as well."

"That is true."

"You found something else, didn't you?" I clench my hands together. "Inspector Tucci mentioned that Brian was trying to get into my room for a reason. That he was targeting me for something."

He's jaw tightens. "Where did he hear this?"

"He wouldn't tell me. But he said he had a source."

"I see."

"So?"

"We did find something when we searched his room. It might be easier to show you." He takes a phone out of his pocket and opens an app. He flicks through some photos and rests on one. He turns the phone to me, and it takes me a minute to figure out what I'm looking it.

Because it's crazy.

Literally. It's a crazy wall. Someone made an actual crazy wall about me. Like with pictures and string and newspaper clippings.

"Are you all right, Ms. Dash?"

"I . . . this was in his room?"

"Yes."

"But it must've taken him a long time to put this together."

"I agree." He looks at me, reaching out a hand to steady me as I sway on the pool patio stones. "When did you agree to come here?"

"A couple of months ago."

It was in the aftermath of everything that happened at Emma's wedding. But the days bled together. The shock, the fever of writing our book, the loss of so many things, the media attention. It was too much. Too much to hold onto the details. The conference seemed like a good idea. To get out of Dodge. To go back to normalcy. To think about something other than myself for a while.

Ha ha ha.

I never do that, right?

That's what you're thinking.

And I get it. All you're hearing are my innermost thoughts and insecurities. But there's more to me than that.

"When was Brian hired?" I ask.

"Also a couple of months ago."

"Where is he from?"

"His application said he lived in New York."

"So he applied for a job here after I confirmed I was attending, and he put up his crazy wall?"

"Yes."

I knew I should've run when I had the chance.

Would've, could've, should've.

Why do people *always* want to kill me?

"How did he know I'd be here? How did he get the job?" I ask.

"We do not have the answers to those questions yet. But we are investigating."

"Was he stalking me?"

"We do not know."

"Why would he want to harm me?"

"We will find out."

"But he's dead. Not me."

"Yes," Officer Rolle says. "I noticed."

"No, I mean . . . If he was here to kill me. If he somehow arranged for me to be here or found out I was coming and got a job here to kill me, then how did he end up dead before I even got here?"

Officer Rolle strokes his chin. "He was working with someone."

"Someone he pissed off?"

"Potentially."

"Who?"

"I suspect you have an idea who."

It doesn't take my brain long to get there. "You mean Guy?"

"He, too, arrived at around the same time. That is . . . suspicious."

"I agree, but everything Guy does is suspicious. And he's known me a long time. Why kill me now?"

"Do you know something, perhaps? Something about his past that he's worried is going to come out?"

Is this what Inspector Tucci was talking about when he mentioned Guy's gun? Was he implying that it was Guy's gun that killed Brian?

That *Guy* was the killer?

And if that's the case, it can only mean one thing.

This fucking play *is* about us.

CHAPTER 11

Is Time Really a Flat Circle?

Have you ever been in one of those moments where time moves at an odd pace?

Like the last days of summer when you're a child. How you milk every second out of the longer days, waiting for the sun to drain from the day, letting the mosquitoes feast on your legs because if you go inside, you have to go to bed, and then it's one day less of freedom.

Or those Sundays when you're an adult. How they can creep by when you're on your own. When you're suffering from the heartbreak of waiting on someone to call. How it all seems like an eternity. How you have to hide your phone sometimes to keep from checking it because you know there won't be the message you're waiting for, and that's too painful to contemplate?

I've felt all those highs and lows and many more in my life, and I'm feeling them all at once at this dinner.

We're in the Mediterranean restaurant. It's another indoor/outdoor space that has frescoes on the cream-washed walls with scenes from the Italian Renaissance and an eclectic mix of French and Greek cuisine on the menu. Classic green beans and tzatziki. Steak and lemon Greek potatoes. Moussaka made with scalloped potatoes. I already know it's not going to taste as good as it smells, but I pointed to something when the polite waiter asked. I doubt I'll be able to eat any of it.

A hundred voices are clattering along with the silverware, but all I can hear is Officer Rolle's warning to me to watch out for myself. Those were his parting words as I left the pool to come here.

I'm sitting between Oliver and Guy. Harper's on the other side of Oliver. Connor, Sandrine, Ravi, Stefano the TikTok guy, and Vicki round out our table, because who else would I be sitting with at this point?

At least I can keep an eye on them.

We're not at the main table tonight—I don't care about that—but I'm not sure how Guy has gone from head of security to a guest.

I could just ask.

I'm asking. I promise.

But first, I'm going to down this glass of what I assume is grog because it tastes like those drinks they used to make at fraternity parties—a mix of every alcohol on hand and fruit punch.

It's gross, but I honestly don't care at this point.

Where was I?

Guy.

Officer Rolle raised some good questions. Questions I asked Guy not that long ago on this day that never seems to end. I accepted Guy's earlier answers, but that was before I saw the photos from Brian's room.

A web I can't unsee. I'm caught in it and I can't get out.

"What are you *really* doing here?" I say to Guy, leaning in close enough that I get a whiff of his aftershave. It's strong and medicinal, and I can't imagine it's meant to attract anyone.

Not that I've ever seen Guy with a member of either sex in a romantic way.

Not that I've ever asked.

Is *he* Sandrine's latest conquest? I've never understood why she doesn't just get divorced, but maybe her husband doesn't care what she gets up to. He's a nice, unassuming man who must know exactly what Sandrine's capable of.

But back to my interrogation.

"Cough it up, Guy. It's time."

Guy takes a sip of his water and puts it down. He's wearing his trademark black T-shirt and pants, the only color in the vibrant tattoos on his arms. "Am I not allowed to eat dinner?"

"You're not part of the conference."

His brown eyes turn to mine with a small sigh. "I thought I should keep an eye on things, given everything."

"So, you're working."

"What else would I be doing?"

"Why always so hostile, Eleanor?" Sandrine says, leaning across Guy. She's got a sneaky smile on her face like she's plotting something, and maybe she is.

My murder? My downfall? To steal my peace?

Mission accomplished. That doesn't mean she doesn't have a point, though.

I *am* generally hostile. It's something I don't like about myself.

"I . . . I'm sorry," I say. "You're right. I received some disturbing news right before dinner and it's getting to me."

I feel Oliver tense next to me. "What?"

Me and my stupid mouth.

"I'll tell you later."

He reaches under the table and takes my hand. "What is it?"

I try to speak quietly so only he hears me, but it's loud in here. "The guy who died in our room had a crazy wall about me."

"A what?" Harper says, her fork clattering against her plate. "Seriously?"

"Officer Rolle showed me a photo." I turn to Guy. He doesn't seem surprised. "You knew about this?"

He turns his hands over to show me his palms. "I was there when they examined his room."

"Is it as bad as it looked in the photo?"

"It wasn't good."

"Fantastic."

"I'll keep you safe," Guy says in a reassuring voice.

"Wait. Is that why you're sitting next to me?"

He tilts his head to the side but doesn't say anything. Guy isn't sentimental, but he's also never been my enemy. Not that I know of.

"Should we be worried?" Oliver asks Guy.

"Obviously, yes, Oli."

"I mean immediately. Tonight. Is there a threat against Eleanor?"

Guy frowns. "I haven't heard anything specific. But given that whoever killed Brian is still on the loose . . ."

"Wait, *what*?" Harper says. "Killed?"

"Did I not tell you that?" I say.

"No. You arrived, sat down, and started drinking."

That tracks.

"Sorry. Officer Rolle just told me. Well, Inspector Tucci said it first, but you know how that goes, anyway, here's what I know . . ."

I fill them in on what I learned from Inspector Tucci and Officer Rolle, and I don't have any trouble capturing their attention. Everyone hears what I have to say, each of their conversations stopping as silence descends on our table.

I've always been good at telling stories.

"Why would this man be stalking you?" Connor asks when I finish. He's wearing a white linen shirt, the first three buttons open, revealing a tawny thatch of chest hair. He's at his most attractive when he's showing concern for someone other than himself.

Which he knows.

"I have no idea."

"Have you ever been to the Bahamas before?" Connor says.

"No."

"Did the man look familiar?"

"Again, no. But it was hard to tell in the circumstances . . ."

"It can't be a coincidence that he died in your room."

"Obviously."

"Something is afoot," Connor says. "And if he *was* killed, then that means a murderer is on the loose."

That stops all of us. Someone here is a murderer.

And by the looks of it, they want to kill me.

The note, the body, the crazy wall, surrounded by enemies, almost drowned. A carousel of fear that I try to push away, but who are we kidding?

Who is it? Who, who, who?

I've spun this roulette wheel before, so I can eliminate some people right off the bat.

It's not Harper. Even if she knew I was about to fire her, that's not a reason to murder me. And she wouldn't do it here. Harper's great at executing detailed instructions, but coming up with plots is not her strong suit. It's why her books don't sell.

Ugh, I know, okay, I *know*. But it's not my fault. And she can't hear me right now. I'm telling *you*.

So it's not Harper.

Or Oli.

I hate how I always have to exclude the people I love the most from the list of people who want me dead.

But now that *that's* over with, let's move on to the real suspects, shall we?

Connor. Sandrine. Guy. Ravi. Cathy. Stefano. Who's said not one word since he joined this table, just stalked everyone with his eyes like he's researching his next TikTok.

That's how you make TikToks, yes?

He seems unlikely as someone who wants to kill me, though.

If *he* ended up dead, then *I'd* be a suspect.

Though I did cut off his NetGalley access from a major publisher. Which is catching. Once you've been banned by one publisher, the others soon find out (don't ask me how, they just *do*), and his entire business model depends on his ability to get early (free) copies of books, so maybe he has more of a motive than I originally thought.

So keep him on the list.

You're keeping a list, yes? No? Start one. I'll wait.

Ready? Let's continue.

Anyway, as much as I hate to admit it, Connor is probably out, too.

Though if I died, I'm sure my books would see a huge surge in sales and he still gets a cut of the money those titles make.

But no. He makes his own money, now. He got a major deal for his books. Plus sold the movie rights. He doesn't need to kill me to make money.

He *does* like planning crimes, though . . .

No, no, it's not him. He has a good life. There's no reason to put that in jeopardy by killing me *and* Brian.

I mean it *could* be him, but I'd put him in the last spot, just below Stefano.

Besides, there are much more obvious suspects.

Like Sandrine. She can plot something like this *and* she hates me. And I have threatened to reveal her secrets in the not too distant past. Before I blocked her and put us both out of our misery.

And Ravi threatened me a couple of hours ago, if today is still today.

And Guy is here on some flimsy made-up excuse, so what is he up to exactly?[47]

"El?"

I turn to Oliver. He has that look on his face that he reserves for when he's worried I've gone completely off the deep end.

---

[47] If I were you, my list would be like this: 1. Sandrine, 2. Ravi, 3. Guy, 4. Stefano, 5. Connor. Oh, wait, I forgot Crazy Cathy. Put her in between Guy and Stefano.

"You okay?"

"Probably not."

He squeezes my hand. "I'll keep you safe."

"I know you'll try." I sigh. "Why does this keep happening? Am I that bad of a person?"

"Maybe it isn't about you," Connor says.

"What's that?"

"Just a theory I'm working on."

"Someone wants to kill me, but it's not about me? How?"

"It could be a strategic move."

"Explain."

He picks up his napkin and wipes a small dot of sauce from the corner of his mouth. "The man who died—he wasn't acting alone. So it's a conspiracy. And in all conspiracies, some calculations are made that aren't always apparent to those outside the conspiracy."

"You should know," Harper says, and part of me wants to clap.

"Exactly," Connor says. "I *do* know. So if you're trying to puzzle this out, Eleanor, which I know you're going to try to do, my advice is, don't."

"Just sit here and wait for the phone to ring, then?"

Like my words have magical powers, Harper's phone buzzes on the table, loud enough to hear despite the chatter.

She picks it up reflexively, then blanches.

"What?"

"I'll tell you later."

"No, tell me now."

She sighs, then leans across Oliver. "He's getting out."

"Who?"

"*Him.* John Hart."

I feel a moment of confusion before the name clicks into place. "What?"

"His parole got approved."

"I thought he got twenty years."

"Our justice system sucks."

My hand grips Oliver's, and it feels like I might pass out.

Because John Hart is the man who killed my parents. When I was eighteen, he drove his drunk ass into their car and ended their lives in an instant.

Mine, too. And Harper's.

He'd gotten twenty years because of how fast he was driving, because it wasn't his first drunk driving offense, and because they also found drugs in his car.

I tried not to think about the fact that it was the drugs that made his sentence longer. That the lives ended weren't enough. I tried not to think about him at all.

I went to the trial, and once the sentence was handed down, I caught his eye in the courtroom and vowed never to think about the man again.

I mostly succeeded because I can put my mind to things when I want to. But why is this coming up now, today?

And why is Connor looking at me sympathetically like he knows exactly who John Hart is? I've never talked to him about Hart.

"Why do you even know this?" I ask Harper.

"I have a Google Alert on his name. I knew he was coming up for parole. I tried to stop it."

"*What?*"

"I went and spoke at his parole hearing."

"Why didn't you—"

A glass clinks at the head table, and all eyes turn toward it.

Elizabeth is clinking the glass. She waits for the room to silence and stands. "I hope everyone is enjoying their meal and that your sessions this afternoon were productive. I, for, one greatly enjoyed my small group—Rope. If you're looking for some extra credit, the writing prompt I gave to my group is on the seating chart outside. As I always say, more writing, more better."

A trickle of laughter runs through the room.

"I wanted to share a tradition that's built up over the years at this festival—telling ghost stories. Because that's what all good murders are about. The ghosts we live with every day. Those things unseen that haunt us. That keep us up at night like a fingernail scratching at a door. That go *bump*."

She gets the frisson she's looking for.

Of course she does. She's the best.

"When I was researching what to talk about, I was reminded of the island's oldest ghost story, its most famous one. That of Blackbeard's ghost. As the kids say—I *know*, right? Well, yes. The fort at Old Nassau was built to withstand him. And it did. It fended off the pirates who attacked from the sea. But there are other enemies to fear. Ones sent here in exile. And this very site is haunted by that terrible man who abdicated the throne of England. Edward VIII. *He* was sent here in shame because of his Nazi sympathies. Instead of tending to his duties, he partied and took it all lightly. An inconsequential man.

"I met him once in France. He was *odious*. But there was a certain group around him, you know the type, brought in by celebrity. Looking for favors. Looking for *his* favor."

She pauses. "Why do I bring this up? Because it's a lesson for all of us. That there are enemies within and we need to stay vigilant against even our friends."

I meet Sandrine's eyes across the table. She's been silent, listening, observing—*plotting?* I wish I knew what it was that she thinks I did to her because the stolen book plot thing is thin.

I can't ask right now, but she holds steady on my gaze, then has the decency to look away.

"But I was speaking about Blackbeard," Elizabeth says. "An interesting fellow. But wait . . . We need the lights off for this part." She gestures to someone on the side of the room—Mark, the hotel manager. As his hand reaches up to flip the switch, I'm about to say something to stop him.

Plunging us into darkness seems risky.

But it's too late. The room is almost inky black, just the silhouettes of people visible.

I have a bad feeling about this.

You?

Elizabeth picks up a small pen light, which she holds under her chin. Her face is illuminated as she speaks.

"Did you know that Blackbeard liked to place slow-burning fuses into his beard and *light them on fire* as he went into battle? His targets would see him standing on the prow, his face aglow, and know that they were done for. What a brilliant man, if I do say so. Evil. But brilliant.

"But that is often true of evil. There's a certain brilliance to it. How else would they get away with it? A stupid criminal is a criminal who gets caught, who leaves clues, who doesn't plan ahead. You cannot *pants* a murder and expect to get away with it."

Against all odds, a weird sense of calm overcomes me as I listen to her melodic voice. I'm safe here. Between Oliver and Guy. Even in darkness. Even if I have an eerie sense of déjà vu, like I've been through this scene before.

Which I have. I've sat in the dark when someone was about to try to kill another person in the room, and it felt like this. That moment of anticipation, like right before it rains. The air shifts, cools, and you can smell it before the first drop hits.

Is that . . .

I turn my head as I feel a rustling behind me; there's the tang of a new scent in the air.

My eyes still haven't adjusted to the dark. But my Spidey senses are working perfectly.

And what they're sensing is freaking me out.

Because as Elizabeth talks of pirates, with all eyes on her, I can feel someone hovering behind me. I flinch reflexively to receive the blow I'm sure they're about to administer.

But that's not what happens.

Instead, the presence behind me eases away as quickly as they came.

I'm safe. Nothing happened. Maybe I imagined it.

I exhale the breath I've been holding.

Elizabeth winds up her ghost story, one I admit I heard nothing of.

The applause starts. The lights come on. And I'm okay. No one hurt me. The hunch I had was a glitch.

Phew.

"Guy? Guy? Are you okay?" Sandrine's voice rises in panic.

Ah, shit.

Oliver pushes past me as he rushes to Guy, who's holding his throat like someone who's choking.

But it's too late. His face is a terrible shade of blue that there's no recovering from.

And all it takes is a moment and one terrible shriek, and then it's over.

Because there's no escaping *this* conclusion about Guy.

He's dead.

First Writing Assignment—Rope

Prompt: What would drive you to murder?

Everyone's always saying there's a book in everyone. I don't think that's true. Writing a book is hard and takes a level of commitment that not everyone has. And maybe they aren't being literal, and what that expression means is that everyone has a story to tell. *That* I believe. Because everyone has had ups and downs and twists and turns and low moments and heights and stakes in their lives.

And also: I think there's a murder in all of us. It just has to be unlocked.

We all have someone we'd kill for. Someone who could drive us over the edge if they tried hard enough. If we thought no one was looking. Like that horrible man in France who invited so many men sexually assault his wife. I bet everyone who knew them says they're good men. That they'd never. But the truth is all they needed was an opportunity. All they needed was to think no one was looking.

So what would drive me to murder? Lots of things, probably. I'd just have to be sure I'd get away with it.

DAY TWO

SATURDAY

CHAPTER 12

Is Downward Dog the Worst Position?

"And breathe out slowly, taking everything in, releasing everything out as you do your sun salutation and flow into downward dog, placing your hands wide, fingers extended. Feel that sand, smell the ocean, what a time to be alive," the yoga instructor says in a melodious voice that matches the tempo of the waves rolling gently into the shore.

It's early. My watch says it's 7:15, but since I'm still on California time, I feel like a two-by-four hit me between the eyes.

And yet here I am doing *yoga* because I couldn't sleep after Guy *died* right next to me last night, and Oliver suggested that yoga might help me to relax.

Um, no.

Putting aside the whole second dead body before the first day of this weekend is over thing, yoga doesn't relax me. Instead, it frees my mind to do what it loves to do the most: act like a hamster on a wheel that's chasing a dangling piece of cheese or whatever the hell it is that hamsters eat.

So, no, yoga *wasn't* a good idea.

And yet here I am in spandex that's making me feel like I've been stuffed into it, in a group of people that likely contains a murderer.

Did you know that once you've committed two murders, you're considered a *serial killer*?

Oh, wait, no, you need to kill or attempt to kill *four* people before you get that label.

Great.

They aren't a serial killer *yet*. Assuming Brian was their first kill (though why I'm assuming that, I have no idea), can we expect two more bodies, or are they going just to quit while they're, um, ahead?

Ha.

No.

Which brings me back to Guy.

Needless to say, no one was interested in ghost stories when we had a real murder to solve.

Not that anyone's said "murder."

The working theory—according to Officer Rolle, who looked *so pleased* to have to come back to the property for the third time and second body that day—is that Guy had a heart attack.

A man in his fifties who hasn't made the best dietary choices in his life in a stressful situation who keels over after a large meal. I get the assumption, I do.

But we know better, don't we?

Because people don't just coincidentally die of heart attacks in these types of situations.

Like how twins are never the answer to a murder mystery.

It's never twins, and it's never a heart attack.

So he was poisoned, and for some reason, the police don't seem that interested in solving it, *even though there's been one murder already*. Instead, Officer Rolle questioned the people at my table for a couple of hours, and most of the conference participants acted like they were in some parlor game. That they'd signed up for one of those fake-murder mystery tours where you're acting out a murder in real time instead of attending a how-to-write-a-perfect-murder-mystery conference.

I guess the two have merged into one. Which I should've seen coming.

Stefano was right in the thick of it, making TikToks about how he had *massive news* to share, but they'd have to come back for the next part because his video was getting too long and he wasn't sure what he was legally allowed to say. Officer Rolle eventually issued him a warning, but unless he confiscates Stefano's phone, he's not going to stop.

I already know him well enough to know that.

Take right now: He's at the yoga class, covertly filming us and narrating who we are. He's several people over from me, so I can only hear snippets.

"...suspect number one... *New York Times*... best works behind her..."

He better not be talking about me.

"And now let's bring up our heart's center and transition into a sun salutation."

The yoga instructor has a perky name, like Cindy or Crystal, and 0 percent body fat. But she also looks happy and peaceful, so I make a half-hearted attempt to mimic her body motion and promise myself for the thousandth time that I'll start stretching more.

"You holding up okay?" Oliver says next to me. He's not a yoga guy, but he is *my* guy, so he came along for the ride or whatever this is.

"I guess? I mean, if the yoga doesn't kill me, then..."

He shakes his head slowly. "Not funny."

"I make jokes to cope with my fears."

"I know."

We share a shy smile, and I flash back to the scene when we arrived back at our room last night. It was close to midnight, and I was keyed up and exhausted, and all I wanted to do was swan dive into my bed. But instead of the crisp white sheets with too many throw pillows I'd imagined, the bed was strewn with rose petals that collected into a large heart in the center. Oliver blanched when he saw them and immediately started clearing them off while I stood there in stunned silence.

Was my proposal interrupted by a murder?

That tracks.

Oliver wouldn't say. He just muttered something about the hotel being confused because we were in the honeymoon suite, and then he locked himself in the bathroom for way longer than it usually takes for him to get ready at night, while I got into my pajamas and took off my makeup like a robot.

But there wasn't any sleeping after that.

I feel like I may never sleep again.

Instead, I crafted fantasy proposal after fantasy proposal where no one was dead and Oliver said romantic things and I said "yes" before he was finished getting the words out.

"I can't believe they didn't question us more," Harper says. Unlike me, she's *very* bendy and has her body folded over in a half-hinge position with her head between her legs. And yet she looks perfectly normal, her face composed, her hair in a perky ponytail.

"I can't believe they think it was a heart attack," Connor says next to her. He's wearing red running shorts that are a little too short and a black tech shirt that you'd wear running.

Only Connor doesn't run unless it's away from responsibility.

"I believe it," Sandrine says, lifting her foot off the ground and holding her hands in a prayer position over her heart. "Guy never turned down a piece of red meat in his life."

"Fat-shaming, nice."

Sandrine shrugs her toned shoulders. She's no stranger to a yoga class. When we were friends, she used to try to convince me to go with her, but after I pretended, once, that it was a pole dancing class and cracked jokes through the whole thing, she stopped asking.

Or the instructor told her I was banned.

Same, same.

"I call them like I see them," Sandrine says. "Unlike you."

"What's that supposed to mean?"

"You've never had an original thought about anything."

"For the love of God, Sandrine, I did *not* steal your book plot."

"So *you* say."

"Explain to me how I did this. I want the details. Which book? Which plot? Which book of *yours*?"

"Ladies!" The yoga instructor claps her hands together loudly. "Please. This is *not* the Zen I was hoping for in this class."

We both mutter "Sorry," and I try to focus on the instructions the instructor gives for the next ten minutes and get into the flow. But it's no use. All I can see is Guy's distended face and the way his eyes accused me before he was removed to the floor and covered with a sheet by the medical tech.

Because *I* was supposed to be the victim.

He drank a poisoned soup that was meant for me.

Metaphorically, I mean.

Soup wasn't on the menu.

I was.

How do I know this?

Well . . . remember that thing back there about how to write a murder and what's supposed to happen in the first act? That technique of showing the reader all the reasons the assembled suspects would want them dead?

That was me, right?

I'm the one with a list of suspects who want me dead.

Sandrine, Stefano, Ravi, Connor, Cathy—I can't even remember which order I placed them in because I'm exhausted . . . If they *all* hate one person, it's me.

But I'm not dead. Maybe there's another explanation.

Maybe it *was* Guy who was the target after all.

Because I'm not believing this heart attack shit for one minute.

I said that before, didn't I?

This is not good. I remember reading once that if you get less than six hours of sleep, you lose ten IQ points for every hour. So if you start with a 120 IQ, for example, and you get no sleep, you are operating at 60, which is somewhere below primate, I believe.

The science might not be exact on this, but I do feel deeply dumb.

Still, I'm going to press on, because remember that thing about hamster-wheel brain that I also mentioned back there?

ANYWAY, bear with me.

Can I make a list of people who hated Guy?

Not that hate is the only motive for murder. There are lots of reasons to kill someone. Greed. Fear. Love. Revenge. But something about this feels personal.

Which means that if Guy was the intended victim, then Connor is suspect number one.

Why is Guy here? Why would he take a job as head of security if it wasn't to get close to me? Was it to get close to Connor? But why?

Brian was blackmailing guests, according to Guy. Or was that Inspector Tucci? Regardless, nothing Guy said is reliable, and for all I know, *he* was Inspector Tucci's source.

Guy doesn't need to spy on Connor to get information to blackmail him with. I'm sure he has more than enough fodder for that.

So what was he up to? Maybe they were working together? Him and Brian, the other dead guy. Right, that makes sense. They're both dead. They have to be connected. But—they're both dead, so there's someone else involved.

So how did it work? I've been fed some facts, but I don't have to accept any of them.

I shouldn't.

Maybe the crazy wall in Brian's room was a distraction put there by Guy to throw everyone off his trail. I didn't get that good a look at it, but there are lots of pictures of me on the internet. It wouldn't be that hard to print some up and post them in Brian's room and make it look like he'd been stalking me.

Guy could've lured Brian to my room to kill him. He could've erased himself from the camera footage. And maybe there's another way into the room so it's not a locked-room murder at all; it just looks like one.

But why would he kill Brian? Was he going to give up the plot? Which was what? To kill Connor? After all this time? Why?

"Breathe, El," Oliver says, touching my arm.

"What?"

"You're bright red. I don't think you've taken a breath in two minutes."

I breathe in slowly, the oxygen flooding my brain. Oliver's right. My heart is racing, and my mind feels like it's about to descend into mania.

"Did you do it?" I say to Connor. He's struggling to stand on one leg while his left foot is resting against his right calf. I'd laugh if I weren't too tired to think straight.

But this. I think I'm right about this.

He gives up trying to balance and lowers his foot to the sand. "Did I do what?"

"Kill Guy."

"What? No."

"I don't believe you."

His eyes look up toward the sky. "This again. You always think I'm up to no good."

"Because you are."

"El, leave it," Oliver says. "We're all tired."

I stare at him for a minute, then pull Oliver aside. "What is going on with you?"

"Nothing."

"No, it's something. Usually, you're right there with me in hating on Connor. But ever since we got here, you've been chill. Why?"

"Don't you think we need to move on from Connor? He's taken up too much space in our relationship."

"I agree."

"I let it go. Him. All of it."

My eyes feel like they're going to bug out of my head. "Like Elsa?"

"What?"

"You know that song from that kids' movie."

"What are you talking about?"

"It doesn't matter. Go on."

Oliver takes my hand and squeezes it. "I found peace with it. He's in your life. He's in mine. Are we going to be best friends? No. But I can't change that, so I'm choosing to accept it and keep it from impacting me."

"Wow."

"You should try it."

"Right. Only . . . what if he killed Guy?"

Oliver frowns. "What evidence do you have for that?"

"He's the only one here with a motive to kill him."

"You sure about that? And what about the other victim?"

"I have an explanation for that. I mean, I think I do."

"I know you're scared." Oliver puts his hands on my shoulders and gazes into my eyes. "We're going to get to the bottom of this."

"Will we?"

"Yes. And in the meantime, I won't let you out of my sight."

"You still think I'm the intended victim?"

"Regardless, we need to figure it out."

"Obvi."

He smiles. "This class blows. Should we get some breakfast?"

"Good idea." I turn toward the rest of the class, all of whom have stopped doing their exercises and are looking at us expectantly. Stefano has his phone facing me at his hip, probably hoping I won't notice he's filming. "All eyes on us, I guess."

"I'd expect nothing less."

And that's where Oliver and I are different. Because he's always expecting the best. In us, in himself, in me.

But me?

I'm always braced for impact.

Act 2

THE THIRD AND FOURTH SEQUENCES

Central Question: How are you going to continue to ratchet up the stakes, tension, and action toward the midpoint of the story?

Third Sequence: The third sequence is where your investigation truly begins. Your protagonist has been drawn out of her usual life and can't ignore the fact that someone in her orbit has been murdered. So, what's a girl to do?

THINGS TO KEEP IN MIND:

A. a. How are you going to raise the stakes for your protagonist? (And it can't *just* be killing someone else.)

B. b. What subplots are you going to employ to keep your murder from sagging?

Fourth Sequence: The fourth sequence ends with the midpoint. This is both literally the middle of your story AND a significant moment where something must occur to change the course of your protagonist's life again.

THINGS TO KEEP IN MIND:

A. a. What twist will you throw in at the midpoint of your murder to keep the reader guessing and turning the pages?

B. b. Your subplots should also all be established at this point.

Final thought (for now): Put as much action on the page as possible. Show, don't tell.

CHAPTER 13

Can I Break My Fast Without Someone Trying to Kill Me?

"Any updates?" I ask Harper thirty minutes later, after I've eaten my way through a tall stack of pancakes drowned in maple syrup and gone back for seconds.

And yes, I had some fruit, too, okay. Geez.

"How would I have updates you don't?"

Okay, tone. But we're all on edge so I'm not going to call it out.

Just to you.

"I mean on John Hart."

Harper's eyes shift guiltily. "Oh."

"I have a lot of questions."

She puts her fork down. "Go ahead."

"Why didn't you tell me about any of this?"

"Because I knew you'd tell me not to involve myself. To stay out of it."

"And that would've been good advice."

"I didn't want to take it, though. You don't understand. I didn't get the trial."

"You think I should've let you go? You were sixteen."

"No, that was the right decision. I was too young. But I needed that closure."

"How is going to a parole hearing closure?" I ask.

As she looks at me, her eyes fill with tears, and I feel like a jerk for bringing this up at all. "I wanted to see what he looked like. What he sounded like. If he was going to say anything about being sorry."

"And?"

"He's just a man in his fifties. Unremarkable."

"And did he say sorry?"

"No."

"And now he's getting out? I'd rather not know that."

Harper bites her lip. "Fair enough."

"And you told *Connor* about all of this?"

"Is that why you're upset?" She glances at Oliver, who's also on his second helping of pancakes because, as he said earlier, he's never said no to a meal, and these pancakes are delicious.

"You don't have to worry about talking about Connor in front of him."

"I don't?"

"No, apparently he's Zen about Connor now."

"Really?"

"Yep. And also, in case you were wondering, we're not talking about the fact that our bed was strewn with rose petals in a heart-shaped pattern last night."

Oliver's fork drops to his plate. "I . . ."

"It's fine. It was the hotel, apparently. So Oliver says anyway, but I'm not sure I believe him."

Harper narrows her eyes at me. "Are you drunk?"

"It's eight a.m. Absolutely not."

"Something's up."

"I haven't slept, and two people are dead. There's half a serial killer on the loose."

"What in the hell?"

"Sorry," I say. "I'm just very, very tired and a little terrified."

"That, I buy."

"So tell me about Connor."

Harper reaches for her coffee. "What about him?"

"Have you been . . . hanging out. Again?"

One of the things I can't erase from my brain is that Harper hooked up with Connor last year. She was feeling low, and I know she regrets it, but I don't think we've ever really processed what it means between us that she slept with one of my exes.

"Not like that. But what does it matter?"

"You know why. Guy is dead. Who else would want to kill him?"

"I have no idea."

"Exactly. Except Connor."

"I don't think so."

I grip the edge of the table. "So it's just a coincidence that Guy and the other dead guy, Brian, arrived here at about the same time, and now Connor's here, and they're both dead?"

Harper shrugs. "Did Connor know Brian?"

"He could have. He used to live in the US. He only arrived in the Bahamas recently."

"You have evidence of a connection between them?"

"Well, no, but . . ."

Harper looks up as Connor walks toward the buffet. He waves to her, then rolls his eyes. She smiles, then looks away.

"This is what I'm talking about," I say. "You and Connor, what is up with *that*?"

"Nothing, we're friendly."

"And you're working for him again?"

"I've been working on book two with him, yes."

Harper worked as a beta reader for Connor on his first manuscript. I hadn't asked for the details about their arrangement when I found out, probably because, I was jealous she was using her editing time on anyone but me.

But like so many things I ignore in my life until it's too late, now that I *am* looking at it, something occurs to me. There was a certain familiarity to Connor's book, and not just because it followed the tried-and-true rom-com formula.

It was well written. Like Emily Henry–level written. *Too* well written for it to be Connor.

"Wait, wait, wait. Are *you* writing his books?"

Harper's eyes slide away from mine. "Why would I do that?"

Oh. My. God. She didn't deny it.

Plus, if someone answers your question with a question, they're covering something up.

"I don't know, but it makes more sense than Connor writing a good rom-com."

She still won't make eye contact, but her cheeks are turning pink like they do when she's pleased. "You read it?"

"I did. It was surprisingly good."

The corner of her mouth turns up, then down again.

Holy shit.

I *knew* it.

Okay, I didn't. But a lot of things make sense now.

"You underestimate him, El."

"Please. I think I have his full measure. But you haven't answered the question."

She finally looks at me. "I didn't write it. I just edited it. Like I do for you. That's what I'm good at, El."

And she is. She's very good at finding the weakness in someone else's work. And yet I don't believe her. But she doesn't want to tell me the truth right now, which is kind of freaking me out. Maybe, if she did write it, Connor got her to sign an ironclad legal agreement with a confidentiality clause.

Connor *loves* his binding legal agreements.[48]

I change topics. "Why did you tell Connor about John Hart?"

---

[48] He'd blackmailed me into signing several when he found out he was starring in my book series.

Her cheeks turn redder. How many secrets does she have from me? No. I don't want to know the answer to that. Everyone has secrets.

Even me.

"He helped me do some research into Hart."

"What kind of research?"

"His life. What he was doing that night."

"Why do you want to know that?"

Harper's voice rises in anguish. "Because we know nothing about him. The only thing is that he killed Mom and Dad. And he never said anything about it. He didn't say it was a mistake. He said he couldn't speak about it at the parole board. He's spent all that time in jail, and he can't come up with a good answer."

"What is there to say? He was drunk. He ran a light. He killed two people."

"I tried googling him and nothing came up except articles about the case. And he wasn't even from LA. There's no explanation of why he was in town. And *then* I found this article about how there was a passenger in his car, a woman, but she's not in the arrest papers, and I can't find anything else out about her."

"This was a long time ago, Harper. Maybe he didn't have a digital footprint. It happens."

"And the woman?"

"If she was the passenger, she didn't do anything wrong. I'd want to keep my name out of it, too. I can't imagine being put in that situation, can you?"

Harper turns her eyes down to the table. I look at Oliver. He's stopped eating and is listening but is wisely staying out of this. Because it's between me and Harper. And if I'm being honest,[49] I'm pretty mad at her right now for bringing John Hart back into my life.

"Connor agrees with me," Harper says. "That it's suspicious."

I take in a slow breath. "Leave it alone, Harper."

---

[49] I feel like I've used this expression more than once, which is a <u>tell</u>.

"Why?"

"Don't we have enough drama right now?" I motion around us. "Why go looking for more of it?"

Harper slumps down in her seat. "You're right."

I stare at the remnants of breakfast. I've lost my appetite.

"Did Connor ever say anything to you about Guy?" Oliver asks Harper.

Harper blinks rapidly. "Like what?"

"How they met? What their business was? If they've been in touch? Why they fell out?" He pauses, then smiles. "For starters."

"I know they met in Europe, but not much more than that."

"Does it say anything in Guy's book?" I ask. "It must."

"I never read it," Harper says.

"Me either."

"I'm sure we can get a copy on Amazon or something, right, Vicki?" Oliver says.

I look up. Vicki's approaching our table with an overfilled plate in one hand and a mimosa in the other. She's wearing a white cotton midi-dress today, with an orange sweater tied over her shoulders. Her outfit says relaxation, but her face is a different story. "A copy of?"

"Guy's book," I supply.

"That poor man. I've never had one of my authors die right in front of me before."

"It's not your fault. But we don't need to read his book, we have you, right, Vick?" I say. "You edited it."

Her lips form a thin line. "I did."

"Not good?"

"Not my decision. Capitalizing at a corporate level. You get it."

Capitalizing on me, she means. And my success. Which was fair game, of course. Only it never sat right with me.

"Sure, but do you remember it?"

"Some."

"Does it say how Guy and Connor met?"

She puts her plate down, then takes a sip of her mimosa. I feel a slight longing for one and check myself. I do not need to add alcohol to the exhaustion I'm already feeling.

"Ask Connor?"

"He's not a reliable witness."

"I wouldn't count on Guy being one either. He was so difficult to fact-check we almost couldn't publish."

"What was the story he was pushing, then?"

"They met in Europe. Connor had just started his detective agency. He needed muscle. Enter Guy."

"So Connor *was* a detective?"

Vicki laughs. "That's what *your* books say."

"Sure, but that was me making him the hero. Reality is different."

Especially where Connor is concerned.

"I think that part is true. Not sure what they specialized in. Guy alluded to some close-to-the-line cases. They were based in London. Then Italy."

"Which is weird, right? Like why are two Americans operating in Italy?"

"Guy is from Montreal," Harper says.

"Canada?"

"Is there another Montreal?"[50]

"So Guy is French?"[51]

"He's Canadian."

---

[50] Why, *yes*, since you asked. There are <u>thirteen</u> places in the world named Montreal! Three in Canada, four in the US, four in Europe, one in Jordan, and <u>one right here in the Bahamas</u>, though it's called Montreal Lane. That's a weird coincidence.

[51] This should not have come as a surprise to me. Guy, pronounced "gi," is a French name, popular in Normandy and brought to England during the Norman invasion. And his last name is Charles, which is the French spelling of the Germanic name Karl. So, very French.

"You know what I meant."

Harper rolls her eyes. "He had a francophone father, English mother."

"He speaks French?" I feel like my voice is rising with each one of these questions.

"Spoke," Harper says.

"You know what I meant."

"He spoke multiple languages, I believe," Vicki says.

"Curioser and curioser."

"Anything else?" Vicki finishes her drink and signals to the waiter to bring her another.

"A bit early for that, no?"

"I'm stressed."

"We all are."

"Not about . . . Yes, that is stressful. It's these meetings in New York."

"What meetings?"

She takes another sip of her drink, finishing it. "The powers that be. They're meeting with the VC. Rumors of cuts are afoot."

"VC?"

"Venture capitalists. They bought the company two years ago."

"They're not cutting you, are they, Vicki?" Harper asks.

"Only time will tell."

"But you have all the bestselling authors," I say.

"And the not-so-bestselling authors."

"Sorry, Vick," Oliver says.

"Oh, Oliver, I didn't mean you."

He nods and looks away. Vicki and I share a glance. I feel bad that I didn't know this and also some panic for me. I've never worked with another editor. Vicki knows me. My highs and lows and how to cajole me when she needs to. She's also a memory palace for the characters in my books. I literally don't know what I'd do without her.

"Anyway," I say quickly, "I'm sure they're not stupid enough to get rid of you, and if you want me to call Simon, I will."

Simon's Vicki's boss.

"That is not necessary. Did you have more questions about Guy?"

"I'm sure there are a million I'm forgetting."

"Did he talk about any enemies in the book?" Oliver asks.

"Not that I recall. But they solved a lot of cases. Put some people in jail. Broke up a lot of marriages. Maybe someone waited till now to take their revenge."

"They'd have to know he was working here," Oliver says. "And it must be one of the attendees because it happened at dinner."

"Or one of the staff," Harper points out.

"*Another* member of the staff who just started working here?" I say.

Oliver nods his head. "Resorts are transient places. I'm sure it's not hard to get a job as one of the waitstaff."

"But then who killed Brian? That wasn't some random waiter."

"True."

"We don't even know if Guy was killed, though," Harper says.

"He definitely was."

"How?"

"Probably poison," I say. "It was sudden . . . Maybe it was in his food?"

"So it *was* one of the waitstaff?" Harper says.

"No, I agree with El," Oliver says. "But the lights were off. Anyone could've dropped something into his plate or drink."

"Yes!" I say. "Sorry, that was loud. But I did feel someone near me in the dark. I just remembered."

"You should tell Officer Rolle," Oliver says.

"I will." I push my plate away. "None of this makes any sense."

"It never does in the beginning."

"Are we at the beginning? Two people dead? Feels like we're in the second act to me. And we're just going on with the conference as if nothing is wrong."

"The financial repercussions of canceling are too great," Vicki says. "And no one at the conference has been harmed."

"Not *yet*."

"I bet half of the participants think it's a stunt," Harper says. "Look at Stefano."

We follow where she's pointing. He's near the buffet, talking into his phone. Has he moved on to suspect number two yet? I should check his TikTok, but that feels like a distraction.

Like this.

Everything we've been discussing. Maybe it's a distraction.

"It does feel like that," I say.

"What do you mean?" Oliver says.

"I can't explain it. But something feels off. Different but familiar."

"You'll figure it out," Vicki says, patting my arm. "You always do."

I appreciate the vote of confidence, but why, though? Why do *I* have to figure anything out? Why can't I just go somewhere nice and not be plagued by unhappiness and murder? What did I do to deserve this?

Okay, okay, I know. I'm making everything about me again. And right after I decided that it wasn't about me, but about Guy and Connor.

But I *am* the star of my own life. We all are. And I have this feeling in my chest. This tight feeling that makes me think something is going to happen at any moment.

I tense up, waiting for something to go BOOM.

But instead, all that happens is Crazy Cathy appears wearing a garish summer dress with lemons all over it.

"Eleanor! Up, up, up. You'll be late for class."

Oliver puts his hand on my back. "I'll go with you."

"You have your own class to teach."

"We could combine them?"

"No, it's all right. I'll be all right."

But how many times does one have to say that to make it true? Is it like Beetlejuice?

Am I the curse or the cure?

Guess we'll find out eventually.

CHAPTER 14

Is This a Trope?

When I get to my classroom at ten on the dot as per the schedule that we are apparently *still* following even though bodies are dropping left and right, everyone is in their places, sitting at attention, the notebooks open to a crisp fresh page.

Well, not everyone. We've been joined by Crazy Cathy, as her coming to find me back there suggests. Apparently she was put into the wrong group yesterday (*can you imagine?*) and insisted that she be moved to my group.

So that happened.

Stefano is back in the first row, and the minute I enter, his hand shoots into the air like an eager fifth grader's. He's wearing a loud Hawaiian shirt whose print is made up of book covers and matching statement glasses I suspect he doesn't need.

I scan his shirt, but none of my book covers are there.[52]

"Yes, Stefano?"

"I assume we'll be spending our time this morning trying to determine whether or not that man was murdered?"

---

[52] Little insider tip: Authors are trained to scan ANY photo or movie or TV scene depicting books for their book cover.

"That was *not* the plan, no."

"But we have to know," one of the unnamed participants says.

"Yes, I agree," another one says, and this sets off the rest of them.

"We can't just sit here and do nothing."

"Wait, that wasn't a *real* murder, was it? It's part of the conference, right?"

"Don't be stupid, Harold."

"I heard he had a heart attack."

"That could be, only it would be a funny coincidence."

"There are no coincidences. Eleanor says that all the time."

"Yes, thank you, Cathy."

She smiles sweetly at me. It's eerie sometimes how much she looks like Kathy Bates in *Misery*. Only this morning, instead of a shapeless tunic with a turtleneck under it, she's wearing a pair of capris and a sleeveless shirt that does, in fact, have one of my book covers on it.[53]

"Well?" Stefano says. "Are we addressing it or not? My audience is waiting for the next installment."

"Of what?"

"My I'm-stuck-at-a-subpar-resort-and-someone's-been-murdered series, obvi."

"So you *have* been filming."

"So?"

"Did you get permission from Officer Rolle?"

"For what? I have the right to *express myself.*"

Do not roll your eyes.

Do. Not. Roll. Your. Eyes.

"Stefano's right," Cathy says. "This is much more interesting than some boring lecture."

I glance down at my carefully prepared lecture notes. Because I might

---

[53] Does it matter which one? Probably not, but it's <u>Amalfi Made Me Do It</u>. Significant? Stay tuned to find out!

seem like I fly by the seat of my pants—and you wouldn't be wrong in thinking that—but when I commit to teaching about writing, I commit. So I have notes, themes, examples.

"What do you suggest, Stefano?"

"Well," he says in an imperious voice, "first we have to investigate the victim."

"Don't we have to decide if there *is* a victim, first?" Sandrine says, because yep, she's changed out of her yoga clothes and slithered into another effortless outfit meant to make me feel frumpy and dowdy and all the things your much cooler ex–best friend can make you feel when you're not on speaking terms.

And yes, if you're curious, I'm sure that's exactly what she was thinking when she chose her carefully tailored white shorts, blue linen shirt, and spotless espadrilles this morning.

"Yes, that would be the—"

"Let's do that, then," Stefano says. "How do we proceed?" He rises and approaches me. "We should use the chalkboard. That's what I've always see done."

"Always see done where?"

"TV, movies."

"That's a trope."

"What's that?" Cathy asks.

"It's a recurring plot device. Like the third-act breakup in romance novels."

"But police use them, too," Stefano says.

"How would you know?" Cathy asks, and I can't help but smile. She's crazy, but she's *my* crazy.

Unless she's finally trying to kill me.

I'm not claiming her then.

"I'd humor him, El," Sandrine says. "Don't want another bad review."

Stefano's eyes darken. "I was just expressing my *personal* opinion. When did that become a crime?"

I grit my teeth. "It's fine, Stefano, no book is for everyone."

"You didn't like one of her books?" Cathy says. "What is wrong with you?"

"Leave it, Cathy."

"I want to hear his case against it. Which book was it?"

"*Amalfi Made Me Do It,*" I say.

"That's not even out yet, and you trashed it?"

"As I said in my review, I felt that the plot was tired and—"

I clear my throat loudly. "I thought you wanted to solve a potential murder?"

His face clouds with confusion. "Yes, of course. Sorry, got carried away."

"Cathy does that to people."

"I was only defending *you*, Eleanor."

"I know, Cathy, thank you. Take a seat, Stefano."

He returns reluctantly to his seat, and I wait for a minute, because fuck it. If I'm doing this, I'm doing this, you know?

Dramatic pauses and all.

I pick up a piece of chalk and shiver. Something about the feel of it, the feel of *this*, is ringing alarm bells.

I write "Guy Charles, 55" on the chalkboard. I'm not sure of his exact age, but fifty-five is close enough and unlikely to be related to why he's currently lying in a refrigerated room waiting to be dissected.

Sorry, that went dark there for a moment.

"Can I film this?" Stefano asks.

"How about you not for now? I'm sure you'll audience will survive without constant updates."

"But my views. You don't understand how the algorithm works. You have to keep feeding it or—"

"What's more important? Your TikTok Creator Fund money or solving this murder?"

"So it *is* a murder," Sandrine says.

I grit my teeth. "I didn't say that. Anyway, Guy. What do we know about him?"

"He worked with Connor Smith!"

"Yes, thank you, Cathy."

I write "Connor Smith" on the chalkboard.

What are three things I know about Guy? I write them down on the chalkboard.

1. *Born in Montreal, Canada. Speaks English, French, and other languages.*
2. *Worked as a detective in the UK and Italy with Connor for ten years. Worked both sides of the law.*
3. *Wrote a book called* The Guy Behind the Man in Rome.

What else? Turns out I know more than three things about him.

4. *Began working at Footprints six weeks ago.*
5. *May be in a relationship with Sandrine.*

"Wait, what?" Sandrine says. "That's slanderous."

"You didn't deny it."

"Eleanor, please. Be serious."

"Fine."

6. ~~5. May be in a relationship with Sandrine.~~
7. *5. Knows Sandrine, was in contact with her before the conference, suggested she attend.*

"Happy?"

I'm met with silence.

8. *Knows how to get a gun into a country illegally.*
9. *Knows people high up in Italy—wasn't interrogated when he should've been about his gun.*

"What is all this about Italy?" Stefano says. "Aren't we in the Bahamas?"

"Obviously."

"Well, then?"

"I'm putting down everything I know about Guy. This is what I know about him."

"What does it mean, though?"

"That he's sus."

"Talking in Gen Z now, El?" Sandrine says. "*Mon dieu.*"

I don't turn around. Instead, I look at the words on the chalkboard.

So many things I know about Guy relate back to when I met him and Connor in Italy and we solved a series of robberies and a murder that I memorialized in *When in Rome.* That story wasn't over, as I found out when I went to Italy for my tenth-anniversary book tour six months ago, because murder has roots and murder leaves traces and murder will out. But that doesn't mean it's relevant to what's happening here.

What we need to determine is what he was doing in the Bahamas. That will be the solution.

Remember that.

I turn around. "Does anyone know why Guy was in the Bahamas? Sandrine?"

"Why would *I* know?"

"Because you've been in touch with him?"

"You keep saying that, but what is your evidence?"

"Guy."

"Please. That man was *not* trustworthy."

"So how did you end up at this conference, then?"

"I thought we were investigating *Guy*, not *moi.*"

I sigh. Having Sandrine here is like being trapped with your ex-boyfriend on vacation.

Which I *also* am.

"Moving on. Another thing we need to determine is whether he was murdered," I say, tossing the chalk up and down in my hand.

"I thought we were assuming that?" Stefano says.

"Yes, but what's our evidence?"

"Um, he's *D-E-A-D*."

"People do die, even suddenly."

"If it was a murder, how could it have been done?" Cathy says.

"The lights were turned off—that was deliberate," Stefano says.

"Or someone used it as a cover," I suggest.

"Was he stabbed?"

"No, Stefano, *imbécile*," Sandrine says. "There wasn't any blood."

"I wasn't close enough to see."

"Why would you want to be close enough to see?"

"I'm just saying . . ."

"Well," I say, "you were at our table, so you definitely were close enough. Unless . . . were you filming? Is there a TikTok of Guy's . . . uh . . . death?"

"I was filming Elizabeth's speech."

"That's all? Your phone didn't wander?"

"You can check for yourself. I stopped filming when the lights came up."

I make a mental note to check his TikTok.

"If we're done with that," Sandrine says, "the only thing that makes sense is poison, given the way he looked and how suddenly he died."

"That's the name of *our* group," Cathy says.

"So, the murderer is in this room?" Stefano says.

Sandrine's chin lifts in a way it does when she's been personally insulted. "Why would they be stupid enough to murder someone in the way their group is named?"

"Murderers are stupid," I find myself saying. "That's how they get caught."

I shiver. Someone else has already said that to me on this trip. Too many things are repeating. Like an echo. Or wait, maybe that's a bad analogy. An echo is distorted, right?

No, it's an imitation or repetition of a sound. But this was a soundless murder.

My God, I need a nap.

"What do you think, Eleanor?" Cathy asks.

"I agree that if he was murdered, he must've been poisoned. There was no blood and he died suddenly. So how do you poison someone?"

"In his food?" one of the participants suggest.

"I didn't see him eat right before it happened," Sandrine says.

"Me either," Stefano adds.

"I thought you were filming?"

"Well, yes, but before that. Anyway, he was talking to *you*. What were you talking about?"

"That's not relevant."

"We can't know that at this point," Stefano says. "We have to assume *everything* is relevant."

Ugh. He's right. What were Guy and I talking about? I'll have to search the memory tape for that one. But in the meantime . . . "Let's focus on the task at hand, shall we? Poison. Any thoughts there?"

"Maybe it was a slow-acting poison and it was given earlier in the day," Cathy says.

"Do those exist?" one of the men says.

"You know they do, Harold," the woman sitting next to him says. "Remember? That's how someone in your third book dies."

"According to Google," Stefano says, holding up his phone, "the classic form of a slow-acting poison is lead."

"He wasn't killed with lead, surely," I say.

"What about polonium?" Cathy says.

"The one the Russians use? Very dangerous to transport. I'd rule that out," Sandrine says.

"Sucrose is a poison," Stefano says. "It says here that even Poirot wouldn't have been able to figure it out."

Sandrine reads over his shoulder. "Because it's what made Poirot fat. It was a self-poisoning."

"Like alcohol."

"What's that, El?" Cathy says.

"Nothing. Anything more likely to be used?"

"Someone has helpfully made a list," Stefano said. "How did people write books before the Internet?"

Excellent question.

"What's on it?"

"Arsenic, belladonna, botulinum, cyanide."

"That last one acts quickly," Cathy says. "And don't you end up foaming blue at the mouth? Is that how Guy looked, Eleanor? You got a good look, didn't you?"

"Too good."

"So?"

"I don't think so. And I don't think this is productive, after all. There are many ways to poison a person, and it didn't have to be when the lights were out, though those two events juxtaposed together are too much of a coincidence. So, I'd assume it was a fast-acting poison administered in the dark by someone who took advantage of it or knew it was going to happen."

"How would they know?" Stefano says.

"I don't know, but I'd guess they'd need to have proximity to him. And no, I didn't do it, but I did hear someone near me when the lights were out."

"Interesting," Sandrine says. "So it could've been anyone at the tables nearby or a waiter or one of the other staff."

"Who was sitting at *your* table?" Cathy says. "They should be on the list."

"And the table next to it," the woman who spoke before says, her voice tumbling out quickly. "How long were the lights out? It felt like a long time, but that's because I'm scared of the dark."

"Figures you would be," Harold says.

"Enough out of you, Harold."

"Let's keep these two apart, shall we, so there isn't another body," Sandrine says. "What we really have to figure out is why anyone would want to kill Guy."

"Let's go through the usual list of motives." I turn back to the board. "Jealousy, fear, revenge, anger."

"What about love?"

"We can add that, though I doubt that's what's at play here."

"Why? You don't think anyone loved Guy?" Sandrine asks.

"No, I'm sure *someone* did . . ."

"So judgy, El."

"So you've said."

"Leave Eleanor alone, Sandrine," Cathy says.

"Anyway," I say, "those are our options. But there are a lot of facts we don't know yet."

And one crucial one I'm keeping back from the group. Because they don't know about Brian. And that must be the key to this mystery. Their connection, what Guy was doing here in the first place.

I can't put my finger on it, but I know it's the soft spot I need to probe and keep on probing.

"Who here knew the victim?" Stefano says.

"Me. Connor. Harper. Oliver. Vicki. Sandrine. Elizabeth may have met him before."

"And me," Cathy says. "Don't forget me."

I try to smile. "How could I ever do that?"

"Anyone else?"

"Potentially," I say. "I don't know everyone here."

"So that's a lot of suspects," Stefano says.

"We don't all have a motive to kill him."

"Does anyone?"

"He was in business with Connor," Cathy supplies. "They had a falling-out."

"How do you know that?"

"I read his book."

"Ah."

"I've read everything about you."

"Great."

"That's creepy, Cathy," Sandrine says, surprising me.

"I'm a fan."

"More like a fanatic."

"It's okay, Sandrine, thank you."

"If you're okay with your stalker being here, I guess that's your choice."

"I'm not a stalker!"

"Excuse me, weren't you arrested for just that?"

I start to feel choked up. And not about Cathy, but about Sandrine, because she's defending me. Advocating for me.

And it hurts.

Damn it.

"*Laissez-faire*, Sandrine."

She makes a *pfft* noise with her lips. "Fine."

"So did Cathy kill Guy?" Stefano asks. "I'm confused."

"No."

"But she's a criminal."

"She's not . . ." I stop myself from saying she's not dangerous, because do I know that? Not really. She could be.

"I have another question," Stefano says.

"Go ahead."

"Did Guy really write that book?"

"I . . ." This has never occurred to me. I'm not sure why, but it makes sense that a ghostwriter would've been used. I try to remember when his book was published and whether I heard any whispers about it then. I guess I can ask Vicki, but I'm not sure what the relevance of that is to his murder.

Only, when someone dies, everything about their life becomes relevant.

You just have to find the pattern and connect the dots, and all those euphemisms we use for figuring out why someone would think that killing someone is the solution to their problems.

"Why did you ask that, Stefano?"

"I guess I just have good deductive instincts."

"More fodder for your TikTok series," Sandrine drawls.

"That, too. Either way, Connor Smith is at the top of my suspect list."

I sigh as I glance at the clock. "I think we're almost out of time."

"But we don't know who the killer is," Stefano says.

"It's too early for that."

"Too early?"

"In the book. I'm trying to wrap this back into the lecture. You can find my notes on the website in the user portal. But this is just the investigatory phase. Unless the killer was very careless, we aren't going to know who did it for a while."

Something catches my eye. Officer Rolle is in the doorway.

"If we find out who did it at all. Assuming it was a crime. Now, before we have our meetings this afternoon to talk over your pages, you should all do the next writing prompt. Thanks, everyone. I'll see you at lunch."

Stefano harrumphs, then walks to the board and takes out his phone.

"Not for public consumption, Stefano."

"It's just for *my* investigation."

"Put your phone away."

He glares at me as he slips it into his pocket, then exits with the rest of the class.

I try not to roll my eyes as I walk toward Officer Rolle. His face is stern, and I know without having to ask that he's here to deliver *more* bad news.

"He was murdered?"

He nods.

"Was it poison?"

He nods again.

"Do you know what kind?"

"Pathology will take a while, but the preliminary determination is that it was something fast-acting."

"So, it was administered right before he died."

"Yes."

"His food is being tested?"

"Of course, but the medical examiner found a prick point on his left shoulder. His determination is that it was administered there. Especially since we found this."

He takes a plastic evidence envelope out of his pocket, and as my eyes take in what it is, I start to feel faint.

"Have you seen something like this before?"

I nod wordlessly.

"I thought so. You'll be coming with me, then."

"What . . . what for?"

"Questioning."

Second Writing Assignment—Poison

Prompt: Write a scene from the POV of one of your characters after the body has been discovered.

I didn't think it would be like this.

I'm not sure what I imagined, but not this.

It's not the guilt. I'm sure that will set in eventually. But for now, I feel . . . relief? So much planning, anxiety, and uncertainty around the who, what, where, and when of it all. And now that the shoe has dropped, I can go back to thinking of other things. I can eat and sleep without the details of the plan intruding.

Because I think I'm getting away with it.

I've crossed all the t's and dotted all the i's, and no one's looking in my direction. I made sure of that. Why would they? Why would anyone suspect little old me?

People have always underestimated me. Ever since I was a child, they thought I'd never achieve anything. No one ever said that. But it was always implied. In the silence when I asked for things. In the surprised when I achieved them. In the rejections when they gave them. Like they knew they'd say "no" before considering it.

But it's the quiet ones you have to be careful about. You have to watch the corners and see who's standing there, or you might get surprised. And when I get away with this—I'm getting away with it, I am—then they'll see.

The haters. The deniers. The naysayers.

It will all be worth it for me to know I've pulled one over on all of them.

I just have to stop thinking about that terrible moment when the life drained out of his eyes. The shock of it all. And the smell that no amount of showers will erase. Poe wrote "The Tell-Tale Heart," but it's not the heart that remembers. It's a muscle that goes on beating unless it's stopped.

It's the memory that's the problem. The Eternal Sunshine of the Spotless Mind of it all. But I think I know what to do.

I just have to act like I forget.

CHAPTER 15

Should You Say the First Thing That Comes to Mind When You're Being Questioned?

As I follow Officer Rolle through the hotel complex to the room he's been given to conduct his investigation, I'm calm.

I've been here before.

A suspect. Interrogated.

Is that what this is?

I haven't been detained. I've only been asked to follow him in a way that was so discreet I'm almost certain no one in my class noticed.

Ha ha.

Did you fall for that *again*?

They *all* noticed. And I'm pretty sure Stefano started a TikTok Live as soon as I was out of earshot, which is not my problem but is not *not* a problem, you know?

Cathy, Sandrine, and a few of the others started following us, but I shooed them away. Sandrine looked at me with something like sympathy, then determined on some course of action and walked in the opposite direction. I don't know what she was thinking, but I know her looks like I know Oliver's. That's the way it is with close friendships. Even when they're over, it doesn't mean you stop knowing that person.

So Sandrine is up to something, which I assume I'll find out about at some point.

In the meantime, Officer Rolle leads me into a smallish room near the front offices and motions for me to sit down at a table where, to my surprise, Elizabeth Ben is also sitting.

"Elizabeth. What are you doing here?"

"I'm your representative." Her hair is in its perfect coif, as always, her cane resting against the wall.

"I don't need a lawyer."

"That's good to hear, my dear, and I am not an attorney. But you do need a representative."

"What do you mean?"

"Someone who can listen for you. When you've had a shock, you don't take in information properly. Such as when you receive bad news in a doctor's office. It's important to have a neutral third party there to take notes, ask questions, and explain everything to you once you've had a chance to absorb the news."

"I . . . Um, thank you." I glance at Officer Rolle. He doesn't seem surprised that Elizabeth is here, nor concerned. I assume she asked his permission beforehand.

But . . .

"How did you know I was here?"

"Officer Rolle asked me where you were located. It only took a couple of questions to ascertain why he was looking for you, and I suggested I attend your . . ." She moves her hand around. "Whatever this is."

"I have some questions," Officer Rolle says. "Please sit, Ms. Dash."

I take a seat in a puffy leather chair. The faux-leather fabric immediately sucks against my thighs, and I know I'm going to be sweating behind my knees any minute. This bizarre day is just getting weirder, but I'm still oddly calm.

I've been here before.

I've *been* here before.

My mind is trying to tell me something.

And you too, of course.

"Am I being investigated?"

Officer Rolle laces his hands on the desk in front of him. "Everyone is being investigated. Someone was murdered and you were sitting next to him."

"I didn't do it."

"Of course, you didn't, my dear." Elizabeth pats me on the leg with a veined hand. "I'm sure you simply have questions for her, right, Officer Rolle? Whether she saw anything. What she might know about who wanted to kill this man. Mr. Charles, is it?"

Officer Rolle blinks at her slowly, then turns to me. "Do you know anything?"

"I might. I felt someone behind me just before it happened."

"Did you see them?"

"No, the lights were out."

"My fault, I'm afraid," Elizabeth says. "I was commissioned to tell a ghost story and I like to create an atmosphere."

Officer Rolle's eyes shift back to her. "Did you turn them off?"

"Certainly not. I was at the podium and nowhere near the light switches."

"Who did it, then?"

"I'm not sure, I asked my concierge to arrange it."

"Concierge?"

Elizabeth shrugs. "A kind young man who's been waiting on me hand and foot since I arrived, I'm afraid. Being old is not for the faint of heart."

Officer Rolle opens a notebook and makes a note with a ballpoint pen. "And he was the one who turned them off?"

"I do not know. I only know that they went off at the precise time I asked them to."

"Which was?"

"I meant the precise time in my story, not the literal time."

"What is the concierge's name?"

"Christian."

Officer Rolle writes it down. "How long were the lights off?"

"A couple of minutes," I say. "And I think it was Mark who turned them off." I close my eyes, thinking back to the scene. "Yes, I'm almost certain it was him."

"Hmmm," Elizabeth says. "Who is Mark? And it was four minutes exactly."

"Mark Knowles, the hotel manager."

"Ah. I have not had the pleasure of meeting him."

"How do you know how long it was?" Officer Rolle asks.

"I time all of my speeches."

"Oh," I say. "Wow. I never do that. Never even thought to."

"Enough time for someone to cross the room, use the device, then return to their seat," Officer Rolle says.

"The device?" Elizabeth asks.

He lifts up the plastic bag he'd shown me earlier. It's holding a small cream-colored ring that looks like one of those ring pops I used to get as a kid. Only this one has a needle attached with a little cylinder above it, and I know exactly how it works. You wear it so the needle extends out from your palm, and when you push it into someone's body, it releases the poison it contains.

Okay, wait. That sounds bad.

I haven't used one of them before. I've just seen the results.

"My goodness," Elizabeth says with some fascination. "What *is* that?"

"It's a poison-administration system," I say. "Right?"

Officer Rolle's face is impassive. "Yes, that is what we believe."

"How do you know that, Eleanor?"

I clear the lump that's formed in my throat. "I've seen it before. Or not that one, I assume, as it's sitting in an evidence locker in Italy. But something very similar."

"You've seen this device used before?" Officer Rolle asks.

"It was what was used to kill Abishek Botha six months ago in Italy."

Elizabeth stirs next to me as he consults his notebook. "Any relation to Ravi Botha?"

"Yes. His brother. Ravi's taken over writing his crime series since he died."

"Has someone been arrested for this crime?"

"Yes. Though I'm not sure they ever determined who it was who used the device . . . He was killed on a boat in the Mediterranean. At first, we thought he'd been poisoned when he drank a glass of Champagne that was meant for Connor Smith. But then the device was found and . . ."

Officer Rolle leans forward. "Yes, Ms. Dash?"

"It was found in *my* bag, but of course I had nothing to do with it."

He doesn't look very convinced by my "of course."

And I get it. It's one thing to be involved in multiple murder plots, but having the same device show up at two of them begs credulity.

Which, I assume, is the point.

"Was Mr. Charles in Italy when this happened?"

"Yes, he was."

"Could he have had something to with Mr. Botha's murder?"

"I . . . No, I don't think so."

"You don't sound sure, dear."

I bite my lip. It's not that I don't want to speak ill of the dead—clearly, I have no problem doing that—but the case in Italy was put to bed. The murderers were identified, and one of them died.

And though there is *one* loose thread—a missing co-conspirator named Marta—that wasn't Guy.

"There are some things about that case that were never explained. One of the suspects still hasn't been caught, but it's a woman. And then Inspector Tucci was just reminding me of a few other details that might still be unresolved."

"What has he got to do with this?"

"He was the police inspector who investigated Shek's death."

Officer Rolle sits back. "What is he doing at this conference?"

"He says his superiors ordered him to be here when the first detective fell through."

"Who was?"

"I don't know. I assume someone local?"

"Who organized this conference?" Officer Rolle asks.

"There's a committee," I say. "My editor, Vicki, is on it. Not sure about the others."

He makes another note. "Is he the only one here with ties to Italy besides yourself?"

"There are several others: Connor, Oliver, Harper. Oh, and Cr— Cathy. One of the participants. And Guy was there. We were all on tour together."

"A book tour, I assume?"

I nod.

"Why was Mr. Charles on your book tour?"

"He's part of the Vacation Mysteries Extended Universe."

"Which is?"

"This term my publisher came up with . . . Connor Smith is the pro-tagonist of my book series. Guy wrote a book about his years working with him as a private detective."

"What do you know about their relationship?"

I explain what I know of Connor's background, but I've already told you about that, so I'll just skip over it here.

"And you were involved with this man?" I can feel Elizabeth's judg-ment from her stiff posture next to me, but my bad romantic choices seem the least of my worries right now.

"I *was*, yes."

"But you still write about him?" Officer Rolle asks.

"I do."

"And he and Mr. Charles were on the outs?"

"Yes."

"Over what?"

"You'd have to ask him."

"But you have a theory?"

I pause.

"Do you, dear? You must."

"I . . . They were on the outs already when we were in Italy. I asked Connor why, but he wouldn't tell me. But I think it had something to do with us being there. Guy had a gun with him—he smuggled it into the country illegally. Inspector Tucci told me that he tried to question him about it but was prevented from doing so by his bosses. He implied Guy was connected, somehow. Maybe to the Mafia. And then he intimated that the Mafia was also in the Bahamas. Is that true?"

Officer Rolle nods briefly. "I must talk to this Inspector Tucci."

"I'm sure he'll be all too happy to give you his opinion."

He puts his pen down. "You do not like this man?"

"He isn't my favorite person on earth, no. And I have some major reservations about his competency. But he could tell you more than I can about that device. Maybe they tracked down the manufacturer, for example."

Elizabeth picks up the evidence bag. "It looks like something that was 3D-printed. Perhaps from a plan found on the dark web."

"How do you know about such things?" Officer Rolle asks.

"Book research," we say together.

"Eleanor is correct. A hazard of our profession, I'm afraid. One has to go to some of the darkest places to find ideas, plug plot holes, and fill in details."

"I see. And you've seen these plans?"

"Not at all. I'm merely saying that there are many things like that available at the end of a few keyword searches. I'm sure it will have occurred to you that anyone who knows the details of that previous case would know about this device."

"I don't think that particular detail is public, though," I say.

"How would you know?" Officer Rolle says.

"Because of my book. *Amalfi Made Me Do It*. It's coming out in a few weeks, and it's a fictionalized account of what happened in Italy. I read all the news reports to make sure I got the details right, then used creative license where I needed to turn it into fiction. The news reports don't mention it. But . . ."

"Yes?"

"It *is* in the book. That device. I included that detail."

"But this book isn't out yet?"

"No, but there are lots of advance reader copies around."

"What is that?"

"Before a book comes out, the publisher distributes early copies to reviewers and other authors to get endorsements."

"Who did they send it to?"

"I don't have the list. Vicki would have it."

"Anyone here?"

"My sister has read it, and Oliver. Vicki, of course, she's my editor. That TikTok guy, Stefano. And Sandrine, I think. Not sure about anyone else."

So, basically everyone.

"I received a copy, I believe," Elizabeth says. "Never got to it, though, I'm afraid."

"That's fine, Elizabeth. It doesn't matter."

"I will get a copy of this list." Officer Rolle marks it down. "Anything else?"

"I'd look into how Guy got the job here."

"Yes, I plan to."

"What happened to the previous person?"

"Mr. Knowles said he'd received a better offer."

"Is he still in the Bahamas?"

"Not that I am aware of."

"And the other victim, Brian? There must be a connection between him and Guy."

Officer Rolle sits back again and strokes his chin. "If Mr. Charles was the intended victim."

"*If?*"

"You said before, it was dark. Perhaps they made a mistake. Tell me more about what happened. What did you see, exactly?"

I do my best to think back. "I only heard them. I felt them, really. You know how you can feel someone standing behind you sometimes?"

"So, they were behind you?"

"Yes, but . . ."

"Could they have mistaken you and Mr. Charles? Was it dark enough?"

"It was very dark. And it was hard for your eyes to adjust because of the light that Elizabeth was holding."

"A light?"

"For effect," Elizabeth says. "It's a technique Blackbeard used."

"The pirate?"

"To draw attention."

"Did anyone know you intended to do this? Use the light?"

"I may have mentioned it, I don't recall." She gives a small cough. "But what does this have to do with how Eleanor might have been the intended victim?"

"I need to explore the possibility. Particularly given what we found in the first victim's room."

"Which was?" Elizabeth asks.

Officer Rolle looks at me. "Confidential."

My hands start to prick again, and I clutch them against my thighs. "Am I in danger?"

"I think everyone here is in danger."

"We should cancel the conference."

"You can do so if you wish. However, you will not be able to leave

Nassau until we discover who the perpetrator is. And we do not have the resources to monitor everyone."

"I'm sure Mr. Knowles will be pleased to have so many guests staying on . . ." I say.

"For now, we might as well press on," Elizabeth says. "Let the participants get their money's worth."

"And get murdered?"

"I doubt any of them is a target."

"You don't always have to be the target to catch a stray bullet."

"An excellent point, Ms. Dash. And hopefully, we have eliminated any more guns from this campus."

"Any more?"

"One was found in Mr. Charles's room."

"He seems to have a way with bringing weapons into countries where they do not belong."

"Another point to investigate. But this one was not used, thankfully."

"Not yet," I say. "You've heard of Chekhov's gun?"[54]

"Was that a joke, Ms. Dash?"

"I hope so."

"Can you think of any reason why someone here might want you dead?"

I hesitate. Wasn't I making a list of potential suspects just a few pages ago? I was, I was. But I don't have any evidence. "There are people here who do not like me. Mr. Botha did express that he blamed me for his brother's death. And Sandrine is angry at me over something I didn't do."

"Which is?"

"She said I stole her book plot. Which I did not do."

"Anyone else?"

I glance at Elizabeth. She's watching me with curiosity. "Not that I can think of. Well, I guess you should put Cathy on the list. Though she's

---

[54] If there's a gun in the first act, it has to go off by the third. But we're in the <u>second act</u>, so who the fuck knows what's going to happen with this gun.

been stalking me for years, so I don't know why she'd decide to kill me now, after all this time."

"Is that all?"

"Stefano may have a bone or two to pick with me."

So, again, basically everyone.

"About?"

I explain about the bad review. My cutting off his access to review copies. It sounds petty to say it out loud.

Do people kill people for petty reasons?

They do.

But do they put together a whole plan of attack to do it? It seems too much. It doesn't make sense. Not unless I'm missing something major here.[55]

So it must be Guy who was the intended victim. That makes more sense. Because one thing in books that's different from life is that the victim is often a villain.

And Guy *is* a villain.

Hmmm. Do you even know when you're a villain? What's that thing the kids say? "My villain origin story"? If I have one, it was meeting Connor. But that was a long time ago in another country. Italy. A country that keeps showing up here like a bad penny.

"Are we done here?" I ask.

"For now."

I stand and hold back Elizabeth's chair, then help her up. "I'll let you know if I think of anything more."

"Yes, please do. And Ms. Dash? You're not planning on investigating this on your own, are you?"

"Of course not."

Wow. Look how easily that lie slipped out.

You should remember that, too.[56]

---

[55] I am. Are you?

[56] I've said that a lot. Maybe you should be keeping a list?

CHAPTER 16

Are We Going to Talk About It?

I see Elizabeth to her table in the buffet dining room because apparently it's time to eat again, though I'm oddly unhungry, which is not a state I am used to being in. We don't talk on the way there. Maybe we're both thinking about the same thing: the murders, who's behind them, and whether I was the intended target.

Or maybe I'm projecting. It's what I was thinking about. Elizabeth was probably contemplating her lunch choices, secure in the knowledge that no one's ever wanted to murder her.

Don't get too smug, though. Someone might want *you* dead. Only they never acted on it, so you haven't been confronted with the evidence of your ability to create enmity.

ANYWAY.

I make sure Elizabeth gets to a good seat, then scan the room, looking for a friendly face I can eat with. Or push food around on the plate with. But I'm coming up empty when Oliver approaches.

"There you are," he says with something that sounds like relief. He's wearing a pair of tan slacks, a polo shirt, and a blazer. His "teacher uniform," he called it when he was packing for the trip. I hadn't planned on dressing up to teach, but I repacked my bag and put some more appropriate clothing in after I saw what he was including. Teaching a murder class in a beach cover-up probably wouldn't get me the respect I was going for. Hence my demure summer dress and cardigan, because every conference room I've ever been in is ten degrees too cold for a woman,[57] and today's was no exception.

"Where were you?"

"I was speaking to Officer Rolle." I tell him what Officer Rolle has discovered. The device that killed Guy. The potential that it was meant for me. His eyes widen as I tell him about it, his brain coming to the same conclusion as mine.

This is not a coincidence.

I mean, obviously.

"I knew I shouldn't have let you out of my sight," Oliver says.

"I'm okay. Why were you looking for me?"

He motions for me to follow him through the dining room. We pass several animated tables of conference-goers, catching clips of their conversations about what I assume are their WIPs.[58]

Or there are a lot of people plotting murders here.

Both are possible.

We stop, and Oliver points to a table in the corner. Connor is sitting at a round table, and the members of my small group surround him. I could be mistaken, but it looks like an interrogation, which Stefano is leading. Cathy is holding his phone, recording, and he's taking notes. And Connor looks . . . not annoyed, exactly. A mix of nonchalant and wary.

It's a look I've seen before.

"Did you assign your class to investigate the murder?" Oliver asks.

"They wouldn't let me give my lecture. They insisted we talk about it."

"And Connor?"

"Stefano think he's the prime suspect. He's 'on the case' or making some Storytime or whatever. For his TikTok."

"Yeah, I've watched them."

---

[57] They're set for the comfort of <u>men</u>. I'm sure you're shocked to learn this!
[58] Works in progress. Writer slang.

"Stefano's TikTok?"

"I wanted to know what he was up to, filming all the time."

"And?"

Oliver tosses his head back and holds his hand up like he's holding his phone. "POV. You're at a resort that's supposed to be five-star, but it's more like two point five, three tops. You're here to learn how to write a perfect murder from the best writers in the business. Or whoever they could get to show up to this conference. Samesies. And then—Storytime, guys—someone is dead! They're saying it's a heart attack, but I'm not falling for that. Come back for part two, where I reveal who the dead guy is and why I *knew* he was going to die."

I snort. "Wow. That was . . . very accurate."

"Thank you."

"I think Stefano was recording a Live when the murder happened."

"I didn't see that on his page."

"He said he was recording Elizabeth's lecture . . . but I don't think a Live ends up on your feed? There must be some way to retrieve it."

"I'm sure there is."

"How much time do you spend on TikTok, anyway?" I ask. "I didn't even know you had an account."

He shakes his head. "It's for research purposes."

"Sure."

"I write contemporary stories. I have to stay involved with the culture."

"Keep telling yourself that. What's on your FYP?"

"My what?"

"For You Page. It's the page that you see when you open up TikTok. The videos the algorithm pushes you."

"Eleanor."

"What?"

He shakes his head at me. "Why does Stefano think Connor murdered Guy?"

"He's not wrong. If Guy was murdered on purpose, Connor *is* suspect number one."

"Why?"

"They know too much about one another."

"That's not usually a reason for murder, is it?"

"It can be," I say. "They've both been keeping secrets. About Italy. About their business. All of it."

"If I remember correctly," Oliver says, "Connor didn't even know Guy was going to be here."

"So *he* says."

He wrinkles his forehead because he doesn't do Botox and still has facial expressions.

Me too. I don't do Botox.

Yet.

"Connor used the device that killed Shek to kill Guy?"

"It's not information that's in the public domain. So, it's someone who was in Italy with us or who's read the book that did it. Only it's the advance reader copy they have to have read, which is a limited number of people. But Connor was there. On the spot. So it doesn't matter if he read the book or not."

"Did he?" Oliver asks.

"I have no idea."

"If he didn't, he'd be pretty stupid to use that method."

"Maybe he thought it was public?"

"Still . . ." Oliver purses his mouth. "Why would he kill Guy? Why now? Why here?"

"It has to be related to why Guy was here. I don't buy this 'job opening' nonsense for a minute." I look over at the table, where Connor's turning red in the face. It looks like the interrogation is being led by the man named Harold.

Okay, I lied about not telling you everyone's names in my group, that they'd all be background players. But I told you Harold's name a couple of chapters back, and Harold has some things to say.

Here are three facts about Harold so you can envision him:

1. He's about sixty, with a gray half-circle of hair on his head.
2. He's the one I mentioned a while back who's been to more than one writer's conference I've attended, and has self-published his books,[59] which he talks about like they're *New York Times* bestsellers to anyone who'll listen.
3. He uses large hand gestures and likes pointing his pen when he's mansplaining the book business.

I'm sure you've met a Harold or two in your lifetime.

Especially if you're a writer.

And the woman standing next to him, who I assume is his wife from the way she was saying his name in class, seems a little too used to seeing Harold act this way.

I wouldn't want to be her if I screwed something up for him.

But I *am* enjoying watching Connor squirm.

"What do you think they're asking him about?" Oliver says.

"No idea. No one seemed that bright in my class. What? It's true."

"You can't say things like that out loud."

"I'm only saying them to you."

He smiles. "Lucky me."

I smile back. "You *are* lucky. I mean, look at how many times you've almost died because of me, and yet you're still alive."

"Not sure *my* life was ever in danger."

"Potayto, potahto."

"Still making jokes, I see."

---

[59] For the record, I have nothing against self-publishing. If you do it right, it's even harder than regular publishing.

"It's my coping mechanism."

"How about doing something more concrete?" Oliver says.

"Such as?"

"A little light breaking and entry?"

"Now you're talking."

"Where are we going?" I ask Oliver a few minutes later as he leads me through the compound.

When I signed on to come here, I thought I'd be spending most of my time in a lounge chair sipping cocktails while Oliver did our copyedits, not getting my knees scraped up by overgrown fronds.

Alas, alas.

"Where do you think?" Oliver says.

"I don't know, that's why I asked."

"Patience."

"You know I'm not patient."

"Shhh." He holds his finger to his lips as we approach the low-lying buildings where the staff quarters are. The white paint has yellowed and is chipping, and one of the roofs has a small tree growing out of it. The brush is encroaching, too. It hasn't been cut back in a while. The resort has seen better days, but this part looks like it hasn't been touched since the last century.

"Guy's office?"

He nods.

"Won't they be locked or under watch?"

"Locked, yes. Under watch, no. They aren't a crime scene."

"How do you know?"

"I checked earlier."

I cock my head to the side. "You've been investigating."

"I have."

"Why?"

"Not sure if you've noticed, but two people are dead?"

"Clever boy."

"I try," he says. "This way."

At first, I think he's made a mistake, but then I notice there's a small path—a shortcut the staff must use. When we come to the edge of it, he stops me again. We're standing directly in front of the door to Guy's office. There's no one around.

"Is this a good idea?" I ask.

"Probably not."

"Shouldn't we leave the investigating to the police?"

He gives me a look over his shoulder. "Duh."

I laugh quietly. "Did you bring your breaking and entering tools?"

"I did."

"Why?"

"I was going to use them in class as a visual aid."

"Well, this is a much better use for them."

He takes a small black case out of the pocket of his blazer and unzips it. Inside are a bunch of thin tools I know can be used for picking locks. I don't have the skill to do it, but this isn't the first time Oliver's shown me that he can.

Last time he did this, he used a credit card, but he was improvising.

We weren't expecting murder that time.

Silly us.

"Keep a lookout," he says as he crouches down by the door.

I stand behind him and look left, then right. We're all alone, only the birds twittering, but I'm starting to sweat, even though I don't imagine anything really bad would happen to us if we got caught. A light scolding, maybe?

Or wait. Is this obstruction of justice? It might be obstruction.[60]

"I'm in." Oliver stands and opens the door, ushering me inside.

I turn on the light as he closes the door behind us. The office looks

---

[60] It's definitely obstruction.

like I remember it. Neat and tidy, with a desk, some bookshelves, and a filing cabinet.

"Did you just touch the light switch with an ungloved hand?" Oliver asks.

"We're not committing a crime."

"You sure about that?"

"Okay, okay. I didn't bring gloves."

He reaches into his pocket and produces two pairs.

"More visual aids?"

"Yep."

"What else you got in there?"

"Wouldn't you like to know?"

I take a pair of gloves from him and put them on. "What are we looking for?"

"Anything that will give us some insight into what Guy was doing here."

"Wouldn't the police have already taken that?"

"We know him better than they do. Maybe they overlooked something."

I look around. Guy's laptop is gone, but everything else is in order.

"I'll take the filing cabinet," I say.

"I'll check the books."

I go to the filing cabinet while he goes to the bookshelf. I open the top drawer. There are lots of files in it, some that look quite old. I take my time flipping through them while Oliver takes each book out and makes sure it doesn't have anything in it or behind it.

Which leaves way too much time for my exhausted brain to wander.

"So, are we going to talk about it?" I ask.

"What?"

"The rose petals on the bed last night."

"Oh, that."

I want to look at him, but I don't. "Yeah, that."

"There were rose petals on the bed."

"I noticed. How did they get there?"

He clears his throat. "Harper put them there."

My heart starts to accelerate. "Is this the surprise you two had planned for me?"

"Yep."

"Just that?"

"Nope."

"I see."

I can hear him put a book down gently on the table, and then he's standing behind me. He places his hands on my shoulders. "Not how I wanted this to go."

I take a deep breath, taking him in. "I can imagine."

"And it doesn't seem like the right time."

"No."

"You're saying no?"

I turn around quickly and catch his hands in the air. I feel a jolt like the first time we ever touched. It's something that's never gone away, the current that runs between us. "I would never say no to you."

"Are you sure?"

"Yes."

He brings his gloved hands to my face and pulls me in slowly. He brushes his lips against mine, once, twice, a third time, and I want to pull him into an embrace, but this is his show.

I'm letting him lead.

For once.

He deepens the kiss, probing my lips open with his tongue. My body responds, melting into him, feeling how well we match each another, the temperature rising as the world falls away and it's just us.

His lips drop down to my collarbone, and a moan escapes me. He pulls back, looking deeply into my eyes in a way that's always been hard to turn away from and to take. Like he's looking into my heart and can see everything I hide from everyone.

"I want to ask you properly when your life isn't in danger," he says.

"You haven't asked me anything yet."

"You know what I mean."

"I do."

"I think you're supposed to say that part at the altar."

"I can say it again then, too."

"Eleanor."

"Yes?"

He smiles. "I see what you did there."

"You don't have to ask now. Here."

"I'm not."

My voice catches in my throat. "Oh, okay."

"How can I? With everything that's happening?"

"I know."

"I want it to be memorable."

I gesture to the plain office. "More memorable than this?"

"Ha."

I step away from him. The last thing I want to do. But the first thing isn't something we should be doing in broad daylight in Guy's office.

Though the possibility of getting caught *in flagrante delicto* is hot.

To me, anyway.

"We should get back to our search," I say. "We don't have that much time before people are going to start asking where we are."

"Right. The schedule. Lunch, then activities."

"No way I'm doing any of those activities after yesterday."

He smiles. "That seems wise." He kisses me briefly, then goes back to his books. I watch him for a minute, then turn reluctantly back to the filing cabinet.

Am I engaged now?

I mean, maybe?

There's no ring, and he didn't ask me, but he was going to ask me last night, so he must have the ring here. Something to search for later.

But for now, it's back to these files.

It's all information about past guests. A missing locket. A concern about a break-in. A near-drowning. All the things you'd expect in a resort over the years. I stop on a file named "Death" and pull it out. It's got a police report in it from the man who died here earlier this year. As Officer Rolle said, he died in his sleep. Nothing suspicious about it. I close the file and put it back.

I try to reach for the next file, but it's stuck on something. I pull at it, and I realize a file has slipped down underneath the others. I push the files aside in both directions and fish it out. It's a personnel file for a man named Karl Johnson.[61] I open it. It belongs to the former head of security.

"Found something," I say, holding it up.

"Me too," Oliver says. He holds a book out to me that has a hollow cavity in it. Inside, there's a USB stick.

"Excellent."

He glances at his watch. "We should go. We've been here too long."

"What do I do with this? I can't just walk around with it."

"Leave the file, give me the papers."

I do as he instructs. He folds them in two and puts them inside his blazer.

"That thing is handy."

"We're totally nuts," he says.

"No shit," I say. "Let's go."

I turn off the light and we go outside. Oliver drops to his knees again and relocks the door while I keep a lookout. Then he stands and grabs my hand. We both still have our gloves on, and I'm about to suggest we take them off when a voice stops us.

"And just what have *you* two been up to?"

Busted.

---

[61] Johnson is the second most common surname in the Bahamas.

CHAPTER 17

Is This the Midpoint Reveal?

"Connor," I say, "what are you doing here?"

Connor takes a step closer, his cologne tickling my nose. He's wearing a cream linen suit and a black fedora with white trim. It looks almost . . . Mafia-esque. "I'm the one asking the questions."

I drop Oliver's hand, our moment of complicity evaporating. "On whose authority?"

"Please. You just sicced your students on me. That man Harold got three inches from my face. Not to mention Stefano. I did *not* consent to being videoed."

"I didn't tell them to go after you."

"Sandrine told me all about it. How you said I was suspect number one in Guy's murder."

"Sandrine loves making trouble for me."

His eyes darken. "Was it a lie? Did you have some *other* suspect in mind?"

"Do *you* have a better suggestion?" Oliver says with a trace of menace.

Come on, Oliver.

I knew your hatred of Connor hasn't been erased.

Connor's eyes track slowly to Oliver's. "I might, yes."

"Are you going to tell us?"

"Not until you tell me what you two were doing in Guy's office." He points at us like he's scolding a child.

"Who says we were in there?"

"You're still wearing gloves, Eleanor. And whatever file you swiped is half hanging out of your coat, Oliver."

I pull the gloves off and stuff them in my pocket—amateur mistake. In my defense, I'm still operating on half of my brain cells. "We're investigating Guy's death."

"You mean his *murder*. That's what Officer Rolle told you after your class, wasn't it?"

How does he . . . ? Sandrine. Again.

Damn it.

"Yes, he was murdered. Poisoned. We don't know more than that."

No point telling him about the device.

Let's see if he slips up, shall we?

"What did you find in his office?"

"Not sure yet."

"Why don't you show me?"

"Why should we?"

Connor sighs, then rolls his eyes for good measure. "Are we going to go through this *again*?"

"What?"

"We're better as a team. You, me, even Oliver."

"Excuse me?"

"I am simply stating the fact that we've had some success in solving murders."

"Define 'success,'" I say.

"Whether you ever cared to learn the details or not, Eleanor, I *have* been a detective for over twenty years. I've solved a multitude of crimes you don't know about—"

"Pretty sure you've also *gotten away with* a multitude of crimes, only some of which I know about."

He pauses. "Even if that's true, my experience is still relevant to our current situation."

"How exactly?" Oliver asks.

"I think like a criminal." He taps the side of his head. "Which is exactly what's needed here."

"And you know Guy. Knew him," Oliver says, then sighs. "He has a point, El, much as I hate to admit it."

"I hate it when he does."

"I know, but we aren't getting anywhere. Let's pool our resources before someone else dies."

"Fine."

Connor rubs his hands together. "Excellent. Shall we go somewhere a little less exposed?"

"Such as?"

He cocks his finger and invites us to follow him. Oliver and I share a glance, then relent. I won't say *What's the worst that could happen?* because you know what it is.

This could be a trap. Connor could be luring us to our deaths.

But given the number of pages we still have ahead of us, that's unlikely at this juncture.

So.

In a few short minutes, we're in Connor's room. It's smaller than our current suite, more like the first room we were shown to, the one Brian died in. A bit tired and in need of a refresh, like the rest of this resort.

A sad place to die, when you think about it.

Connor goes to the mini fridge and gets out a bottle of generic fizzy water but doesn't offer any to us. Which tracks.

Oliver and I take a seat at the small dining table. The top is chipped in the corner, and I can't help picking at it.

Connor twists the cap off his water and paces. It's a thing he does. He thinks better standing up, I remember him telling me years ago, when I found it thrilling to be caught up in one of his cases instead of slightly sick to my stomach.

"What did you find?" Connor asks.

Oliver opens his jacket and pulls out the pieces of paper from the filing cabinet. He glances through them, handing them one by one to Connor. "This is the personnel file of the person who had Guy's job before him."

"Anything interesting?"

"He worked here for eight years," Oliver says.

"Why did he leave?"

"He got offered another job." Oliver shows me his exit interview. "An offer he couldn't refuse, it seems like."

"Like in *The Godfather*?" I say.

"Um," Connor says. "Funny you should say that."

"What do you know?"

He starts to guzzle down his water, then wipes his mouth while we wait.

"Spill it, Connor."

"I haven't been entirely truthful with you."

I *knew* it.

"You don't say . . ."

"Guy reached out to me a couple of months ago."

"And?"

"He told me he'd tracked down Marta."

My heart skips a beat. "*Marta?* Marta Giuseppe?"

He nods.

Marta is the youngest daughter of the Italian capo who Connor crossed ten years ago in Italy. She's also the one the police didn't catch in Italy after she was involved in a plot to kill Connor and me.

"Where is she?" Oliver asks between clenched teeth.

"Here. In the Bahamas."

"*What?*"

I grab Oliver's hand. "Why?"

"The Giuseppes have parked a lot of money here. They own property. Hotels. You name it."[62]

"*This* hotel?" Something twigs in the back of my brain. What is it? What is it?

Oh! The cocktail party last night.

Those overheard conversations about the book business and *Yellowface* and . . . someone was saying something about the property being owned by the Mafia. And Inspector Tucci. He *also* said the Mafia was here, which I should've focused on more, but I didn't because . . . well, I don't have any excuse, really.

Now it's just one more thing to add to the list of I-can't-believe-this-is-happening.

Again.

"What?" Oliver says. "Is that true?"

"He thought so."

"So, that's why he was here?"

"Yes.

"So, let me get this straight," Oliver says. "You've known this the entire time and said nothing about it?"

"Connor operates on a need-to-know basis."

Oliver shoots me a look. "This isn't funny, El. Two people are dead. You might be in danger, too. Especially if Marta's here. We all are."

"No need to raise your voice, mate."

"I've told you more than once that I'm not your mate." Oliver's standing now, his fists clenched, and as much as I'd enjoy him knocking Connor to the ground, it's a misfocus.

"Oli, he's not worth it."

---

[62] The Bahamas is a tax haven, with good banking secrecy, Google AI tells me. No, as I said previously, and apparently bears repeating, I didn't use AI to write this. AI could <u>never</u>.

"You've said that before." Connor sneers.

"Still true."

I turn my back on him and face Oliver. "Remember how you said you were chill about him. Zen, even?"

"That's before I was stuck in another murder investigation with him."

I smile. "I get it. Trust me. But let's find out what he knows and then deal with him?"

"Pardon me? Deal with me how?"

"Yeah, okay," Oliver said. He squeezes my hand and takes a deep breath.

"Hello? Are you listening to me?"

"How could we ignore you?" I say and turn with a fake smile. "Carry on. Why did Guy want to find Marta?"

Connor looks confused for a moment, then puts his water bottle down. "Don't we all want to find Marta?"

"Yes, but . . . why Guy specifically? She didn't want to kill him."

"He *was* part of the original plan that landed her father in jail."

"Okay, fair. They never seemed that fussed about him, though. Which, now that I think about it, is odd, right?" I look at Oliver. "Inspector Tucci told me Guy didn't get questioned about the gun he brought into Italy. The higher-ups called him off. He implied that Guy was connected."

"Connected, connected?"

"Must be, right? Why would he be connected in the police department otherwise?"

"We had contacts there," Connor says. "Through our work."

"Enough to get you out of a gun charge? I mean, clearly not. *You* had to come to a plea agreement for your thing."

"Thanks to you, I'm not allowed in Italy ever again."

"Thanks to me? That's rich."

"Don't get distracted, El," Oliver says. "You're on to something."

"Right, sorry, where was I? Oh, right, the police. Guy's ties. The way Guy got off with nothing. He's connected to the Mafia, which must mean . . . he's connected to the Giuseppes."

I turn back to Connor. He isn't reacting. This isn't new information to him.

"Right, Connor?"

He hesitates, then . . . "Yes."

"Since when?"

"Since always."

"*Always?*"

"As long as I've known him."

"And you knew this the whole time?"

Connor is choosing his words carefully. "Not at first, but did it never occur to you to ask how I met the Giuseppes and planned all of those heists?"

It didn't. It never occurred to me to ask that question at all.

The TL;DR is that Connor and Guy planned a series of audacious bank robberies, with Gianni Giuseppe, the capo's son. Connor and Guy then got hired to solve *those same robberies* by several insurance companies. Then someone killed Gianni Giuseppe, the capo's son, and things got serious. Connor, Guy, and I solved the murder—his father had ordered his killing after he discovered Gianni was involved because he hadn't asked permission—and the capo went to jail for twenty years, but died before he could get out.

Which set the stage for his family to plot revenge against me and Connor.

"*Guy* introduced you to Gianni?" I ask.

"Yes."

"So he knew him before you did?"

"Also yes."

"Why do I have to drag this out of you? Just tell us already."

He sighs. "Where do you want me to start?"

"At the beginning. Obvi."

Connor nods slowly. "I met Guy in London. We ran in the same circles."

"Bad circles?"

"What do you think?"

"I don't know what to think anymore."

"I grew up . . . not great. Passed around from sister to step-parent to brother . . . That doesn't matter. I learned a lot of skills along the way, and when I was in my twenties, I found myself in London trying to make my way in the world. I realized I was good at figuring things out, mysteries, and don't give me that look, Eleanor, it's true. But I was also good at planning things, illegal things, so I found myself doing both."

"You were a hired gun?" Oliver suggests.

"Of sorts. So much of private detective work is . . . frankly, boring. Following around errant husbands and wives, it's enough to make one cynical about love."

I start to choke.

"You okay, El?"

"I'm fine, please go ahead."

"Surveillance is hell, as they say. But it does give one time to think."

"About how to pull off crimes?"

The side of his mouth curls up. "Among other things. It became a game of sorts. Guy and I would pick a target and work out a plan to break in. An art museum. A diamond store. You get the idea."

"Did you commit these crimes?"

"We did *not*."

"But something happened. Why did you leave London?"

"I met Allison."

"And she made you see the error of your ways?"

He smirks. "Something like that."

"Please. What really happened?"

"She was working as an actress on various locations. I started traveling with her. Guy kept up the business, and I'd assist when I was around."

"And Guy got bored?"

"I wouldn't say bored, exactly. He decided to try one of the small jobs we'd planned. A bar that took in a lot of cash receipts."

"He pissed off the wrong people?" I guess.

"He did."

"So you had to pay the money back?"

"A little more than that. These types of people don't just let you return the money and go on your merry way."

"What, then?" Oliver asks.

"We had to do certain tasks for them. Provide a different kind of surveillance. Keep an eye on their enemies."

"Sounds dangerous."

"It was. And we had to keep up the business as a cover."

"But then you left. What happened?"

Connor considers his answer. "The details aren't important, but let's just say we performed a task that was big enough to satisfy our debt."

"They let you go?"

"They did. On condition that we avoid London in the future."

"Was it a robbery?" Oliver asks.

Connor nods slowly.

"What did you take?"

"I'm not going to tell you. But needless to say, it was at a great cost. Allison was not happy with my life choices, and Guy and I no longer had a business."

"What did you do?"

"Allison got a role in a film that was shooting in the US. So we went there. To LA. I liked it. The sunshine, the beach. It was soothing."

I almost choke again. I've spent years of my life with this man, in one way or another, and yet this is all news to me.

In the books, I gave Connor a more sympathetic backstory. An orphan at a young age—which might be the truth, who knows—who'd been sent to a private boarding school by a rich but distant uncle. It was giving *The Secret Garden* as a literary device to build up empathy. It also explained why he was in England and how he started his investigative business, which was also a lot cleaner than the reality. He's not quite Sherlock Holmes in the books, but he's not *not* Sherlock Holmes. A keen observer, quirky, charming with women.

"When was this?"

"Eleven years ago."

"But then you went to Italy?"

"Allison and I were having problems, and Guy reached out. He had work for us, he said."

"Legal work?"

"I thought so until I got there."

"And then?"

"And then I found out that he'd somehow gotten into bed with the Giuseppes and had promised Gianni we'd help him pull off the robberies."

"Why didn't you just leave?"

Connor clenches his hands into fists. "Have you learned nothing? It doesn't work like that. They have tentacles everywhere."

"So you did it."

"I *planned* it, but I extracted a promise that they'd let me leave when it was done."

"Did you think they were going to hold to that promise?"

"I had no idea, but I had to try."

"What was the plan?"

"You know the plan, Eleanor. You wrote a whole book about it."

"No, I mean the plan for afterward."

"I was going to come back to America and get on the straight and narrow."

"With Allison?"

He holds his hands out. "If she'd have me."

"But things didn't go according to plan," Oliver says.

"They bloody well did not."

"What happened?"

"I never trusted Gianni from the minute I met him. And when he found out about it, the capo was not fond of the plan to say the least. And then . . ."

"Yes?"

"I met you."

A lump forms in my throat. I've been waiting to get to this part. All the questions I never asked. All the things I've wondered about.

Am I finally going to get those answers?

In front of Oliver?

"I've always wondered why you involved me in the case."

"You were good at investigating."

"But you were the *perpetrator*."

"Not of the murder. I needed to find out who did it before they killed me, too."

Of course, of course. It's all so clear now. "So you put my life in danger."

He gives me a rueful smile. "Sorry about that. Couldn't be helped."

"Really?"

"I did try to walk away. To keep you out of it. But you were so insistent."

That does sound like me.

I glance at Oliver. He's listening, fighting to keep his face in a neutral tone.

Which is better than I'm doing, if I'm being honest.

Which is an expression I keep using. And if you've been paying attention, this should put you on your guard.

Am I only being honest when I say I am? Or is that my tell for when I'm lying?

"You didn't have to listen to me," I say.

"I was smitten."

"No. There was something else going on. Something you're not telling us."

Our eyes meet and I try to see into his brain. Why did he start something with me when he was in the middle of a huge crime? What makes sense? What was *his* plan?

To pull off the robberies, get his finder's fee from the insurance companies for "solving" the robberies, and then retire.

For which he needed money. Because the finder's fee was no guarantee.

So what did he know about *me*?

That my parents were dead. That I was there taking a luxury vacation in the very nice hotel where he was hanging out in the bar. That I came from LA, a place he loved. That I was young, naive, and alone.

"You thought I was rich, didn't you? When you met me. You were at the bar at the St. Regis. What were you doing there? Trying to pick up rich divorcées? That's it, isn't it? You were thinking of your future. A soft place to land. But instead, you caught me. I was your escape plan. You were going to leave Allison and marry me and take me for all I was worth, which, joke's on you, wasn't much because I spent the last of the inheritance on that trip. But you didn't know that. And then, joke's on me, you did end up using me as a financial escape hatch when I wrote about you."

His mouth turns up. "Have I ever thanked you for that?"

"Thank me? Are you serious?"

"El."

"What?"

"What does this have to do with Guy and why he's in the Bahamas? With Marta?"

I take a deep breath. Oliver's right. Like always. I can deal with yet another betrayal from Connor later.

"Good point. Why *was* Guy looking for Marta?"

"My guess? To protect himself."

"Why?"

"Because he was in on it with them."

"In on *what* with them?"

Connor pauses again, and if he doesn't answer me soon, I am *not* going to hold back on the urge to put my hands around his throat and throttle him.

"The plot to kill us in Italy."

"Are you kidding me?" I say.

"How do you know that?" Oliver says at the same time.

"Please. I know Guy's handiwork when I see it."

"He confessed to you?" I guess.

"Eventually."

I put some more of the pieces together. "So you knew Marta was here before you came?"

"I did."

"But . . . how did *that* happen? How did this conference end up being scheduled at a hotel owned by the Giuseppes where Martha was hiding out?"

"That's a hell of a coincidence," Oliver says.

"There are no coincidences," I say.

"Good girl."

"Don't call me that."

"Apologies. See, I told you you're good at this."

I think it through, trying to see through the haze of my anger.

"You set this up. *You're* the reason the conference is here?"

"Yes."

"All to catch Marta."

"Yes."

"So *you* killed Guy."

He grimaces. "Absolutely not. That was *not* the plan."

"So, what's going on then?"

"I don't know. But my guess is . . . someone's on to us."

Act 2—Continued

The Fifth and Sixth Sequences

FIFTH SEQUENCE

The fifth sequence of your murder is where the subplots come to the fore. The action continues to rise toward the sixth sequence, where we will have a culminating series of events that directly impacts the main plot.

THINGS TO CONSIDER:

- Have you put a touch of romance into your mystery? Here's where you need to develop it, but that development needs to be in furtherance of the overall plot.

- Have you set up a major conflict between two of your main characters? How is that going to interfere with the investigation and/or resolve it?

- The sequence should end with the answer to the question you've set up in this part of the novel—will they get together, will a fight break out, will that tropical storm turn into a hurricane?—and then pose another question to lead us into the last sequence of Act 2.

SIXTH SEQUENCE

This sequence ends in the culmination of Act 2. It's where all of the rising action you've been creating till now comes to a head at the 70 percent mark of your book.

It should feel like the tension is increasing throughout this sequence, as is the pace.

THINGS TO CONSIDER:

- Have you given each of your main characters significant secrets? Now is the time to start revealing them!

- I also think it's important to start going through your list of suspects and convincing the reader, in turn, that each of them is a plausible killer.

This sequence will end with your main character reaching a low point—a dark night of the soul where all seems lost and hopeless.

It's from the ashes of the sixth sequence that they'll rise to begin to unravel the true nature of the plot they've been embroiled in.

This sequence should end with a NEW twist that will take us away from the solution you've been convincing your readers of until this point.

And also: Someone else needs to die.

CHAPTER 18

Is This a Subplot?

This is a lot to process.

I'm sure your head is reeling a bit. I know mine is.

Connor and Guy arranged for this conference to be in the Bahamas to discover where Marta was hiding when they knew where Marta was hiding.

Wait.

That doesn't make sense.

Which shouldn't surprise me, because when has anything Connor's ever done made any sense? Not on the surface, anyway. You have to dig down to get to the truth.

Like an excavation of an ancient civilization.

So, let the digging begin.

"If you knew where Marta was," I ask, "why did you need to bring the rest of us into it?"

Connor answers in the same tone he did in the last chapter. "We needed a plausible excuse to be here so we didn't spook her."

"Bullshit."

"It's the truth."

I put my hands on my hips. "Give me a break. The minute Guy showed up, or before, even, when Marta learned who was coming to the conference, she'd be out of here."

"Isn't she an international fugitive?" Oliver says. "She'd need some time to arrange new papers if she wanted to leave . . . Wait. Did Guy tell her he could get her papers?"

Connor touches his nose with his index finger and points to Oliver.

"Do *not* say 'Winner, winner, chicken dinner,'" I say.

"I wasn't going to."

"Uh-huh."

"That was his way of trapping her here?" Oliver says. "He wasn't getting the papers; he was just waiting until everyone was in place."

"Yes."

"What was the plan then? Where's Marta?"

"I don't know."

"What do you mean?" I say. "I thought you said she was here."

"Marta's *here?*" Harper says from the doorway. "What?"

I turn in surprise. "How did you find us?"

She shakes the phone she's carrying, showing me her Find My Friends app.

"You're *still* tracking me? I thought I told you to turn that off months ago."

"Excuse me, it saved your life already once."

"Did you find them, Harp—" Sandrine says, stopping behind Harper. "Oh, are we interrupting?"

"You're hanging out with her? Again?"

Harper looks momentarily guilty, then sheds it. "What has that got to do with Marta being here?"

"Nothing. Or wait, maybe it does. Did *you* know she was here, Sandrine?"

Sandrine brings her hand up to her heart in pretend offense. "I don't even know who Marta is."

Wait. Is that true?

Sandrine wasn't in Italy. And I changed her name in the book I wrote about it, so, maybe.

But something else is bothering me.

And it's not just that she's hanging out with Harper!

"You've been in touch with Guy, though. He told me. He implied you were involved romantically, and—what is it, Harper? Why do you start coughing every time I say that?"

"Nothing. Go on."

I look at her, but I can't let myself get distracted. "Anyway, as I was saying, Guy said you were here because he'd suggested it. But why would he do that? Why would he suggest that you come to an event he knew a murderer was at? Or any of us?" I turn to Connor. "Explain."

"Guy told me he'd established communication with Marta before he got here. He made the offer of giving her new papers so she could leave and go somewhere where no one could find her. He told her he'd bring them to her. That he'd applied for the job here as cover so he could help her without raising suspicion. He told me he made contact again when he got here, but not where she was specifically."

"Is she on staff?" Harper asks.

"I don't know. I just know the family owns this place."

"So the real plan was what?" I ask. "Come here, flush her out, and turn her in?"

Connor bites his lip.

"Oh, no, you didn't."

"What?"

"You were using *me* as bait, weren't you? All of us. That's why the conference is here. You figured she wouldn't be able to resist exposing herself if I was this close to her."

Oliver moves across the room like a shot, pushing Connor up against the wall, his arm across Connor's throat. It happens so fast it takes us all by surprise, including Connor.

"Is she right, Connor? Is that what you've done? You've put Eleanor in danger?"

"Take a step back, old boy."

"Answer the question."

Connor tries to wriggle free, but Oliver's got him in an iron grip. "Okay, yes, that was the plan. It was Guy's idea."

"And you went along with it?"

"He didn't leave me much choice."

"How's that?"

Connor tries to move again, but Oliver holds him fast. "Will you let me go already?"

Oliver glances back at me and I nod. He releases him.

Connor steps away and pulls his shirt down where it rose up out of his trousers. "That wasn't necessary."

"I'll decide that. Enough of your lies and deceptions, Connor. Tell us what's going on."

Connor looks at me, then Harper.

A duo of women he's slept with. Disappointed. Lied to.

Does he even care about that? Did he ever care about *me*?

Ah, now we're getting to it, aren't we?

Anyway, that's not important right now.

"Let's go, Connor," I say. "Out with it."

"As I told you, Guy found out that this resort is owned by the Giuseppes and that Marta was here. He reached out to me to ask me—no, insist—that I help him capture her."

"Capture or kill?"

"He said capture."

"And you believed him?"

"Guy has never killed anyone to my knowledge."

"That's so reassuring."

"Let him talk, Eleanor," Sandrine says. "It's just getting good."

I resist the urge to roll my eyes, but I do notice that she and Harper are standing awfully close to one another and . . . no. No, no, no, no.

Harper and *Sandrine*?

Seriously?

Sandrine's married. Not that this has stopped her before, but Harper is my *sister*. Which is probably the point. The better to screw with me, so to speak.

And Harper? What does this say about her? She keeps sleeping with my sloppy seconds—Connor, Sandrine. Who else?

I shake myself, trying to regain my focus because everyone is watching me, waiting for me to say something.

"Uh . . . Why didn't you just call Inspector Tucci and be done with it?"

"He doesn't have jurisdiction here."

"He could get her extradited, I'm sure."

Connor flaps his hand in dismissal. "That is a whole long, involved process, and she might disappear before it was complete. Like I said, the plan was to get her to commit to staying, then come here and capture her ourselves and deliver her to Inspector Tucci."

"So that's why Inspector Tucci is here?"

"Yes."

"How did you arrange that? Wasn't someone else supposed to be on the faculty?"

"Guy took care of it."

"And that didn't make you suspicious? That he could pull strings and get a member of the Italian police force to the Bahamas?" I say.

Connor pulls in and exhales a long breath. "I didn't ask sufficient questions, I grant you."

"Too busy thinking about saving your own skin," Oliver says.

"How do you reckon?"

"Marta wants *you* dead, too. If she's behind bars, you're safe."

"Right," I say. "And me, Oliver, Harper—we're all here to tempt her to act. To pull her out of her hidey-hole."

"Yes."

"But it backfired somehow."

"Clearly."

"Marta killed Guy."

"That's my working theory."

"She was in the dining room?"

"I didn't see her," Harper says.

"Are you sure you'd recognize her?" I ask.

"I spent a lot of time with her when she was working in the marketing department."

"You didn't . . . You weren't involved with *her*, with you?"

"What? No. Why would you ask that?"

My eyes travel to her hand, which is now holding Sandrine's. She drops it as her cheeks redden. "I spent a lot of time with her because I was working for *you*. Setting up your tours, and events, and appearances. So yeah, I'd recognize her."

"Fine, sorry."

"Honestly."

"Maybe she's wearing a disguise," Oliver offers. "And it was dark. She might've slipped in and done it and then slipped out again."

"That could work. But why kill Guy? I was sitting right next to him. Did she make a mistake?"

"I have a theory about that," Connor says.

"Which is?"

"Marta figured out what he was up to. So she took the opportunity to kill him."

"Why not you?"

"She must not know we were working together."

"Or she has other plans for you."

Connor smirks. "You'd like that, wouldn't you?"

"What do *you* think?"

"I have a question," Sandrine says. "How did you get the conference put *here*, exactly?"

"I volunteered to be on the organizing committee."

"*You're* on the organizing committee?" I say.

"Always the tone of surprise."

"Using your own time to work on something that benefits people other than you? Doesn't sound like Connor Smith."

"He was working for himself," Oliver points out. "Zero surprise."

"I was doing it for *all* of us."

"And Guy's predecessor?" Oliver asks. "How did that factor in?"

"Guy arranged it. I'm not sure who he convinced to make him an offer to leave—someone, obviously."

"How can you not know?"

Connor looks at me. "Aren't you tired of this, El? Same old argument."

"She gets off on it."

"Harper!"

"What? It's true."

"We should find Inspector Tucci," Oliver says. "And Officer Rolle."

"That, I agree with," I say. "But wait. What about Brian?"

"Who's Brian?" Sandrine asks.

"The dead guy that was in our room," Harper says.

"Ah."

"You told her?"

Harper shrugs.

How long have they been in contact? How long has this been going on? Back to when Sandrine and I were still friends?

I. Have. So. Many. Questions.

"Why would Marta kill Brian?" I ask. "Was Guy working with him?"

"Not that I know of," Connor says.

"We've established that you don't know much."

"See, I told you she gets off on it. Good thing you didn't propose, Oliver."

"Harper! What's gotten into you?"

"Couple of cocktails at lunch," Sandrine says with a slightly wicked grin.

"You had them, too!"

"*Bien sûr.* A murderer on the loose. Bodies dropping. That'll drive anyone to drink."

"That's what I've been saying," I say.

"Have we forgotten anything?" Oliver asks.

Connor lifts his hand. Sitting in the palm of it is the USB stick. How did he get his hands on that? Last time I saw it, Oliver was holding it.

"What's that?" Harper asks.

"It was hidden in a book in Guy's office."

Oliver pats his pockets down. "You lifted it off of me."

Connor shrugs. "Old habits."

"Let's look at it," Harper says.

"It's evidence," I say.

"When has that ever stopped you before?"

"That's enough out of you, Harper."

"You can't just order me around. I mean, you can, because you're my boss and all, but it kind of sucks that you do."

"You're right." This isn't the right time to do this, but when has that ever stopped me? "Harper, you're fired."

"Ha ha."

"No, you're free. I release you."

Her face falls. Maybe in relief. "Are you being serious right now?"

"Yes."

"Wow, Eleanor. Firing your own sister. Nice."

"Shut it, Sandrine." I look at Harper to see how she's taking the news. She seems suspended between shock and ... happiness? "Harper? You okay?"

She lifts her chin, but her eyes are glistening. "I'm fine."

"It's for your own good."

"Gee, thanks."

"You know it is. You're miserable. Stuck in *my* life. Making bad personal decisions." I try not to look at Sandrine, but I don't quite manage it. "It's time for you to figure out what you want to do in *your* life."

"Sounds like a good idea for everyone," Oliver says. "But in the meantime, how about we figure out what's going on and then we can make big life decisions, yeah?"

I nod. "Where were we?"

"The USB," Harper offers.

"Anyone have a laptop?"

"I do," Connor says. "Writing deadlines, you know how it is. Give me a moment."

My eyes shift to Harper. Her face reddens again.

I *knew* it.

Connor returns with a silver laptop. He puts the USB into the slot on the side of the computer. He clicks on the icon and finds one folder.

It's called Novel.

"Oh God," I say. "Not *another* writer."

Connor clicks again on the icon, but it won't open. Instead, a pop-up appears with a prompt for a password.

"Any idea what his password is?" Sandrine asks.

"Your guess is as good as mine," I say. "Connor?"

"It would be something obvious. Subtlety wasn't his strong suit."

I think about it for a moment, and then something flashes into my mind. The key to all of this. I reach forward and type:

Giuseppe.

Open sesame.

INTERLUDE

Because We All Need a Minute to Breathe

Hi, folks, Eleanor again.

I mean, I've been here the whole time, obvi, but I thought it was time for you and me to have a little chat. Because some of you might need a refresher on where we are and a clue to where we're going.

I know *I* do.

Did I mention that I'm not a very good detective? No? Well, I'm not. You've probably noticed that by now.

So, where are we?

Trapped in some mirror version of my life with two dead bodies in a resort owned by the Giuseppes, a family that's tried to kill me more than once. And I've been lured somewhere *again*. This time by Guy and Connor, who cooked up some harebrained scheme to catch Marta by using me, Harper, Oliver, and themselves as bait.

What could go wrong?

Those idiots.

ANYWAY, Guy paid for his stupidity with his life. Which I guess he deserved because he was part of their evil plans going all the way back to Italy.

So it's looking like Marta killed Brian *and* Guy.

That's the simple explanation.

But remember back there where I said it was *never* the simple explanation? And remember also when I said things come in threes? Like bodies?

Plus, we're not even in the third act. So I've only uncovered the first layer of the onion I'm currently peeling, and there are going to be a lot of tears before I get to the middle of it.

Okay, that was a bad metaphor, but you get the idea.

But I promised you a hint so—

Here are three things that don't make sense to me yet:

1. Guy and Connor setting a trap for Marta by luring me, Harper, Oliver, and Inspector Tucci to the Bahamas makes a certain kind of messed-up Connor sense. Like how idiots might use humans for shark bait instead of chum. Because right now, *we're the chum*. But why is Sandrine here? Ravi? Stefano? Cathy? Why is there still a plausible list of suspects who'd want to kill *me*?

2. If I were Marta, I'd hightail it for the hills the *minute* Guy showed up, I don't care how difficult it might be. I certainly wouldn't hang around and wait for him to expose me or buy some stupid story about how he wanted to help me escape with new papers. So is Marta even at this resort? And if she isn't, why did Guy and Connor go through with their plan? Because I'm not buying that Guy hadn't identified her yet for one minute.

3. Why would Brian have a crazy wall about *me*? If he was working with Guy and the plan was to expose Marta, I shouldn't have had anything to do with him. And while I might've said Guy put that wall up after Brian died to divert suspicion, that's not a Guy kind of thing to do. It's too subtle for him. So either the wall is *real*—in which case, *yikes*—or it's fake, and it was put there by *someone else*.

How are these things clues, you might be wondering? It'll all become clear in time.

You can bookmark this page and come back to it later. And yes, it's okay to turn down the corner of a book you own. That's right. *I said it.* But if you're reading electronically, then just use that bookmark function thing.

Okay, interlude over.

Let's get back to it.

Because the sixth sequence is always the most interesting one, in my view.

CHAPTER 19

What Does "Tl;Dr" Mean, Anyway?

Will it surprise you to learn that we don't read Guy's novel?

After shooing Sandrine away, we start to, but it's *very* long and boring and starts with the main character's childhood. He's just a very thinly disguised Guy and he hasn't even bothered to change most of the names because when we do a few keyword searches for "Giuseppe" it has over two thousand hits. But the name "Marta" is nowhere. We try to read the last chapter, but it's just a series of cryptic notes that we might be able to puzzle out if we had more time, which it doesn't feel like there's enough time to do.

So, it's a bust.

But why would Guy keep the manuscript on a USB in a book hidden in his office? It feels significant. Maybe it's useless to our current predicament. We can't decide that, though. Instead, after a short discussion, we persuade Connor to find Officer Rolle and Inspector Tucci and come clean about all of it.

The plan to unearth Martha.

The USB.

Guy's connection to the Giuseppe family.

Whatever there is in their past that could be relevant to the crimes we're in the middle of.

It's not going to be easy for him, but I think he sees the importance of not holding anything back, even if it puts him in legal jeopardy.

Ha ha.

It's Connor.

He's going to hold something back. Probably a lot of things. He's most certainly not going to confess to anything illegal.

Let's just hope that whatever he withholds isn't something that ends up getting someone *else* killed.

Because that's what usually happens. Someone keeps a crucial detail to themselves for reasons they can't quite explain other than to drive the narrative forward, and before you know it, *they're* dead, or someone else is dead, and if they'd just come clean in the beginning, that wouldn't have happened.

Is that just a fictional thing, or do people act like that in real life?

Of course they do.

We *all* have secrets.

Imagine you died suddenly. What's the thing you're most worried about someone finding out about you?

Don't panic. I'm not going to ask you what it is. It's just an exercise to show you what I mean. But yeah, you *should* erase those emails and texts. Like immediately. And not just a simple delete either. Go into your sent messages. Go into your drafts. Go into your deleted emails and your archives. *Be smart about it.*

Anyway.

Connor's off to tell his story, and I am starving and craving a drink.

But I'm giving up drinking for the rest of this trip.

What? I'm serious.

Maybe I haven't been hiding it from you, but my mind has been clouded since I got here.

Notice how I said "maybe" back there? Good. You're getting the hang of this.

ANYWAY, Oliver goes to forage some lunch for us as I walk into the rotunda by the pool. It's a covered white structure with metal bistro tables around it. The white paint is chipped, and the bistro tables are rusted in spots. Like the rest of this resort, it's a bit tired.

Like me.

Sandrine, Ravi, and Stefano are sitting at one of the tables, a pitcher of something on the table. Maybe the grog they've been serving nonstop since we got here. Because why else would all of my enemies be sitting at one table together, like they're lying in wait for me?

"El-ea-nor!" Sandrine calls with a ringing laugh that reminds me of better times but puts me on my guard immediately, which is probably the point. "Come join us!"

"Yes!" Stefano says with gusto. "Do!"

This is *not* a table I want to join, but if I walk away, it would be like declaring war.

So instead, I avoid making eye contact with Ravi—who doesn't seem *quite* as enthused that I'm joining the party—and take a seat.

"Drink?" Sandrine asks, picking up the pitcher. The liquid is dark and dangerous-looking, and as much as I want it, I have to keep my promise to myself.

For today, anyway.

"I think I'll pass, thanks." I look around. The resort has a deserted feel to it, like the day after a big party. "Where is everyone?"

"Excursions," Ravi supplies. "Snorkeling, sailing, the make-up water polo match on that island over there."

I follow his finger out into the ocean. There's a small island just offshore that belongs to the resort. The water between it and the shore is dotted with boats and sunshine. It all looks so *innocent.*

"People went on those?" I ask.

"*Chacun à son goût.*"

"How come you didn't go, Stefano?"

"I've been *investigating,*" Stefano says, as if I should know this.

"Oh, right. I saw you interrogating Connor earlier. How did that go?"

"That man is exasperating."

"I'm aware."

"He's still the top of my list, though."

"Great."

"What about you?" Stefano asks, pointing the drink in his hand at me like an accusation. "Where have *you* been?"

"Researching my next book." This isn't a lie, I realize as I say it. If I survive this, it will all be fodder for the next installment in the Vacation Mysteries.

Which makes me question myself. Did I subconsciously come on this trip just to have something to write about? Like the yoga class I went to with Sandrine that I turned into a pole dancing class?

Maybe we can all agree that I'm very funny and just leave it at that?

"Any luck?" Sandrine asks, a bit too pointedly.

"Some pieces are coming together. Others remain a mystery."

"Thanks for the details."

"Welcome."

"That was sarcasm."

"I know." I look around. "Have you seen Inspector Tucci?"

Ravi shakes his head. "Not since breakfast. Why?"

"I had some questions for him."

"That man. He has called me Shek *three* times and also advised me that he had a very good idea for a book I should write."

Sandrine laughs. "Welcome to being an author."

"What do you mean?"

"Everyone has a great idea for a book," I say. "And they always want *you* to write it."

"Unless *they're* going to write it when they retire."

"Right. Someday. Someday they'll write a book."

"Because it's so easy. You just do it like this." Sandrine snaps her fingers. "And an amazing book appears at your fingertips and sells at auction for major money."

Ouch. That's a bit close to the bone.

Mine, that is.

"I always wonder why everyone wants to give their amazing book ideas away," I say. "If I had an amazing idea for a book, I'd keep it."

"How do you know if it's an amazing idea?" Stefano says.

"If it won't leave you alone. If you're dying to write it down, then that's a good start."

"Huh."

"What are you planning to write about, Stefano?"

His eyes shift away. "I'm not sure."

"He's writing about a book reviewer who gets embroiled in a murder," Sandrine says.

Stefano's head whips around. "How do you know that?"

"Because everyone's first book is *always* about them. Right, Eleanor?"

"Absolutely." I look at Ravi, tucking into another drink. "Can I ask you a question, Ravi?"

"Go ahead."

"When did you get invited to this conference?"

"Why do you ask?"

"Humor me."

"Several months ago. I've been invited to so many things it's hard to keep track."

"And who asked you?"

"I received an invitation through my publicist. Same as you, I expect."

"Would you still have the invitation?"

"I might do in my emails."

"Could you check?"

He takes out his phone slowly, frowning at the screen. He taps at it and then tilts the screen toward me. He received the invitation at the beginning of November. It's from the conference email address and signed "the Conference Committee." It looks unremarkable. But Connor was on that committee, directing things.

Re-creating the past to flush out Marta, if he's to be believed.

But for that plan to succeed—if that *was* the plan—they needed everyone else to go along with it.

Or maybe they're all in on it together, and I'm the one out in the cold?

"Did you know I'd be here when you accepted?"

"No. It never occurred to me to ask."

I squint at him against the sun. "Would you have accepted if you'd known?"

"Perhaps."

"Even though you hate me and think I'm responsible for your brother's death?"

His eyes narrow. "You *are* responsible."

"I'm not, though."

"The only reason he was on that tour was because he had to go to help save his career. He told me. He told me all about you taking his marketing budget and how it was your fault that his books weren't selling anymore."

This is a gross oversimplification of a complicated issue, but I don't have time to debate the fine details.

"But that's not why he was killed. He was involved—"

The color rises in Ravi's face. "That's *slander*. And if you repeat that again, I will sue you."

"You can ask Inspector Tucci. Your brother tried to kill Connor in LA."

Ravi points his finger at me. "You'll be hearing from my attorney." He pushes back his chair and stalks off, stopping to grab his drink *and* the pitcher of grog.

"That was quite dramatic," Stefano says into the ensuing silence.

"Do *not* take out your phone and make a TikTok about this," I say.

"I wasn't going to."

"I mean it, Stefano."

He smirks at me. "Is that a threat?"

"I—"

"Because I know you had my NetGalley access revoked."

I glance at Sandrine. "What makes you think that?"

"I have my sources. I would've thought an author as big as you could take a little criticism."

"It was more than that."

His eyes narrow behind his fake glasses. "So you *have* seen my Tik-Toks."

"I never denied I did."

"So petty."

I take in a slow breath. "You requested the title after you'd already said numerous times that you didn't like my books. Why would you do that?"

"I was trying to give you another chance to get in my book graces."

"Your . . . what?"

"In my book graces. I like to give an author three strikes."

"Like the penal system?"

His hands flutter in front of him. "See, that's the problem with your books right there. So. Much. Sarcasm. Like, do something new. Do something *novel*."

"You've had that one in your drafts folder for a while, haven't you?"

"I'm entitled to my opinion, aren't I?" Stefano says.

"Why did you come here? To *this* conference?"

"I told you."

"You're writing a book."

"*Yes.*"

"About yourself?"

"It's not about me," he huffs.

"How many words do you have?"

"I haven't started writing it yet, I'm working on the outline."

"And who gets murdered in this book?"

He crosses his arms. "I'm not going to tell you. You'll just take my twist."

"Excuse me?"

"I've heard that's what you do."

"From her?" I point to Sandrine.

He doesn't look at her. "It's commonly known."

"If you repeat *that*, I will sue you."

"More threats."

"I'm serious, Stefano. I've never stolen a plot in my life."[63]

"I have the receipts."

"Such as?"

He pauses like he's not sure he's going to go ahead, but his glee pushes him forward. "I looked into it. A bunch of your books are super similar to others."

"In what way?"

"The murders. The locations."

You'd think I'd be freaking out more, but I'm numb.

I'm also 100 percent certain that what he's saying isn't true. I've never stolen a plot from another author in my life. Who needs to do that when people keep involving me in *their* plots?

Wait . . .

"You didn't answer my question before," I say. "Why are you here? The real reason?"

"What's it to you?"

"It might be a lot to me."

"What's that supposed to mean?"

"Two people have died. Put it together."

He pulls his chin back. "Are you accusing *me* of that? And what do you mean, two people? Who else has died?"

Fork. It's getting too complicated to remember who knows what.

I should just assume no one knows anything.

"That isn't important right now. Answer the question."

---

[63] Except from murderers. If you involve me in your murder plots, I reserve the right to write about it.

"No." He pushes his chair back and stands, his face red, his hands shaking. "This isn't over."

"It didn't even start."

"You think you're funny, but you're really not."

"You're the one who's hiding something."

He shakes his head. "You said it. We're *all* hiding something." He turns and stalks off like Ravi did.

I watch his back, trying to figure out what he's not telling me, other than the bare hatred he seems to have of me from reading my books.

"And then there were two," Sandrine drawls.

"Don't start."

"I haven't started anything."

"Really? Why are you here? Why come somewhere you knew I'd be?"

"It's not for me to go."

"Are you quoting from *Pride and Prejudice*?"

"Always with the accusations."

I slump in my chair. "I feel like I'm going crazy."

"You made your bed."

"I didn't do anything!"

"You know you did. The common denominator of these stories is you."

Didn't I say that? I'm sure I did. Or at least thought it.

"So I'm that terrible, huh? I can't go anywhere without being faced by enemies, and that's just because I have so many of them?"

"If the description fits."

"You can say whatever you want. It doesn't hurt me anymore. But don't think I haven't noticed that you're not answering the question. I'm not some journalist on CNN who can be distracted by denying something three times."

"And *you* haven't answered why it matters."

"It matters because someone's brought a bunch of people to this resort who have reason to kill me and two people are dead."

"But you're not."

"Not even denying you want me dead, nice."

She purses her lips. "Don't be ridiculous. I'm not a murderer. And I can tell the difference between you and Guy, even in the dark."

"Guy was up to something. It's not a coincidence that we're all here."

"Investigate that, then. Leave me out of it." She stares at me, and though I expect her to get up and stalk out like the others, she doesn't.

So I'm going to do it.

I'm going to stand and leave and go somewhere else, but before I do, Oliver comes to the table holding two plates of food and a grim expression on his face.

"What did I miss?"

SAMPLE PAGES FOR REVIEW BY ELEANOR DASH, HOW
TO WRITE A MURDER CONFERENCE

I've always wondered what would drive someone to
spend their life writing about murder.

There are so many pleasant things to write about.
Happiness. Love. Romance. Why choose death?

It has to be some defect, some trauma mining,
doesn't it? Something that happened to you in the
past that turned your bright world dark. Because
everyone starts out happy, don't they? Babies smile
unless they're cold, hungry, or wet. They're otherwise easy to please because they haven't seen any of
the bad parts of the world yet.

Then something happens to some of us. Maybe most
of us. Bad things. Things I don't like to think
about. And after that, things get twisted. That
bright mind full of happiness turns dark, and eventually, that darkness has to come out somewhere,
sometime, someway.

My mother always used to say, when you see something, you have to do something.

If something isn't right, you have to make it
right.

But I've learned that if *someone* isn't right, they
have to hide that from the world.

You cannot let your freak flag fly, no matter what
they say nowadays. Acceptance is just another lie
they feed you to make adulthood palatable.

You have to hide yourself away, like that song.

What was that song?

Doesn't matter.

The truth is you have to be careful. You can't leave signs.

You can't go around writing "All work and no play makes Jack a dull boy." No way. That's what you write if you want to tell everyone you're a psychopath. Like in that movie with Kathy Bates. She wasn't acting normal. She wasn't keeping it inside.

But that's not how psychopaths operate. They don't leave clues like that. They're right here with us, leading our companies and running our countries and, yes, sometimes, when they have to, eliminating life.

Exterminations are part of the job description, but it's not something to laugh about. Nobody *wants* to be a psychopath, just like no one wants to wipe a smile from a newborn's face.

Life happens, though. Life wears away at your fresh skin until it's rough to the touch. Life takes away your choices and makes a mockery of your freedom.

And in the end, we all die, one way or another.

CHAPTER 20
Does Misery Love Company?

"So, what do you think?" Cathy asks eagerly an hour later. It's the middle of the afternoon, the air-conditioning fighting against the building heat. After the mental scorching by the pool, it feels nice to be inside this hermetically sealed environment, even if it's seen better days.

We're in one of the conference rooms, where the faculty are holding individual meetings with the conference participants who decided to submit pages for their small group leader to review. It looks like most conference rooms do—thick carpet on the floor made of some multicolored fabric meant to hide stains, mottled beige walls, and air that seems to have had the life sucked out of it.

We received the pages from the conference participants weeks ago, anonymized with only a number to identify them. The idea is to read them, provide feedback when they show up for their appointment, and you learn who they are, and avoid making the participant cry. Saying things like *Don't quit your day job* and *They aren't publishing anyone these days unless they're a celebrity* are discouraged.

This is harder than you might think.

I'd already met with Harold, who, it might not surprise *you* to learn, is writing a book about a former FBI agent who discovers that his old boss has been murdered and he's been framed for it. He's called Damien in the book, and Damien/Harold finds this information out on a helicopter for reasons that aren't clear, other than I think Harold wanted to take a helicopter ride and expense it.

After I get the basic plot details out of him—some convoluted story about international espionage, because of course it is—he tells me he writes his books with his wife, but I notice that *her* name isn't on the pages, or on the multiple books he self-published in the last three years.

She's also not in our meeting, and when I point that out, he raises his shoulders, and I can see the thought bubble about *women* forming above his head before he deflates it.

That doesn't stop Harold from telling me that he has a problem with publishing.[64] He's an "old white man," and publishing doesn't care about them anymore, according to Harold. When I try to point out that plenty of men are doing very well in the industry, he gives me the hand. An *actual* hand. But I let it go. Why interfere with his reality? I give him back his pages with their seventeen typos corrected, and he shuffles off.

I make eye contact with Elizabeth at the table nearest to me, who has a bemused smile on her face.

How many of these has she had to suffer through?

So many hopes, dreams, and aspirations in her hands.

Harold's dream is to live in a time when people who look like him are still in charge of everything, i.e., *now*, but he doesn't recognize it. And there's nothing I can or want to do about that because when you had 100 percent of something and now you only have 99 percent, it feels like you lost something, even though you never should've had all of it in the first place.

Elizabeth gets it. She's being talked *at* by a different man in a black blazer and blue slacks, like he's at a corporate retreat. He has the square shoulders of a former soldier and a look in his eyes like he might've killed someone in combat. He reminds me of Guy, which isn't something I want to be thinking about right now, but is also impossible not to think about.

---

[64] Who doesn't?

Because that's what I should be doing, not critiquing pages that will never make it out of the slush pile.

Sigh.

By process of deduction, my next appointment was supposed to be with Stefano, but he never showed, too butthurt from our earlier conversation, I assume. Ironically, his pages weren't bad. He said before that he hadn't started writing his book yet, but that wasn't true.

Everyone's a liar.

That's not a clue; that's just life.

I'm pretty sure I guessed the killer in the first chapter, but that's easy enough to adjust. He just has to cut the part where he tells the story from the killer's perspective because it's a) tired and b) has too many clues to the real killer in it.

But he doesn't want my advice. He spends his career tearing down people who do what he wants to do. And in the tearing down, he's convinced himself that anyone can do it. It's sad because so many in his community just love books and talking about them in a positive light. But Stefano gets up every day and chooses violence.

Which brings me back to Cathy.

"Did you like my pages?" she asks again. She's pulled her chair too close to me, and I can see the fingerprint smudges on the glasses she's put on to read. They magnify her watery eyes in a way that reminds me of a bug.

"They were ... um ... interesting."

They were scary, and weird, and harmless all at the same time. Just like Cathy.

She frowns. "I don't think there are enough books from the psychopath's perspective."

"Okay."

"Don't you think it's original to see an entire book through the eyes of the killer?"

"There are books like that already."

She sits back and crosses her arms. "Like what?"

"*The Murder of Roger Ackroyd*, for one. Others come to mind."

"Yes, well, *one* example which is *old*."

"Only one of the best and most well-known books in the mystery space, but okay."

Cathy isn't listening. "I do think that we don't think about it enough. What makes a murderer."

"Right."

"And obviously, if you kill someone, there's something wrong with you."

Is she asking me or confessing?

I don't get to ask because there's a tinkle of laughter behind me. It's Elizabeth. The carpet must've muffled her steps. "My dear, there are so many reasons someone might choose to kill. Even heroes do it sometimes."

Cathy looks at her with a mix of skepticism and awe. "They do?"

"You were talking of Agatha. Think of *Curtain*, Poirot's last case. He chose to bring someone to death before his own."

"Wasn't that because he couldn't catch the murderer otherwise?" I ask.

Elizabeth gives me a gentle smile. "Yes, of course. But that proves my point exactly. There are sometimes *rational* reasons for murder."

"If someone's wronged you," Cathy says like an eager student.

"That might be one motive. This is always where you should start. With the *why*."

"The why?"

"The *mens rea*. What propels someone to violate the ultimate norm? Once you understand that, then you can begin your story."

Cathy cocks her head to the side. "So you're saying everyone has a murder in them?"

"Perhaps."

"I think that's right. There has to be someone that everyone hates enough to kill." Cathy points at me. "Like Eleanor. She might murder the man who killed her parents when he gets out of prison."

A chill goes down my spine. "How do you know about that?"

Elizabeth pats me on the shoulder. "I'll leave you to it." She turns and walks away, her cane ticking silently against the floor.

I try to compose myself, because right now, if I *was* going to commit a murder, it would be Cathy. "Explain yourself, Cathy."

"Why are you taking that tone?"

"Because you keep violating my privacy."

"It's public information."

"That doesn't explain why *you* know about it."

She shrugs. "I follow his case."

"Why?"

"Because it's about you."

I feel sick to my stomach. "You have to stop."

"What?"

"Me. You have to quit me. Move on. Find another target."

"You're not a target. I'm a *fan.*"

"It's too much, Cathy. We've talked about this before! Showing up every time I leave the country. Switching into my small group. Researching things about me. The recording in my house? I should've turned you in to the police for that. I'm too soft on you."

Cathy takes off her glasses slowly. "Excuse me?"

"I—"

"Who are *you* to tell me how to behave?" Her eyes are flashing, and for the first time in a long time, I'm a bit frightened of Cathy.

Which might have *you* laughing. Or shaking your head in disbelief. Because she's been frightening this whole time, even if I've made her into a joke. That's what I do for things I'm frightened of. I cut them down into bite-sized soundbites so they don't scare me as much as they should. But these are just the lies I tell myself to get through.

The truth is that Cathy should be at the top of any list I make of someone who might see getting rid of me as some kind of solace. As a solution to her illness. And maybe these pages that I'm still holding in my hands are a roadmap to what she wants to do.

Kill *me*. Maybe she's using this event as the *opportunity* to do that. Taking advantage of an existing situation and the chaos that seems to follow me and striking when she can.

It wouldn't be a bad idea. I mean, I assume by now that people just figure I'm going to be surrounded by murders and chaos, and they aren't wrong about that, it turns out.

It's why *you're here*, after all, isn't it?

So, is Cathy the killer? Did she somehow find out that the Giuseppes owned this resort or that Marta was here and manipulate the circumstances to get me here so she could strike?

But wait. No. Cathy doesn't have that kind of power. And it doesn't explain what Guy is doing here, or Connor, or why Brian is dead, though the crazy wall *does* reek of Cathy.

There has to be another explanation for that.

I'm not safe around Cathy, but that doesn't mean she's behind the current events.

I take a deep breath and hand Cathy her pages. "You can write, but I don't think you should try to mine the depths of a psychopath. I think that's been done before, like I said, and that you should try to find a more original way of telling this story."

Cathy takes the pages and holds them against her chest. "You're not going to give the pages to Vicki?"

"No."

"I thought that's what I paid for."

"You paid for my feedback, and I've given it."

She stands, her hands fluttering against the pages. "We'll see."

"What, Cathy? We'll see what?"

"I'm not going to tell you. I don't want to spoil the ending."

✻   ✻   ✻

I feel like I've spent too much time wandering through this resort, lost in my thoughts. This afternoon is no different. After Cathy leaves, I find myself wandering again. Out of the conference center, through the pool area, and toward the beach. Stefano's standing with Harold and a few others from my small group near the snack bar, poking a finger at Mark, who's tugging on his collar in discomfort.

Oh God. What are they up to now? Stefano doesn't think he can solve this, does he?

I approach slowly with caution till I can catch their conversation.

"—unacceptable. It wasn't even cooked."

"We could die of food poisoning."

"—left in the sun."

"—and the pool is cold. Like freezing."

"My room wasn't cleaned this morning—"

That doesn't sound like a murder investigation. Should I intervene and rescue Mark? No, he won't be killed because someone had to reuse their towels.

There are bigger problems in life.

Like death.

I walk away, aimless.

Okay, that's a lie.

I'm headed to the bar. I'm *at* the bar.

Even though I was *just* promising myself I wasn't going to drink today. Yikes.

But I want a moment of peace. Where the questions, doubts, and fears quiet down in my brain, and I'm alone with myself. Only, my brain seems to hate me. It seems to want me dead. Because it won't let me sleep or think straight or want ordinary things. Like Oliver. Like happiness.

So I'm going to have a drink.

One drink.

"That's what I always say," Vicki says, turning to greet me with pink cheeks as I plunk down on the barstool next to her.

"Was I talking out loud?"

"You were."

"I need to fix that."

The bartender asks me what I want, and I hesitate, but in the end, I ask for an Arnold Palmer.

"Changed your mind?" Vicki asks.

"I thought it best to."

"You don't mind if I have another?"

"Of course not."

Vicki nods to the bartender, pointing to her glass. Looks like she's drinking vodka on the rocks, which doesn't seem like the best life decision.

"You okay?" I ask.

"Been better."

"The murders?"

"What? Oh, yes."

"And?" I prod.

"I spoke to Elizabeth at lunch."

"Oh, no."

"Yeah."

"How did she take it?"

Vicki glances at me. "How would you take being forced into retirement?"

"Badly?"

She smiles, but it's sad. "Yep."

"Fuck."

"That's what she said. Which is surprising because I've never heard her swear in the twenty years I've been working with her."

"Maybe she could go to another publisher?"

"They'll all look at her sales numbers and come to the same conclusion."

"So it's over?"

"It's over. And you know what the worst part is? She's sick. She just told me. She's been feeling run down and lost some weight and . . ."

"Cancer?"

"She'll get the results next week."

I shudder as the bartender passes me my Arnold Palmer. It's tart and sweet and does nothing to calm the nagging in my brain. But I have to stay sharp. There are pitfalls all around me, more than the ones I know about.

"Maybe you could cancel Connor's book deal and give it to Elizabeth instead?"

"It doesn't work like that."

"It should. That idiot put us all in danger."

"How?"

"By suggesting we come here, for one."

Vicki's face clouds, then clears. "You mean on the committee?"

"Why didn't you tell me he was on it when I asked before?"

"I knew you wouldn't like it."

"Okay, true, but why would you ever let him on that committee in the first place?"

"We always need volunteers."

"But Connor? He never does anything for himself. You must've known he had an ulterior motive."

"I did wonder. But he was so helpful. He even found this place."

"Exactly. That was part of his plan."

"Plan?"

I explain to her what we learned. How Connor suggested that the conference happen here to act as a trap for Marta. How it's owned by the Giuseppes. How we still don't know who killed Brian and Guy, but it was probably Marta, who's on the loose.

Vicki's face goes white as she listens; then she gulps down her drink. "I should've seen it."

"It's not your fault. He's very charming and persuasive when he wants to be."

"He put us all in danger."

"I'm sure you're fine. No one wants *you* dead."

"Don't be so sure of that."

"Elizabeth? She wouldn't hurt a fly."

"No, I . . ." She stares off into the middle distance. Then she reaches for her glass in a distracted way and gulps the rest of it down.

"Careful," I say.

"What's that?"

"Don't drink too much. We still have dinner to get through."

"Right. I should go change." She stands up on wobbly feet, knocking over the chair behind her. "Damn it."

"It's okay, I'll help." I bend down and bring the chair up. "See, all better now."

Vicki's eyes fill with tears. "You are sweet."

"It'll be okay. Elizabeth will enjoy retirement. Never having to hear another person complain about her books again? No more deadlines? And she doesn't even have to retire. She can rest on her laurels. Still go to conferences. Nothing has to change for her in the grand scheme of things."

Vicki just shakes her head, unsteady on her feet.

I put my hands on her arms. "You'll be okay to make it back to your room?"

"What? Oh, yes, I'll be okay."

"Skip dinner if you don't want to go."

"I might."

"I'll cover for you."

She forces a smile and drifts off, swaying through the chairs.

"You should make sure she gets back to her room," the bartender says to me.

"She'll be fine. It's just over there."

He shakes his head. "She's in trouble."

"Did she say something?"

"She didn't have to. In this business, you see all kinds of things. Learn a lot, too. If you take the time to listen."

I look at him properly for the first time, because that's what we do, right? Ignore the people on staff? They fade into the walls.

He's in his mid-twenties, is a local, and is wearing a blue staff polo. He has a kind face, but appearances can be deceiving.

"She had a lot to drink," I say. "And a stressful day."

"Can I be honest with you, madam?"

"Sure."

"Is that lady your friend?"

"Business associate and friend."

He picks up a glass and starts wiping it with his bar towel. "If I had to guess, I'd say she's afraid of something."

"There have been a couple of deaths here, as I'm sure you've heard."

"I don't think it's that," he says.

"What, then?"

"You're one of those mystery authors, aren't you? I guess you'll figure it out."

"Thanks so much for your help." I turn around and away. I feel like I'm being judged by someone I don't even know.

And I know you're judging me, too. Because I haven't figured out what's going on, and this is supposed to be my job. I'm supposed to see around corners, and figure out plots, and have insight into the people around me.

But all I want to do is crawl into bed and rot away for the next forty-eight hours, even though I can feel the ticking clock of these murders all around me.

Is it ticking down to midnight or dawn?

There's the rub.

CHAPTER 21

Is the Shit About to Hit the Fan?

"Can you zip me up?" I say to Oliver as the sun sets through the windows to our bedroom. It looks so innocent outside, so peaceful, but it's the opposite of peaceful in my brain.

I should be used to that by now, though. Anxious is my default setting.

Which would explain why I spent the first twenty minutes back in this room searching it for listening devices. I came up empty, but I'm not a spy. From what I've read on the internet for book research, those things are pretty easy to hide.

So, instead, I'll just have to pretend like they aren't here, because the alternative is not good for my paranoia.

I feel Oliver come up behind me and gather my hair in his hands. He lifts it, then reaches down and slides the zipper for my dress up like a sigh.

"Thank you."

He lets my hair go and puts his hands on my shoulders. His fingers automatically start to massage the hard knot of muscles there, and God, that feels good. Too good.

Because what I want to do is turn around and wrap my arms around his neck and let our bodies meld together until I can blot out everything but him. His mouth. His hands. The way our bodies fit together, not perfectly, but perfect for us.

Now is not the time to get all hot and bothered, though.

Besides, this is a closed-door mystery.[65] Cozy adjacent.[66]

"I'm sorry," I say.

"About what?"

"You know. The way I was acting earlier."

His eyes meet mine in the mirror. "When you were flirting with Connor?"

"I wasn't . . . No, sorry, you're right. I was doing that thing where we vibe when we're trying to solve something. It's this thing we have. I don't want to do it."

"I know."

"But I do."

"Yes."

I lean back against him. We look good together, like one of those couples that you meet, and you think, *Oh, right, that makes sense.* "I feel like we've had this conversation before."

"Have we?"

"Trapped on an island, our relationship in question, a murderer on the loose."

"When you put it like that." Oliver steps away.

I shiver, the air-conditioning caressing my bare shoulders the way I wish Oliver would.

"I'm sorry," I say again.

"Are you?"

"Yes, of course I am."

I hear a sound in the other room. I freeze.

"It's just Harper," Oliver says.

---

[65] Which is different than a locked-room murder. I think.
[66] Can sex be cozy? I'm thinking no.

"Oh, right. I haven't seen her all afternoon."

Oliver raises his eyebrows. "I'm sure the whole firing thing is going to take a minute to sink in."

"Did I really do that?"

"You did."

"Good."

Oliver turns around in surprise. "Pardon?"

"It needed to be done. She can't live her life in my shadow anymore."

"I wondered when you'd come around to that."

"Eventually. My timing wasn't the best, though," I say.

"Timing doesn't seem to be our strong suit."

"No." I take a step toward him. "But I want it to be. I want to put everything else aside, and I don't want to pretend that you didn't almost propose last night."

"I'm not sure we can do that."

"Yes, we can. Remember what we promised?"

"Remind me."

I smile at him, trying not to cry. "That we'd work it out. That'd we make sure we were the most important things in each other's lives."

"I don't remember you saying that."

"Maybe I used different words, but that's what I meant. You know I did. Hasn't it been good between us lately? Writing the book together. Living together?"

"Hiding from the media."

"Okay, but together we got through it." I reach for him. He hesitates for a moment, then takes my hand. I wind my fingers through his, squeezing tight. "Marry me."

"What?"

"Marry me. I don't care about the perfect moment or having a ring or any of it. Let's do it. We can even do it here. Just get on a boat and go out to sea and have the captain marry us."

"You're serious?"

"I couldn't be more serious."

He looks into my eyes, and I start to sink into my shoes. He's going to say no, he's going to say no, he's going to say no. And my heart is breaking into a million pieces.

"Please say yes."

"I want to."

"It's easy. You can. Yes. See?"

"What about Connor?"

"He's not important."

"How can you say that?"

"Because he isn't. I don't want to be with him. He's a liar and a cheat, and he put all of our lives in danger. Again. He doesn't care about me. He never did. Yes, I have residual feelings for him. I think when you love someone, that never goes away entirely. And as much as it pains me to admit it, I did love him. Not like you, but I did. And I know you were with people before me. We've never run into any of them, but it wouldn't surprise me if something leftover came up if you were around them. I wouldn't take it personally."

The corner of his mouth turns up. "Uh-huh."

"Okay, I would. But I'd know it didn't mean anything. Not in here." I bring his hand to my chest, right over my heart. "You must feel it. I know you do."

"I do."

"So don't quit on us, please."

"I'm not going to. But there's a big space between that and getting married."

"I know. And I'm asking you to leap into it. To leap across it. With me. Because I know we can make it. Look at what we've overcome. Look at everything thrown our way, and we're still together. That has to mean something."

"You don't believe in fate."

"You're right, I don't. But I also don't believe in coincidences. So it's not just happenstance that we're together. That we broke apart and got back together."

"No, it's Connor's fault, in both instances."

"So we have Connor to thank, then."

He laughs. "I'll pass on that."

"I thought you'd made your peace with him?"

"I decided not to let him bother me anymore, but that doesn't mean I like the guy."

"I know." I take another step toward him, and now his hand is trapped between us. I'm sure he can feel my heart beating.

Thump, thump, thump, thump. It feels like a clock ticking down. A metronome clicking out the beat of us. Of our ending.

"Eleanor?"

"Yes?"

"Yes."

I gulp. "Yes, yes?"

"Yes."

I launch myself at him, and he meets me in a kiss. Is it a kiss for the ages? I don't know how to rate kisses. I only know I'm going to remember this kiss for a long time, and I try to put all of *my* hopes and dreams, and feelings into it.

I resist the urge to unbutton his shirt.

He flirts with the zipper he just did up, lowering it enough to free my shoulder and shower it with kisses.

Eventually, we break apart, a little breathless.

"Now what?" I ask.

"Thought we always got that part right."

"Yes, but probably not the time right this minute."

"True." He rests his forehead against mine. One of his curls tickles me. "To answer your question, I don't know. I've never been engaged before."

"Me either."

"I don't think we should do that find a boat thing, though."

"No?"

"Last time we were on a boat, someone died. Let's wait until we're back safe in Los Angeles."

"Last time we went to a wedding, someone died, too."

"Are you trying to talk me out of this?" he says.

"No, I . . . I just keep feeling like I'm missing something."

"About us?"

"No. The case. Oh. You never said. What happened with Connor?"

He frowns. "I brought him to Officer Rolle. Hopefully, he did what he said he was going to do."

"And Inspector Tucci?"

"We couldn't find him."

The back of my neck starts to twitch. "That's weird. How hard did you look?"

"I asked around, did a lap of the property . . . He's probably just off trying to find clues in weird places. Someone said they'd seen him taking the little ferry to the island offshore."

"We should go there tomorrow. I hear the beach is nice."

Oliver smiles.

"What?"

"Maybe Connor's going to jail," he says.

"I doubt it."

"He and Guy knew where Marta was and didn't turn her in."

"They heard a rumor. He'll slither out of it like he always does." I twine my hands through his. "Any sign of Marta?"

"Not that I could see. But I never met her. And I assume she's not stupid enough to be wandering around in the open if she's killed two people."

"Assuming she's still here."

"Yes." I go through my mental checklist, all the things I've noted to myself to check up on. I come up empty.

Well, almost.

"We're still missing something," I say.

"What?"

"The ring."

"Oh, that." Oliver laughs. "Why don't we go to this dinner, and I'll give you the ring afterward?"

"Having second thoughts?"

"No, I want a minute to think about how I'm going to do it."

"What?"

"Propose."

"We're already engaged!"

"Yeah, yeah, but I want to do it properly." Oliver's mouth turns up at the corner. "I'm sure Connor's keynote will give me plenty of time to think about it."

"Oh God. What's the topic again?"

"'Can Romance Bloom While Murder is Afoot?'"

"That is the worst title ever. I can't believe Vicki's giving him book deals and dropping Elizabeth."

"What?" Oliver says.

"I didn't tell you? Vicki had to drop her. She told her today."

"That's insane." He lets my hands go and pulls away. "I'm so screwed. If Elizabeth's getting dropped, I'm next."

I want to argue with him, but what's there to say? Vicki basically told me he was getting dropped. And I've kept it from him because I don't want to be the person who delivers that news.

"We have *our* book coming out later this year. Hopefully, it will do well, and that will help?"

He gives me a brief smile. "That would be good."

"I know you want to do it on your own."

"I do. But that's not important right now."

"What is?"

He catches my hand again. "This. Us."

"Oh, that."

"Forgot already?"

"Never." I kiss him, pressing against him again. I feel like I'm always trying to convey my feelings with kisses when I should be much better at doing it with my words. But words fail me.

An alarm sounds in the distance, faint, insistent.

"What's that?" I ask.

"Time for dinner."

"How do you know?"

"It's the sound Harper uses on her phone when you have to be somewhere."

"I should know that." I check the time. "Isn't dinner in thirty minutes?"

He gives me a look.

"I'm not always late."

"Enough times, though."

"How am I going to be on time now that I've fired her?"

"You're not seriously asking that?"

"No, of course not." I mean, I was. But it's not important. Oliver doesn't need to know anything else bad about me. I've told him enough. He's seen enough. And he's still willing to marry me.

I asked him to marry me and he said yes.

Eventually.

That's good, right? I'm happy?

"Let's go to dinner before Harper feels like she has to come in here and remind us to go," I say.

"Are you trying to avoid her?"

"Maybe. For a minute. Is she feeling murderous?"

"I think she's confused and hurt."

I wrap my arms around his neck. "She'll get over it. It's for the best. It's dangerous being around me."

"And yet you've asked me to stay."

"Obviously."

I kiss him again, pushing myself close to him, trying to forget everything else.

But Oliver pulls away. "Are we going to dinner?"

"Can't miss Connor's insights into love," I say, trying to keep my voice teasing and light.

"He got you, didn't he? He can't be doing everything wrong."

Despite Harper's alarm, it feels like we're the last to arrive.

The Italian restaurant where the dinner is happening is buzzing with voices fueled by adrenaline and alcohol. Like all the restaurants here, it's indoor/outdoor, with a pergola above and walls made out of a faded teak lattice. The air is laced with garlic and cooked tomatoes, and I wonder for the first time why there's no Bahamian restaurant in this resort beyond the snack bar, which serves up fried conch.

Not everything's a mystery, Eleanor!

Focus.

The first person we run into is Officer Rolle. He's just stepped away from Mark, who's looking stressed. But you'd be stressed, too, if people were dropping dead at your hotel with regular frequency and a bunch of entitled writers were complaining about the services.

"Good evening," he says. "Have you seen Inspector Tucci?"

"No," I say. "Not since this morning."

He frowns. "We've been looking for him for several hours. I've just been speaking to Mr. Knowles about getting access to his room."

"Why?"

"After that . . . tale Mr. Smith had to tell me, it felt prudent to speak to him. He did not answer his door, and no one has seen him since this morning, as you say."

"I couldn't find him when I looked either," Oliver says. "Have you identified Marta yet?"

"No."

"How can that be?" I say.

"She could be any number of the staff, *if* she's in the resort."

"Are there really that many twenty-something Canadians on staff?"[67] I scan the room as if I might find her. While a lot of the staff appear Bahamian, there's a mix of races, like there's been at every resort I've ever been to. No one who stands out as Marta, though.

Assuming Marta looks like she used to.

Officer Rolle gives me his inscrutable look. "There are eight women who work here or who have worked here recently who match her general description."

"Let's do a lineup, then."

"We cannot simply accuse. And are you certain you'd recognize her?"

"Me, no. Harper, yes."

"We've spoken to Ms. Dash. She did not seem so certain."

"So we're just sitting ducks?"

"We have added security tonight." He points to several officers standing about the room, surveilling us. "They would be foolish to try anything now."

"And yet . . ."

"We'll keep our backs to the wall," Oliver says. "And the Giuseppes? Is it true they own this place?"

"It appears so."

"How can you not know?" I say.

"It is owned by a company that is owned by a company . . . You get the idea. We will sort it out."

"And Brian?"

"We have not yet established a connection between him and Mr. Charles. Or Mr. Smith."

"It has to all be connected."

---

[67] After her father went to jail, Marta's mother moved the family to Canada, where they acquired perfectly unaccented English, among other skills.

Officer Rolle nods. "I agree. Now I must continue the search for Inspector Tucci."

"Are you worried about him?"

"It is not about emotions but facts, Ms. Dash."

I glance at Oliver as the lights dim briefly, which seems like a bad idea, considering. "I guess we should take our seats."

"Good evening." Office Rolle bows in an almost Teutonic manner and turns away.

I watch him go. "None of this makes sense."

"I'm sure it all will in time," Oliver says.

"Hopefully, before it's too late."

"That's always the hope." He picks up my hand and kisses my ring finger.

I smile at him, and then we enter the restaurant properly, then weave our way through the crowd of strangers and acquaintances until we get to our table. Harper's there with Sandrine, her hair pulled back in a severe ponytail that makes her look older than me.

She glances up as we take our seats, makes brief eye contact, then looks away.

I've got work to do here, to repair what I've broken. But it's not just what I said today, or yesterday, or in the last ten years, even. It's from the day our parents died and what that broke in both of us. That's not something you can just recover from.

Like picking up the bottles after the party on New Year's Day. You can't just stuff it in the trash and take it out to the curb. I'm going to try to fix it, but not here, with everyone plus a murderer.

Hold me to it, though.

Anyway, the rest of the table is made up of the usual suspects.

Literally.

Ravi, Stefano, Connor, Cathy.

"Where's Vicki?" I ask as I sit in one of the only two seats left. So much for keeping my back to the wall.

"She must be around here somewhere," Harper says.

"She seemed pretty trashed at the bar earlier," Sandrine says.

"She had a hard day."

Sandrine shrugs and turns back to Harper. I try to catch Harper's eye again, but she's avoiding me. Too dedicated to making bad romantic choices, I guess.

Yep. Snark is firmly in place.

Just checking.

"Officer Rolle said you couldn't identify Marta," I say to Harper. "Did he show you photos?"

"He showed me a bunch of personnel files."

"You seemed so sure you could identify her earlier."

She shrugs. "If I saw her in person, yeah. But on a tiny photo that might not even be a photo of her, no."

"You're not worried."

"*I'm* not her target."

Ouch.

Oliver squeezes my hand under the table as Elizabeth rises at the head table. Which I see we've been demoted from, again. And how did Stefano get here, anyway? He's not an author, just a leech. Or Cathy?

I feel like I've lost control of this plot.

Damn it. There's that feeling again. I'm missing something. The key to it all. I keep brushing up against it like a thought that's on the tip of my tongue. The kind that comes together at two in the morning.

I hope that's not too late by then.

"Welcome, everyone, to night two of our conference," Elizabeth says as I scan the waiters and waitresses as they walk through the room, bringing out the salad course. I don't recognize anyone but Mark Knowles, overseeing the operation nervously. Is it possible that one of these women is Marta?

No, no. She wouldn't be so stupid as to be out in the open knowing Connor and I are here.

Not after killing Guy.

If she killed Guy.

Did she kill Guy?

"It's been a great adventure so far, has it not?" Elizabeth says. "Perhaps more than what some of us asked for. But that's the writing life. It will take you places you never expected. That's why we do this, isn't it? To experience things we couldn't do, or say, or feel in our real lives. To put down on paper our darkest secrets and desires. To put them where they are safe and sound.

"That's the truth of the *real* artist. We're vessels for others' desires, wishes, hopes. We bring them to life and, in so doing, stave off the need for others to do so. I firmly believe that if novels didn't exist, the world would be a darker, more dangerous place. Because in art, we can shine a light, we can laugh, we can explore, we can *mine*, we can relieve stress and distract. We can teach and fail and love and sigh and smile, all inside the covers.

"We can escape." She smiles. "Speaking of escapes, I'd like us all to welcome Connor Smith, who knows a little something about getting out from under the darkness and writing about something lighter. I'm talking, of course, about *love*."

Oliver raises his eyebrows at me while Harper pretends to retch and draws a laugh from Sandrine. I look at Connor properly for the first time as the room applauds. He gets up from the table, reaching inside his jacket for his speech. If I didn't know him better, I'd think he looks nervous.

No, he does.

He's nervous.

And I'm nervous, too, because this feels like a repeat of last night. Someone gets up and gives a speech, and then the lights go out, and then someone's dead.

Maybe this time it's me.

And that's why they've waited until now. Not because they mistook Guy for me or because I wasn't the target. Because of how I'm feeling right now. Nervous. Scared.

That's what they want. They want me to feel my death coming.

But that's not what happens. Instead, just as Connor's about to open his mouth to start telling us how romance can blossom while bodies are dropping, the door to the room bursts open.

It's Officer Rolle. The room hushes as he announces in a somber voice that carries like a theater kid's.

"Inspector Tucci is dead."

And before a thought can even form in my head, he raises a hand and points across the room.

"Stop that man!"

My head's on a swivel trying to figure out who he could be talking about when Mark peels himself off the wall and goes into a full run through the tables and out the back door.

And ... scene.

CHAPTER 22

Should I Be Paying Attention to the Lack of Footnotes?[68]

"Why are we running?" Oliver asks me as we push deck chairs out of the way and follow after Mark through the pool area, Officer Rolle on our heels.

"Seemed like the thing to do?"

"Is Mark the murderer?" Connor asks, slightly out of breath.

Mark is younger than us and surprisingly spry for someone in a suit and dress shoes.

"He must be," I say.

"Why?"

"We'll find out when we catch him."

We reach the edge of the pool and I stop, looking left, then right. "There!" I point as Officer Rolle sprints past me.

"Stay where you are!" he yells at us over his shoulder.

I look at Oliver, a bit red in the face. I guess none of us are that spry. "Are we listening?"

"Maybe we should just walk behind him?"

"Let's circle around the other way so he can't escape down the beach," Connor says.

---

[68] Um, obviously. I'd be very worried right now if I were you.

"That's smart," Oliver says.

I give him a look.

"What, it is."

Connor breaks into a jog again, and Oliver and I follow after him. I'm wearing low heels that are starting to pinch my feet; not the best thing to try to run in, but if a couple of blisters means that this nightmare is over, it's worth it.

We cut past the bar I was at with Vicki earlier and reach the sand. I immediately start to sink into it. I kick off my shoes, and ah, that's better. But it's dark out, darker down here without lights, the ocean a black shimmer to the right of me, the sand lightly golden under my feet. The moon is rising in the sky, a full moon, beaming on us like a flashlight.

"There!" Connor says, pointing at two dark figures sprinting toward us.

Mark is in front, brandishing something that glints in the moonlight. A knife.

"Careful!"

Connor and Oliver form a line, blocking his passage. But Mark either doesn't see them or doesn't care because he doesn't slow down; he just puts his hands in front of him like a human missile and barrels right at Connor.

I scream as Connor ducks out of the way of the knife at the last minute.

Mark doesn't get away, though, because in a move I can only describe as graceful, Connor sticks his leg out and trips Mark, sending Mark and the knife flying toward the sand. The force knocks Connor over, too, flipping him onto his back.

Mark scrambles to get up and retrieve his weapon, but Oliver and Officer Rolle tackle him and bring him to the ground as two other officers arrive on the scene.

It takes a minute or two to subdue him. He's in his mid-twenties and strong.

Or maybe it's just the fear. Whatever he's running from.

From something or someone.

"A little help here," Connor says from the sand.

"Oh, sorry." I reach out my hand and he takes it. He almost pulls me over as I help him up, but eventually, he makes it into a standing position. I tug my hand away, wiping it on the side of my dress.

"Thanks," Connor says in a tone that shows that he saw that.

Whatever. Connor doesn't have real feelings.

I know that better than anyone.

"Might want to work on your ab strength," I hear myself saying, "if you can't get up by yourself anymore."

Connor gives me one of his inscrutable looks. "So helpful as always, Eleanor."

"You're the one always asking for my help—no, I'm not doing this. Let's find out what this is all about."

Connor shrugs, and we turn back to Oliver, Officer Rolle, and the other police officers, who finally seem to have Mark under control, his arms behind his back, held together by zip ties.

One of the officers is holding the knife. It's sharp and glints with menace.

That was too bloody close.

"Let me go!" Mark says, struggling side to side.

"I don't think so, Mr. Knowles. Or should I say Giuseppe?"

Wait, *what*?[69]

"He's a Giuseppe?"

"Yes, Marco Giuseppe."

I look at Mark—Marco—whoever he is—as he stands there, still struggling in the arms of the two officers pinning him in place.

There were two boys in the Giuseppe family—Gianni, dead, and Marco, too young to think about ten years ago. I never met him, but he has the same fair coloring as his mother and sisters. He doesn't look anything

---

[69] I told you to be scared! See!

like his dead brother or his dead father. They were both more stereotypically Italian—olive skin and dark hair.

But I'm feeling pretty stupid anyway.

"*He's* the murderer?" I say to Officer Rolle.

"I didn't kill *anyone*," Marco says. "They're the killers." He points at me, then Connor. "They've murdered half my family."

I want to defend myself, but what can I say? I *did* accidentally kill his mother when she was trying to murder me. And his father *did* die in jail after we exposed him as a murderer. And I guess Gianni maybe never would've died if Connor had simply refused to plan the heists that got him killed . . . so yeah, we are connected to half his family dying.

The math is mathing.

But that doesn't make us responsible. Correlation versus causation. Sometimes it's both.

"Who killed Guy, then?" Oliver asks.

Marco's eyes shift away. "I don't know."

"I don't believe you."

"I don't care."

"Where's Marta?" I ask.

He looks at me briefly, enough for the hatred to come to the surface, then get buried again. "I'm not talking to you. I'm not talking to *anyone*. I want a lawyer."

"That sounds *so* innocent," Connor says.

"I know my rights."

"I thought you weren't talking?" Oliver says.

"Am I under arrest?"

"Yes," Officer Rolle says. "I am arresting you for fleeing from an officer. We will determine other charges in due course. You will be taken to the lockup, where you'll be given a phone call to contact a lawyer."

Marco lifts his chin. "Fine. *Fine.* I accept."

My body floods with a sense of relief, and I almost want to laugh. It's a beautiful night. The sky is clear, a ribbon of stars across the inky black. The moon is reflecting in the ocean, whose waves have quieted to ripples. There are lights around the trunks of the palm trees that line the edge of the beach and the berm behind it.

If I were alone, I'd peel off my clothes and dive into the water and swim out to the island and just sit in the quiet.

It's that kind of evening. But it's also *this* kind of evening. The kind I can't seem to escape.

So I don't laugh. Instead, we all watch as the officers take Mark away. Officer Rolle doesn't leave, though. He stays with us, and an ominous feeling comes over me.

I mean worse than before, which it seems is possible.

Fantastic.

"Did he do it?" I ask.

"I do not know yet. But the fact that he's here . . ."

"It makes sense," Oliver says. "If the family owns the business, they'd need someone to run it. And that must be why Marta chose this location. They thought it was a safe space. Until Guy reached out to Marta . . ."

"What if . . . they figured out why he was really coming here? So they decided to flip the script. And the conference . . ." I look at Connor. "They saw you coming from a *mile* away."

"It was a stupid plan," Oliver says.

"I say, at least we had a plan and—"

"Or wait," I say. "What if Guy was working *with* them?"

Connor looks shaken, not stirred.[70] "I wouldn't put it past him."

"You built a trap and fell into it."

"Yes, thank you *again*, Eleanor."

"Did Guy turn on them?" Oliver asks. "Is *that* why they killed him?"

"It makes sense."

"And Inspector Tucci?"

I follow the trail of breadcrumbs. "He was nosing around. Investigating.

---

[70] Yes, I <u>have</u> been keeping this in my drafts folder.

Maybe he stumbled onto something he shouldn't have. Or they didn't want to wait to find out if he would. Maybe he recognized Marco."

"Why wouldn't he say anything?"

"Why did Inspector Tucci do any of the things he did? Maybe he was in on it, too. Maybe he was on the take."

"Oh, you never said, Officer Rolle. How did he die?"

He clears his throat. "We do not know. He was in his bed. He looked asleep at first, but then, when we checked his pulse . . ."

"No way he died in his sleep," Oliver says.

"I tend to agree with you. The most obvious cause would be poisoning."

"Not *another* poisoning," I say.

"Why not?"

"Because of the small groups . . . One is Gun, and Brian was shot. One is Poison, and Guy was poisoned. Marco just tried to use a knife on us . . . Inspector Tucci's death should follow the pattern." I think it over. "Rope or Heavy Object."

"What are you talking about, Ms. Dash?"

I explain about the small groups. How we were divided into them.

"But what does that have to do with Inspector Tucci's murder?" Connor asks.

"Maybe nothing. If he wasn't part of the plan."

"You think the Giuseppes were following a plan to kill *you?* That they always planned on killing five people?"

Do I have to tell you that Connor's tone is sarcastic?

You're picking that up from context, right?

Just checking.

"No, I guess that doesn't make sense. Inspector Tucci *must've* learned something that set them off," I say, looking at Connor pointedly.

"Not about me." Connor puts his hands up.

"I find it interesting that you said anything."

"This is ridiculous. I didn't kill Tucci. Or any of them."

"You simply set this whole plan in motion."

Connor works his jaw. "I admit we didn't think it through. I didn't know about Marco. And I certainly shouldn't have trusted Guy. But I've told you all that I know."

"Marta has a motive to kill Inspector Tucci," Oliver says. "He put her father and sister in jail."

"And Marco could've done it, too, even though he denies it. How did you get into Inspector Tucci's room?" I ask Officer Rolle. "With *his* master room key, right?"

"Yes."

"Marco has access to everything. Our original room. Brian's room, too."

Oliver rubs at his chin. "But what about Brian? How does he fit into it?"

"I still think he's connected to Guy." I look at Connor. "Right?"

"I've already answered this question multiple times."

"What do you think, Officer Rolle?" Oliver asks.

He's been watching us, silent. "Is this what you always do?"

"What's that?"

"Throw out theories until something sticks?"

"Pretty much," I say. "You don't do that?"

"I follow facts. The facts do not lie. I'm sure it will all be connected," Officer Rolle says. "But, I admit, Brian is the element that I cannot work out."

"What's going to happen now?" I say.

"We will investigate."

"I meant to us."

"I'm going to insist that everyone stay in their rooms until Marta is apprehended. We will go back to the dinner and make the announcement now."

"That's going to go over well."

"Better than dying," Oliver says.

"Totally. But Marta must be long gone by now. I wouldn't hang around if I were her."

"Maybe she doesn't have anywhere to go."

"Certainly not the airport," Officer Rolle says. "It is closed, and when it reopens, she will not get through security."

"What about a smaller airfield?" Oliver says. "A private plane?"

"All flights are canceled because of the solar storm. We will send officers to all of the airfields when they reopen. She will not escape that way."

"By boat?"

He nods. "That is possible. We cannot police all of the private boats. But we will put out a warning to the authorities. It is our highest priority to catch her. Now, if you will return to your rooms."

"Oh!" I say.

"What?"

"It just occurred to me. Vicki didn't make it to dinner . . . We should check if she's okay."

"Are you concerned about her?" Officer Rolle asks. "Is she connected to all of this?"

"No, I mean . . . She had a lot to drink. She probably just fell asleep. But given everything . . ."

He frowns. "Yes, all right."

"Let's go now," I say, my anxiety increasing. An anxiety born from experience. Because if someone goes missing at a resort where there's a murderer on the loose, then it's just common sense to be worried about them.

Especially when that person is three-quarters of the way to being a serial killer.

So let's pick up the pace, shall we?

I lead the way off the beach and through to the villas. I'll come back for my shoes later.

I don't remember how I know what room Vicki's in, but I'm almost certain this is it. I knock. No response. I knock again, harder. No response.

"Are you certain this is her room?"

"No, I . . . Hold on." I take out my phone to text her, and there it is. A text from her yesterday saying she'd checked in and she's in room 114. Which is the room we're standing in front of. "It's her room."

Officer Rolle steps forward and hits the door, hard. He also rattles the door handle.

"I'll go around the back," Oliver says. "Maybe she didn't lock her balcony." He hustles away before anyone can object.

"That would not have been prudent," Officer Rolle says.

"Vicki is a smart person," Connor says.

"What does that have to do with it?" I say.

"She wouldn't leave her balcony door unlocked."

"People do stupid things when they're drunk."

"I wouldn't know."

"How lucky for you."

Officer Rolle makes an impatient noise. "Where did Mr. Forrest get to?"

"I'm sure he'll be back in a second."

His radio crackles at his hip. "Hold on." He steps away so we can't hear him.

"Wonder what's that about?" I ask.

"Maybe someone else is dead," Connor says.

"That's not funny."

"I wasn't trying to be."

I put my hands on my hips. "I am so sick of you."

"You going to fire me, too?"

"I would if I could."

"This again?"

I take a deep breath. "No. Not again. I'm moving past it. We're moving past it."

"We?"

"Me and Oliver."

"Good luck with that."

"What's that supposed to mean?"

"I'm always going to be here," Connor says, tapping the side of my head gently. "And here." He taps my breastbone.

We stare at each other for a beat before I step away as the front door to Vicki's room opens. It's not Vicki, though; it's Oliver.

"Is Vicki there?"

"No," he says.

"Oh, no."

"How did you get in?" Connor asks.

Oliver raises a finger and beckons us inside. We follow him through to the back sliding glass doors. It's open.

"Was it unlocked?

"No. I got in with this." He holds up a slim black rod. "One of the cleaning staff was going by and she had it." He shows us how it works, inserting it into a small hole in the bottom of the door, then twisting it so the lock mechanism is released.

"She just gave it to you?"

"I explained the situation."

"Why did she have this?"

"For when the electronic locks aren't working."

"Wait," I say. "That means there was a way to get into our original room. To kill Brian. They didn't need the key."

"They only needed this." Oliver taps it against his hand. "But that would still mean that you have to be on staff. It's not something just anyone can have access to."

"You got one." Connor points out.

"Yes, but let's assume that before there were a bunch of dead bodies here, the staff knew better than to do that. How would you even know that you could open it like that anyway? It has to be someone on the staff."

"Like Marta," I say.

"Yes."

"So Marta was in my room and found Brian? And killed him?"

"Or lured him there."

"Why?"

Good question. I go back to finding Brian on the floor. The staged suicide. Why would Marta kill him? What was he doing there?

He was probably working with Guy. So he was there at Guy's behest. To bug my room? To lie in wait? Or maybe he wasn't working with Guy. Maybe he was working with Marta. But if so, why kill him right before when we arrived?

Was he waiting to tell on her? And she found out?

Where the hell is she?

Wait.

That girl. That girl with the towels yesterday! *That* was Marta. And wasn't someone complaining earlier about their towels not being replenished? She's here. Oh, shit. She's been here the whole time.

"I saw Marta."

"What?" Oliver says.

"Remember when that girl came to the door with towels? That was her. She's working on the room staff. It's the perfect cover. A reason to go into every room. She'd have the master keys."

"Are you sure?"

"Pretty sure." I look around. There isn't any disturbance in the room, no sign of a struggle. No sign that Vicki's been there recently. "Did you check the bedroom?"

"Yes, the bed's made. Everything looks normal."

"We need to find Vicki."

"Why would Marta want to harm Vicki?" Connor asks.

"She published the books, didn't she? If Marta wants to kill all of us . . . and you served us up on a plate to her . . . We have to find her."

"She is not here?" Officer Rolle says, coming into the room with a preoccupied air.

"No."

He emits a deep sigh.

"What is it?"

"That call I received . . . Vicki is not the only missing person."

"Marta?"

"No, Inspector Tucci."

"But he's dead."

"Someone moved his body."

"Wasn't it under guard?"

"The man guarding it was knocked on the head. Someone snuck up on him."

"What? How?"

He shakes his head slowly, like he can't believe it. "From inside his room."

DAY THREE
SUNDAY

Act 3

The Seventh Sequence

- You've done it now. You've killed all the people you're going to kill (probably), and you've developed your A and B plots. All of your secrets have been placed, and you've dropped your twists at the end of Act 2 to take your story in a new direction.

- You've also brought your protagonist to a low moment, both in terms of solving the case and maybe also personally (though you can bring them to a personal high for contrast). So . . .

- How will your protagonist rise from the ashes and reach the climax of your story, where your NEXT brilliant twist will be revealed? (Yep, you need a lot of twists!)

- You also need to plant some red herrings and examine the suspects that you've seeded to distract the reader from the real solution.

THINGS TO KEEP IN MIND:

- The sequence should end with your characters believing that they've solved the mystery, only to be sent in one final direction at the end of the sequence.

- Writing a mystery is like laying out fishing lines and then pulling each one in slowly so the bait catches what you're after. By the end of this sequence, you should only have a few lines left in the water.

- But while we're talking about fishing . . . be careful <u>not to jump the shark.</u>

CHAPTER 23

Are We to Be Murdered by Every Giuseppe in the Country?

"This is a shit show," Harper says.

"Understatement."

We're back in our room, the three of us alone together. Officer Rolle didn't make a specific announcement to the participants about what was going on. He simply told everyone that, because of events that had transpired in the investigation, everyone had to go to their rooms and remain there until breakfast. There was a curfew, and anyone found outside of their room would be dealt with accordingly.

The two-too-many drink crowd grumbled and complained—I heard Harold's voice from across the room being shushed by his wife—but they eventually got up and moved out of the restaurant and to their rooms. I stopped to update Elizabeth on what was going on—Vicki missing, Tucci's body gone—and she rapped her cane against the ground like Gandalf, maybe hoping she could magic them back into their places.

I hugged her impulsively, and she shooed me away.

And now I'm back in our room, and I've caught Harper up on everything to date.

At least, I think I have.

There is still *something* I feel like I'm forgetting. Missing.

Can *you* tell me what it is??

I thought at first that this feeling I've had all day is about Marta. That I recognized her but didn't, and *that's* what is tugging on my brain.

But it feels like more than that now. Marta isn't enough. She's been identified, but the taste of missing something is still on my mind. Is there a Taylor song for this? There's one for everything, right?

Help me out, Swifties.[71][72]

Anyway.

"So we're just supposed to sit here and wait?" Harper says.

It's late now, somehow already midnight. She's changed into pajamas, a checked pair like the matching ones we used to have when we were kids, opening presents with our parents with fake snow spray-painted on the windows. I probably still have a matching set somewhere, but we stopped doing that whole matching PJs on Christmas morning thing a while ago.

"And not answer the door unless it's an official," I add.

Harper twists her hair into a braid. "We're not just going to do that, though, right?"

"Why do you say that?"

"No way we're sitting here letting the others figure it out.I don't believe that for a second."

Oliver and I exchange a glance. "What did you have in mind?"

"We should find Marta."

"No, that's dangerous. And the police are on it."

"We have to do something."

"We could read Guy's book," Oliver says. "Maybe there are some answers in there?"

"You have it?"

"I made a copy."

---

[71] Do not say "All Too Well." That's a song about not forgetting even when you want to.

[72] Okay, "I Forgot That You Existed" is a strong contender. And weird. I thought of this and then the song went viral on TikTok. Am I magic?

"How?"

"I air-dropped it to my phone."

"Have I told you lately that you're a genius?"

He smiles. "And look what that gets me."

"My undying love and devotion."

"Yuck. Get a room, you two."

I breathe out a sigh of relief. Harper's making jokes with me. We aren't beyond saving.

"Hey, Harp?"

"Yeah?"

"I love you."

She bites her lip. "Is that why you fired me?"

"I did it for your own good."

"Feels like you did it to win an argument."

"Maybe, but I was going to do it anyway. I decided before we came here."

"Why?"

"You know why," I say. "Because you have to go live your own life. It's been too long living mine. Helping me live mine. You have to follow your own dreams, make your own mistakes."

"I've made lots of mistakes."

"You know what I mean. Don't you want to wake up every day and *not* think about me?"

She laughs. "How did you know?"

"I know you better than myself."

"What am I supposed to do now?"

"I can't be the one to tell you what to do. You have to figure this out on your own."

She folds her hands together. "The only thing I'm trained to do is write, and I'm not good enough."

"So train for something else. Or try writing again. Just because it didn't work last time doesn't mean it couldn't work now. Try a new direction."

"You just told me that *Elizabeth's* getting dropped by her publisher. What hope is there for me?"

I don't look at Oliver. "Elizabeth had a long and successful career, but everyone has to pack it up eventually. If you truly want to write, then find the idea that won't leave you alone. Find the idea that you're scared to write about."

"Who says I didn't do that last time?"

"I read it, remember? It was great. Well written. But . . . something was missing."

"What?"

I hesitate because what I have to say might come across as harsh. In for a penny . . .

"*You*, Harper. I didn't feel *you* on the page. Your passion. Your intelligence. Your propensity to date the wrong person in every situation."

She laughs out loud. "Oh, yes, I can see it now. I'll go on *Love Is Blind* and write about that."

I cock my head to the side. "That's not a terrible idea. Is there murder in it?"

"If I had to go on that many bad dates, there would be a murder."

"*Murder Is Blind*,"[73] Oliver suggests.

"Good one."

"I'm not going on *Love Is Blind*," Harper says.

"But you get the idea."

"I think your next lecture has been canceled."

"Yeah, yeah, but you know I'm right."

She gets serious. "And what if I don't have a big idea in me?"

"That's what we're *all* afraid of," I say. "Everyone who writes is afraid

---

[73] TM. You're not allowed to steal this book idea. I might write it one day.

of failure, afraid of not connecting, afraid of not being good enough. But we press on anyway because we love it more than we hate it. It's the job we can't quit."

"I don't know if I feel that way."

"Then don't do it. Walk away. Take a pottery class. Take up running. Take voice lessons. Anything else. Just be spontaneous. What's the first thing that pops into your mind when you don't edit it?"

She smiles, a little dreamy. "A true-crime podcast."

"Why did you just say that?"

"You're not going to like it."

"Tell me."

"If I think about what I had fun doing, like actually enjoyed in the last couple of years, it was investigating John Hart."

"The man who killed our parents? Seriously?"

"It's like a giant puzzle where I'm filling in the pieces one by one. And I'm telling you, El, some things don't add up."

"Like what?"

"Like the missing woman. Why wasn't she found?"

"Maybe they didn't even look for her."

"They asked him. He denied it. But lots of witnesses saw her. So what is he hiding?"

I try to smile at her, even though I don't want to go anywhere near this topic. "I'm glad you have something you're excited about, Harper. I am. But we have one mystery on our plate already, and I cannot handle anything more right now."

"Sorry."

"No, don't be. Start your podcast if that's what you want to do. I just don't need to hear about it if that's your first case."

"I get it."

I hold my arms open. "You forgive me?"

"For what?"

"Firing you?"

She steps into my arms and hugs me. "Depends. You're giving me six months of severance, right?"

I laugh as there's a knock at the door. "I'm giving you a year."

"I'll get it," Oliver says.

He walks to the door as I reach out to stop him. "Careful. Don't open it if we don't know who it is."

"Right." He gets to the door and peers through the peephole. "It's Officer Rolle."

"You're sure?"

He shoots me a look and opens the door. Officer Rolle's shoulders are sagging. "We've found her."

"Who? Marta?"

"Yes."

"And?"

"We would like you to come listen to what she has to say."

"Why?"

"Because she is denying everything."

We're back in the room where Officer Rolle didn't interrogate me, exactly, but kind of did. Me, Oliver, Connor, Officer Rolle, and Marta.

It's late, and I'm tired, but I'm also keyed up like I've had too much coffee. The resort was quiet and beautiful when we walked through it, its flaws covered up by the night.

Harper decided to stay back and read Guy's book. She didn't want to face Marta, she said. She'd had enough of staring into the faces of murderers. And I couldn't blame her for that, but it felt like I had no choice but to go and hear what Marta had to say, so I did.

No surprises here—Marta *is* the maid I remembered from earlier. Early twenties. An innocent face. A *scared* face. She's wearing her maid uniform, and her hair is pulled back.

"Why are *they* here?" Marta asks as we enter. Her voice is high, one of those voices it's hard to hear in a crowded room.

"I think they can help in this investigation," Officer Rolle says.

"I already told you; I didn't do anything."

"You helped plot to murder me and Connor in Italy," I say.

Marta's eyes narrow. "I had nothing to do with that."

"Sure. Right. Did you think killing Inspector Tucci was going to get you out of that?"

"I didn't do that either."

"And stealing his body? That's rich."

Her eyes shift around the room. "What are you talking about?"

"His body is missing. You already know. Where did you put it?"

She just shakes her head.

"Where did you find her, Officer Rolle?"

"She was hiding in the staff quarters' laundry room. Once we knew who she was, we were able to identify which room was hers."

"Did you find anything in her room?"

"Nothing evidently connected to the crimes, but we are continuing our search."

Marta pouts. "Because I didn't do anything, I already told you."

"What about Guy?" I say.

She scoffs. "That *man*. I told Marco not to hire him, not to allow the conference to come here, but he thought he knew better. 'Let them come,' he said. The idiot."

"So Marco killed him?"

"No! My brother's not a murderer."

"Not *that* brother," Connor says.

Marta scowls at him. "I barely even knew Gianni. He moved out when I was six and died when I was twelve."

"Your sister and mother felt differently."

"Mother always had her heart set on revenge, ever since the beginning."

"So the plan was her idea?"

"I didn't say that." She shakes her head again. "I shouldn't say anything."

She wants to talk, I can tell. Does she think she'll convince us if she does?

It's amazing how many people think that. That they can rationalize their hatred. That they can explain away their evil. That you'll see it their way if they have a moment to explain themselves.

But most evil is rooted in selfishness, I've found. Thinking your problems are more important than others'. Thinking that if you choose evil, you won't get bitten.

"Where were you when Guy was killed?" I ask.

"I was cleaning one of the rooms. And I can prove it. We have to keep a detailed time sheet of where we are and when we clean each space. Plus, there are security cameras. Check them. You'll see. My log is on my cleaning cart. I wasn't anywhere near where Guy was killed."

Officer Rolle writes something in his notebook. "We will verify."

"And Brian," I ask. "What about him?"

"I didn't know him before he got here, and I barely talked to him."

"Please."

"Why would I? I was keeping a low profile."

"Working as a maid."

She lifts her chin. "What's wrong with that?"

"Nothing," I say. "I'm just surprised your brother treated you that way."

"I didn't want to just sit around."

"You wanted access to the resort," Oliver says. "It's obvious."

"Marco had all the access he needed."

"Sure, but as a maid, you could be among us, without anyone paying any attention. Because people never pay attention to the help."

"It's smart," Officer Rolle says. "I'll give them that."

"No, you're wrong. I didn't have anything to do with Brian dying. And he wasn't working with Marco. He was brought here by Guy. Of that I'm sure."

"How?"

Marta scoffs. "You think we weren't watching everything Guy did from the moment he got here? Give me a break. My brother's an idiot, but not *that* stupid. *That's* why Brian got fired. Guy found him snooping around in *his* room."

"Brian was spying on Guy?"

"That's what Guy told Marco. He insisted on giving him the boot."

"But you said they were working together?" Oliver says.

"I said Guy brought him here."

"What's the difference?"

She lifts her shoulders. "Brian had his own thing going on. Why else do you think Guy killed him?"

"*Guy* killed Brian?"

"Who else could've done it?"

"You. Marco."

"We didn't."

"Why, then?"

"Brian must've found something in Guy's room. Guy was *not* a good person. You do the math."

She has a point. Guy *is* the most likely suspect to kill Brian if what Marta's saying is true. Guy *wasn't* a good man. But what could he have been hiding that would lead him to kill Brian if it was discovered? If they were working together, then it had to be something that made Brian distrust Guy. Did he confront him about it? Was that why Guy killed him?

But what could it be?

Was Guy a murderer?

He had a gun, Officer Rolle said. Maybe more than one. And everyone knows that if you have a gun, you use it. In these kinds of books, I mean. Don't do that in real life.

So Guy used one of his guns to stage Brian's suicide and told everyone that he'd been fired because he was spying on guests.

But why do that in my room? What did Brian find? What was Guy hiding?

Oh! The USB.

"Was there anything on Guy's USB stick besides his novel?" I ask Officer Rolle. "Or anything in the novel itself that might be the key to all of this?"

"We are still analyzing it."

"That must've been what Brian found . . . But why bring Brian here? What did he need him to do?"

"And someone still killed Guy," Oliver says. "He didn't kill himself."

"Which brings us back to Marco," I say. "I still don't get why you'd let him come here. Even assuming you're telling the truth about the rest of it."

Marta crosses her arms and smirks at me. "I thought you were supposed to be smart."

"What's that supposed to mean?"

"Guy was working *with* Marco."

"Wait, what?"

"Explain yourself," Connor says.

"You really think we just let him come here?"

"You just said you did ten minutes ago."

She shrugs. "I wanted to see if you'd buy that."

"This isn't a game."

"Or a joke, young lady," Officer Rolle says. "Three people are dead and one is missing."

"And I don't have anything to do with that."

"So, tell us the plan, then," I say. "Explain."

I touch Oliver and Connor on the arm, letting them know to keep silent. Because we hate silence as a species. We have to fill it. Preferably by confessing to the things that are top of mind.[74]

---

[74] Try this in your personal life. Something you're wondering about? Ask the other person, talk around it, then sit in uncomfortable silence until they start talking. Just be ready to hear things you didn't want to hear.

Marta sighs, and I know we have her.

"I don't know how Guy found out I was here, but he did. He reached out to Marco. Guy told him that he knew who Marco was and that I was in the country. He said there'd be consequences if we didn't go along with his plan."

"Which was?"

"He wanted to host a writer's conference here. He wanted to bring *you* here," she says, pointing to me, "and *you*," she says, pointing to Connor.

"Why?"

"Why d'you think?"

"Just tell us," I say. "I'm sick of guessing."

"To take care of you once and for all. When it didn't work in Italy . . ."

"When *what* didn't work in Italy?"

"The plan to kill you."

"Guy *was* in on that?" I ask, my voice rising to a squeak.

She gives me a look of disdain. "Of course he was. He's worked for the family for *years*. Who do you think tried to kill Connor in LA?"

"That was Shek," Connor says.

"Ha ha. No. You do this for a living?" She laughs at Connor. "It was *not*."

"Then *you* did it."

"I was in New York. Which I can prove."

"But you were working at my publisher's," I say.

"Yes, I agreed to do that. I didn't know what they were planning. They just said they wanted to keep tabs on you."

"And you believed them?"

"Maybe I was willfully blind. But I wasn't knowingly involved in a plan to murder you. I would never have gone along with that. Way too risky."

"Yet you went along with Guy's plan," I point out.

Marta shakes her head. "No, I didn't. That was Marco. I told him not to do it."

"So why are you here?"

"I'm wanted for murder, hello!"

"You could've turned yourself into the police and explained everything you are telling us," Officer Rolle says.

Her eyes shift back and forth. "Have you *met* the Italian police? Look at what they did to Amanda Knox. No, thank you."

"So you escaped here?" Oliver says.

"Marco's been here ever since he finished hotel school. It was a safe place to land till I figured out my next move."

"Until Guy found you," I say.

"I wanted to leave immediately, but Marco had other ideas."

"Murder."

Marta blinks slowly, catching up to her thoughts. "He didn't say that. He just... We were going to *use* Guy. Guy had access to papers, he told us. He was supposed to bring them. Once I got them, I was going to leave and then..."

"Guy was going to kill Connor and me?"

"Not my concern."

"But Guy is dead," Oliver says. "Which makes Marco the killer."

"I told you he wasn't."

I rap my knuckles on the table. "Three people are dead. Someone did that. And it wasn't Guy. Not the last two. So Marco killed Guy. He was in the room that night. He was the one who was operating the lights. He knew about the timing of Elizabeth's story."

"That's something," Connor says. "No one else knew about that."

"She said she told her concierge," I say.

"He must've told Marco. Makes sense."

"But why kill Guy?" Oliver says. "Why then?"

"He didn't need him anymore," Connor suggests. "We were all in place."

"But that would alert us. Brian's faked suicide was one thing..."

"Guy must've threatened him," I say. "He must've felt like he had to act, whatever the plan was. Right, Marta?"

Marta starts to say something, then stops herself.

"And Inspector Tucci?" Oliver asks. "Why him?"

"Marco would have all the reason in the world to kill Inspector Tucci," Connor says. "As would Marta."

"I *didn't.*"

"And who next, Marta?" I say. "Me? Connor? This has to stop."

Her head hangs low. "I . . . I didn't think he'd do it."

"You just thought he'd lure us here and what? Scare us? Leave us to Guy?"

"That's what he said he was going to do."

"And you believed him?" Connor says. "You ridiculous girl."

"Marco isn't violent. I'm telling you. Maybe Guy was working with someone else? Someone you don't know about yet?"

"How big is this conspiracy?" I ask.

"It's not . . ."

"If I believe you—and that's a big if—what was he planning on doing to scare us?"

"He didn't tell me."

"I got a threatening note," I say slowly. "Right after I got here. Was that part of it?"

"That doesn't seem like the kind of thing Marco would do."

"I don't know why we're taking anything she says at face value," Connor says. "She's admitted that she, Guy, and her brother conspired to bring us here. It wasn't for a garden party. Guy killed Brian, Marco killed Guy, Marta or Mark killed Inspector Tucci, and then moved the body for some reason we'll determine later. It's simple."

"What about Vicki?" I ask, because where the hell is she? I can't think about it too much or I might just lose my mind.

"She'll turn up," he says confidently.

"And if she doesn't?"

"You're wrong about me," Marta says. "You'll see."

"What's that supposed to mean?"

Her eyes flash. "If neither Marco nor I are the killer, then they're still out there. Only no one's on their guard anymore. I'd be careful if I were you."

CHAPTER 24

Can a Good Night's Sleep Help You Solve a Murder?

Where were we? Oh, right, Marta made some threats. That happens so often it barely registers with me. But with that warning, Marta stops talking, and Officer Rolle sends us back to our rooms, telling us—again—to stay there till morning.

When we get back, Harper seems to have gone to sleep, and so we decide to do that, too. And improbably, it works. I tuck myself into my lumpy bed and pull up the comforter that should never be viewed under a black light, and fall into a deep sleep without any effort, something that rarely happens. But tonight, tonight, I swim deep, tumbling through dreams, images, all the people I've met and seen die in the last year. But it's not a nightmare; it's a catalogue. It's my brain going over and over and over the evidence and sifting it through. Putting it into order, seeing the patterns. And eventually, there's a moment of clarity, and I know who did it.

Me.

"El? You okay?" Oliver's shaking me gently.

I blink slowly against the morning light. "I did it."

"What?"

"The murders. It was me."

"Are you serious?"

I rub my eyes with my fists, and the images start to recede. The certainty. "No, I don't think so. I mean, in my dream, it was me, but that doesn't make sense, does it?"

His dark brown eyes cloud with concern. "Are you having a stroke?"

"I don't think so."

"Smile for me."

"Why?"

"Because I want to check if your smile is crooked. That's one of the signs."

I sit up. "I'm not having a stroke. I think it's more of an epiphany."

"Please explain because I'm about to call the staff doctor."

"I'm not sure I can. I just know we haven't solved it yet."

"I don't agree," Oliver says. He runs his hand through his curly hair. How does he look so good and put together after the night we had. After three murders?

I feel like a potato that got half skinned before it was put into boiling water.

"Explain it to me like I was five."

The side of his mouth twists. I bet his breath doesn't even smell. "Guy was involved with the Giuseppes. We know this from two sources now, Connor *and* Marta. He's been pissed at Connor for years. Probably for 'solving' the whole plot in Italy ten years ago. That wasn't the plan. They were *helping* Gianni plan those robberies. They weren't supposed to go to the police. But when the murder happened, Connor decided it was too much. So he found a way to 'solve' the crimes and get the finder's fee, which I bet he didn't share with Guy. And regardless, now they had an enemy. A dangerous one.

"So, Connor and Guy have no choice but to leave Italy. Then you write your book, and they *both* get famous. Guy always said it himself—he couldn't work as a detective anymore because of it. So he writes his book, it doesn't sell, what's he got left? I bet his resentment builds over time. And then Antonio, the capo dies, and maybe Guy reaches out to Sylvie with the idea in the first place."

"But what would he get out of killing Connor?"

"Satisfaction?"

I shudder. "Maybe. So that's why he brought the gun to Italy? To kill Connor."

"Or to defend himself if necessary."

"But we survived."

"You did."

"So he's still pissed, and he figures he'll find the rest of the family to finally get revenge?"

"Sounds like it."

"But why not just kill us in LA? Why bring us here?"

"He'd be a suspect if anything happened to you in LA. But here, *they'd* get blamed. It would come out who Marco and Marta were. So, he gets away with it."

"He tricked them."

"Yes."

"And Brian?"

"He *wasn't* working with Guy," Harper says, coming into the room, her hair a mess and deep circles under her eyes.

"What?"

"I read the book. I stayed up all night, but I did it."

"Did he really write out everything he was doing?"

"Not exactly. I'm not sure *why* he was writing it——he said at one point that it would be like an O. J. Simpson thing, *How I'd Do It*——"

"That's disgusting."

"Yep."

"So what did you find?" I climb out of bed and put on a robe, as Oliver does the same. We don't sleep in the nude, but I don't want to be talking to my sister with both of us in our underwear either.

She catches us up on the details we already figured out: Guy planned to bring me and Connor here so the Giuseppes could kill us off once and for all. He could blame them and then turn them over to Inspector Tucci. He'd get off scot-free and get a book out of it, too. Once he changed enough details "to protect the guilty," which is a line he plagiarized FROM ME.

Guy even cackled about Connor being stupid enough to fall for it. *Again.*[75]

"And Brian?"

"Guy was suspicious of him from the beginning. So he started to look into him. He thought Marco and Marta had hired him to watch him."

"Did they?"

"He couldn't find any connection between them. But when he found Brian snooping in his room, his suspicions were confirmed."

"So Guy killed Brian?"

"Unclear. He told Marco about it, but Marco denied having anything to do with Brian being here. Said he'd just applied for the job."

"Impossible. He was sent here."

"Obviously."

"But by who?"

"It must be Marco and Marta," I say.

"But why?" Harper says. "They were already on the inside. Marco runs the place. He didn't need an inside man."

"Guy, then."

"Then why cover it up in the book? His surprise was genuine. And Guy's not that sophisticated. I mean, his plan is the same plan as they had in Italy."

---

[75] There's that word, again. <u>Again</u>. It's been echoing through this book since the beginning. Patterns should make you suspicious. And yes, I'm back to giving you clues <u>again</u>. Ha!

I freeze in place. "Say that again."

"It's what they planned to do in Italy, isn't it? Get you and Connor together with a bunch of suspects. Kill you off. Blame someone else."

"So, who were Marco and Marta going to blame it on?" I ask. "From their perspective?"

Oliver tucks his head to the side. "Ravi, Sandrine, Stefano, Crazy Cathy—take your pick."

"Crazy Cathy loves me."

He shakes his head. "A crazy thing called love."

"Whatever."

"Okay, yes, they might all be considered viable suspects to kill me, but not Connor."

"Who says Connor was the target?"

"You just said that's what Guy wanted to do."

"But he could blame Marco and Marta."

"*Exactly.* So why are the other people here, then?"

Harper frowns. "I don't follow."

"Why are there other suspects at this conference?"

"Connor made sure they were here."

"Probably. And probably at Guy's suggestion, but *why*? If the plan was to blame Marta and Marco, why bring Sandrine, Stefano, or Ravi into it? And then what about Brian? What's happening now, it isn't Guy's plan."

"Obviously," Harper says. "He's dead."

"I mean, from the moment Brian arrived, it wasn't his plan. It was somebody else's."

"Wait," Harper says. "What?"

"Like you said, we've seen this film before."

"Guy's not the director?" Oliver says.

"Not anymore. Someone else figured out what he was doing and is using it to their advantage. That's why he's dead. That's why Brian's dead. And Inspector Tucci, too."

"So . . . not Marta and Marco?"

"I don't think so. Because if it was their plan, then why are Connor and I still here? No one's even tried to kill Connor. No one's really tried to kill me. So, something else is going on . . . Someone else is in charge here."

"But who?"

I flip through the Rolodex of suspects in my brain but come up blank. "I have no idea."

"How are we going to figure it out?"

"The way we usually do."

"Which is?"

"Gather all the suspects and start asking questions."

"Oh, sure," Harper says. "What could go wrong with that?"

We decide Oliver should find Officer Rolle to tell him the conclusion we've come to while Harper and I get dressed. She leaves, and I root around in the drawers in our room looking for something suitable to wear to the potential unveiling of a murderer.

It's harder than you think.

I'm amazed my things aren't still in their suitcase where I left them, then smile. Oliver. That man. He is the best. And he's right. We're engaged now. I have to find a way to be done with Connor emotionally. I should start by never going on vacation or any other type of trip with him again.

I have a new Connor Smith/Vacation Mysteries book coming out in a couple of weeks, and we'll have a bunch of events together, but once that's done, that's it. My book with Oliver isn't coming out till the fall. I haven't written another Connor Smith mystery. I'm out of contract. I'm free.

I smile as my hand hits something hard in the drawer.

I pull it out. It's a small blue box. You know, one of *those* boxes. I let it sit in my palm for a minute. I shouldn't open this.

Oliver said he wanted to have a moment to give this to me. A proper moment that wasn't tainted by murder and mayhem. And I get that, I do. But I also have low impulse control.

You know that about me, obviously.

So, do you really expect me not to peek? I mean, it's research. And it's in Oliver's best interest. Because what if I don't like the ring? There's still time to change it, and I don't have a great poker face. He'd want me to be happy with it, right?

But wait. Harper. Harper knew about the proposal. He must've consulted her about the ring. So the ring is fine. I can put it back in the drawer and forget about it.

Ha ha.

You didn't fall for that, did you? Not after all this time. Actually, I haven't looked yet. But I am taking it with me to Harper's room to ask her about it.

I enter without knocking, which I should also know better than to do, but did you just read that thing above about my bad impulse control?

"Harper, am I going to like this ring?"

She looks up from where she's sitting on her bed with what looks like a journal on her lap. "Where did you find that?"

"In a drawer."

"Put it back."

"I will, but I want to know if I'm going to like it."

"You'll like it."

"Promise?"

She shakes her head. "You're awful, you know that?"

"But you love me anyway."

She doesn't say anything, which is not a great feeling.

"Are you in love with Sandrine?"

"What? No."

I bite my lip. "But you're together, yes? You've . . . hooked up?"

She blushes, then nods.

"How could you?"

"You want me to draw you a picture?"

"I understand the mechanics—I want to know how come you slept with my ex–best friend."

"We ran into each other at a party. You know I've been down since everything that happened on Catalina. You were even the one who told me to go to the party. You remember, the one Rich was throwing? Anyway . . . one thing led to another."

I take a deep breath. I want to push this and confront her. Tell her how betrayed I feel by her choices. But she knows me better than anyone. She knows how bad I'd feel about it.

That must be why she did it.

And okay, okay, I'm making it about me again, but is there another way to see it?

"Can I give you a bit of advice?" I say.

"Maybe?"

"It seems like you keep ending up getting involved with people in my world. Connor, Shawna, Sandrine. And I know it's none of my business, but this is all related to why I fired you. Go find someone who has nothing to do with me, okay? Untangle your life from mine."

"You think it's easy?"

"I didn't say that."

Harper looks off to the side. "All anyone ever asks me about is *you*. Even Sandrine. You think I don't know why she's interested in me?"

"She's trying to hurt me."

"Yes."

"So why did you go along with it?"

Her eyes brim with tears. "Maybe I was trying to hurt you, too."

My own eyes start to well. "Why?"

"I don't know, El. I ask myself that all of the time."

I gulp down the tears forming. This is not the time or place to have a deep discussion about why my sister wants to hurt me.

Besides, I already know the answer.

"Maybe you can write about it in there." I gesture to the journal she's holding. "But also, since when have you journaled?"

She shrugs, and I reach for it. She pulls it away quickly, but not quickly enough for me. I have great reflexes from years of tennis.

"Give it back."

"I wanna see." I take a step back as she stands and moves toward me. I flip it open.

"Don't read that."

"Why?"

"Because it's *private*."

I glance down. I see the word "murder" before Harper wrenches it from my hand.

"You're journaling about murder?"

"It's just a writing exercise. Like you assign to your students."

"Okay."

She holds the journal against her chest. "You really have a problem with boundaries."

"I know."

"Are you working on it?"

"I fired you, didn't I?"

"Hilarious."

"You're still writing?"

"No."

I make a face.

"Okay, yes. But it's not going anywhere. Like I told you."

"You're going to do that podcast thing?"

"I think so."

"Okay."

"You should put that away before Oliver gets back." She points to the ring box.

"Good idea." I tuck it into the pocket of my skirt for safekeeping.

Harper releases a sigh. "Someone wants to kill you? Again?"

"Seems like it, given all the suspects and everything."

"They've killed so many other people, though . . . Oh! *And Then There Were None?* Maybe that's the plan. To kill all of us."

"Or it's another smokescreen."

"We have no idea what's going on, is what you're telling me."

"Pretty much," I say. "We need to talk to the others."

"I thought that's what we're doing."

"Thanks for the reminder. I'm going to go put this back. Be ready to leave in five. And bring that." I point to her journal.

"Why?"

"I want to try something."

CHAPTER 25

Does Gathering All of the Suspects in a Library Ever Work in Real Life?

"What are we all doing here?" Sandrine asks. She's wearing a wrap dress that yokes around her slim neck and drapes perfectly across her body.

Even in the midst of a murder investigation, I can be jealous.

We're in the resort's library, because of course we are. This is where we've come to solve the mystery. If you're imagining something ritzy, you haven't been paying attending. The shelves look like they came from IKEA (is there IKEA in the Bahamas?—you look it up, I'm busy), and the books are all dog-eared and twenty years old. There's a whole row of Elizabeth's titles next to Shek's series, and the usual scattering of P. D. James, Agatha, and Edwardian romances.

Why does everyone want to read about murder and mayhem on vacation?

A question I might try to answer if I get out of here alive.

Because maybe this *is* our version of *And Then There Were None*, and someone's got a long list of potential kills that they're working their way through.

So I'm on the list, but I'm not *the* list.

But they wanted me to think I was, because why else would they have sent me that note at the beginning of it all? Why else would all of these people who hate me be here?

There's only one way to find out.

I hold up Harper's journal, which I've decided to use because it's more dramatic than bringing the laptop. "Guy left some notes."

"What?" Ravi says, while I avoid looking at Connor.

He knows about the USB drive.

I'm hoping he doesn't interfere with the method to my madness.

In fact, I'm betting on it.

"Yep," I say, looking around the room—Sandrine, Oliver, Connor, Crazy Cathy, Stefano, Ravi. Officer Rolle is in the corner, watching over the proceedings. "There are a couple of facts you should all know."

"Such as?" Sandrine says with a sneer. Her dress is a shade of red associated with scarlet letters.

I'm not surprised. Betrayal is her thing.

"Guy brought us here to expose the owners."

I quiet down the cacophony of voices that erupt after that statement, then explain Guy's plot, without saying how stupid it was.

It's implied, though.

And the scowl on Connor's face says it all. Even though I've left him out of it for now, he's not pleased. When is he ever?

"We were pawns," Sandrine says. She's got a headband keeping her thick hair off her face, and less makeup than usual. It's the first time I've ever thought she looked her age.[76][77]

"I'm not sure. And so glad you brought that up," I say, opening Harper's journal to a page near the end. "You were in touch with Guy, weren't you?"

"Yes, but not . . ." She frowns.

"Not what?"

---

[76] I'm telling you, girls. All that makeup and skin care is aging you. I only started wearing face cream when I turned thirty, and look at me.

[77] Okay, you can't see me, but trust me, there's a reason people often confuse me and Harper, and it's not just because she's the more put together of the two of us.

"We weren't *friends*. He was looking to write a book, and he needed someone to help him. To ghostwrite it, if you will."

"What proof do we have of that?"

"Ask Harper." Sandrine nods toward the chaise where Harper's sitting. "She knows. She's the one who gave me the idea in the first place."

"How?" I ask as Harper makes a slashing motion at her throat.

Sandrine ignores her. "Because she's been ghosting for a while now."

I *knew* it.

"Is that true, Harper?"

She looks down. "Yeah."

"Who have you been writing for?"

"I can't say."

"Why not?"

"Because it's in my contract. I'll get in trouble if I tell."

"Is it Connor?" I say with resignation.

"I'll have you know that I've written every word of my novels *myself*," Connor says indignantly.

"Is it someone here? You can say that, at least."

Her left eye twitches, and I know the answer is yes. "Stop asking me. I can't tell you. And it's not relevant to what's happening."

"How do we know that?"

"You'll have to trust me," she says and makes a *moving on* gesture with her hand. "Why are we here again?"

"Oh, right. Guy's book." I tap the journal, hoping to instill fear in someone in the room. Instead, they're all looking at me like I'm insane.

"Let's go through the revelations one by one, shall we?"

Sandrine laughs. "You'd think you'd be better at this by now."

"Thanks for volunteering to go first. We know Guy was involved with what's happening. He mentions having an accomplice who he strongly hints is female. It's you, isn't it?"

"It isn't."

"But how do you even know him . . . Wait . . . wait . . . He's Canadian. You're Canadian. Marta lived in Canada . . . That's the connection, isn't it?"

Sandrine rolls her eyes. "Not all Canadians know one another, El. *Franchement.*"

"You were always telling me, though, how Canada is like a village. One degree of separation, you always said."

"I did not know Marta."

"And Guy?"

"I met him because of *you.* Conferences like this." She waves her hand around.

"Connor?" I ask. "Is she telling the truth?"

"Sandrine was *not* involved in the decision to come here. Not that Guy told me, anyway."

"Which is not an answer to the question I asked but is an answer."

"You're wrong, Eleanor," Connor says.

"Am I? Maybe *I'm* not the target, and you are. Did you think about that?"

"Who am I supposed to have killed?" Sandrine says. "The man who died before we got here?"

"His name was Brian," I say.

"How am I supposed to have done that?"

Oliver clears his throat. "We don't actually know when you arrived. You weren't on our plane or transport from the airport."

"That's right," I say. "She wasn't. Neither was Ravi, nor most of the rest you. Only Elizabeth was. When did you get here?"

"The night before," Officer Rolle offers. "They came in on the afternoon flight on Thursday."

"So you *were* here when Brian was killed."

"I couldn't even pick him out of a lineup," Sandrine says. "And why would I kill him? You're not making any sense, Eleanor."

"Guy wanted him eliminated for some reason."

"That's convincing. And what about Guy, am I supposed to have killed him? How?"

"He was poisoned just like Shek was."

Ravi gasps. "Pardon me?"

"The same device was used to kill both of them."

"What are you implying?" Ravi asks.

"It would be a good way to get revenge. Killing someone who had a hand in your brother's death in the same way?"

"Now *I'm* supposed to have killed someone?"

"Guy *was* in contact with you," I bluff, patting the notebook again.

"So?"

"Why?"

"He reached out to express sympathy for my brother's death."

"Is that all?"

"He told me he had some information about Shek."

"What kind of information?"

"That's private."

I tap the notebook again, then open it, flipping through the pages like the answer might be within. "He told you Shek was involved in the plot in Italy, didn't he?"

"I don't know what you're talking about," Ravi says.

"The police already suspect him."

"So?"

"You can come clean. You can't hurt him anymore."

"I have his legacy to protect."

"A legacy of being involved in a conspiracy that killed three people?"

Ravi raises his chin in defiance. "You have no proof of that."

"Oh, but I do. Oliver and I found it when we were in Italy. And the police have it. It will all come out at the trial."

"But Guy . . ."

"Promised it wouldn't? Did he tell you there wasn't going to be a trial? Was he . . . was he *blackmailing* you?"

Ravi's teeth click shut. He takes a beat, then speaks slowly. "Whyever would I admit to that?"

"Because, in case you missed it, people are *dying*."

"Tell us, Mr. Botha," Officer Rolle says. "It would be best."

He lets out a long, slow sigh. "Okay, fine, yes, he was."

"How?"

"He had messages between my brother and him . . . compromising messages . . . He said if I didn't pay, then he'd make sure that they found their way to the authorities."

"How did you pay him?"

He gives me a grim smile. "He is getting a percentage of book sales. And I was to help him get a book deal for whatever that is." He points to the journal. "Said he learned from the best."

"Connor."

"Yes?" Connor says.

"It was a statement, not a question." I bite the inside of my cheek. "Did you kill him?"

"What? No."

"A lot of people kill their blackmailers."

"I am *not* a criminal. *He* was the criminal."

"But it can wear at you, can't it? Paying money for something you didn't even do."

I know the feeling. Connor blackmailed me for ten years, and I was close to killing him. But the thing that held me back was that I was responsible for my situation. I'd trusted the wrong person, and I had to pay for that.

That's not Ravi's case. He's paying for his *brother's* crimes. That might break a person.

I hope I never find out.

"How am I supposed to have done this?" Ravi says. "He was sitting next to *you*, not me."

"Good point," Sandrine says.

"Shut it, Sandrine." I let my eyes rove over the room. It's a powerful feeling, I have to admit, being this close to solving it all. But I shouldn't get ahead of myself. I tend to do that. And Sandrine is laughing at me.

"What's your secret?" I ask her.

"Excuse me?"

"That's what Guy traffics in. He hired you to ghostwrite his book for him. Did you start?"

"That's what I came *here* for. He said he had notes and we'd discuss it. But we never got to speak about it."

"What was the book about?"

"All this." She waves her hand around. "*Amalfi Made Me Do It*, the sequel."

"You think it's funny?"

"I think it's ridiculous."

"Did *you* kill him?"

"What? No. Why would I?"

"I don't know. Why are you dating my sister? It's all kind of *Single White Female*, if I'm being honest."[78]

"*You* want to date your sister?"

Harper snorts, and I shoot her a dirty look. "You're part of the problem here."

"Me?" Harper gives me her innocent eyes.

"You should shun her."

"Shunning. Okay. Sure. On it, boss." She frowns because I'm not her boss anymore.

I turn back to Sandrine. "What are you up to? What's your big plan?"

"I don't have a plan, Eleanor. I just want to make a living doing what I love. But you have made that impossible."

"That's exactly what I'd expect you to say. Turning it around on me, when *I'm* the victim."

"No, *Guy* is the victim."

---

[78] There's that expression again.

"And Inspector Tucci," Oliver adds.

"And him," I say. "And Brian. Why'd you have to kill Brian?"

"I cannot believe you let her do this," Sandrine says to Officer Rolle. "This must be a violation of our rights."

"You are not under caution," Officer Rolle says.

"So we don't have to talk," Sandrine says. "Understood."

"Yes, Sandrine. Say less."

"Why? How do you think I did it? I'd love to hear your theory."

"You're a plotter."

"So?"

"We're in a plot. Don't you get that? Or did you know that already?"

"I don't know why you're looking for complicated explanations. It must be Marta and Marco together who have done this with Guy. They killed him for some reason that will be revealed in time. Case closed."

"They deny it."

"Of course they do. But Officer Rolle will investigate, and he'll find the evidence. They have a motive to kill Guy *and* Inspector Tucci. And you, for that matter. *Et* Connor."

"What about Brian?" I ask. "And why are Connor and I are still alive? Why not kill us immediately?"

"I have no idea, Eleanor. But you're fishing." The venom in her voice saps my energy.

"Why do you hate me?"

"I don't hate you. I just got tired of you. Of your selfishness. Of the *me, me, moi* of it all. It's not more complicated than that."

Tears spring to my eyes. "Okay."

"I was suffering, and you didn't even notice. Constantly talking about Oliver and Connor and *your* next book deal. You never cared about my career or that I was drowning. You never tried to help me."

Anger takes over my pain. "What are you talking about? I was there for you when you left your agent. I read your book. I gave notes. I even kept your secrets. You're jealous. That's all. Which I get, okay? I get it.

But you didn't have to break up our friendship over it. You could've just told me."

"And you think I, what? Planned to murder you instead?" She makes a sound in her throat that I can only describe as *French*. "You're ridiculous."

"How did you meet Brian?"

"I don't know him."

"Is he the one you've been having an affair with?"

She pales. "You're mistaken, Eleanor. I do not know Brian. The man you're referring to, who is a *friend*, for the record, is named Daniel. He's in his fifties. He's certainly *not* Brian."

Damn it. I thought I was onto something there.

Stefano raises his hand. "Is it my turn now?"

"You want me to accuse you of planning a murder?"

"It would make great content."

"Oh my God."

He raises his shoulders. "What? You have no idea what it's like. The pressure. Having to produce TikTok after TikTok to feed the algorithm. And the stress of it all being taken away at any moment because one minute it's being banned and the next it's not."

"So get a real job."

"It *is* a real job. See, that's a typical legacy-author attitude."

"Why do you hate authors?"

"I don't."

"Really? Aren't you with the one with the TikTok series called Books That Were Literal Crimes Against My Mind?"

"Sounds like you're a fan of my content."

"That's what you would take from this. I love the book community, but you just tear people down. You've broken careers."

"So you decided to break mine?"

"I spoke up for myself! Why should you get books for free if you're just going to hate them on sight?"

He sneers at me. "*This* is why you're almost getting murdered all the time."

"Thanks a lot."

"It's kind of true, Eleanor," Cathy says. "You *are* the *communis denominator* in these stories."

This stops me. "Wait. Why are you speaking in Latin . . . That's in *Amalfi Made Me Do It*. How do you know that?"

"I read it on NetGalley."

"You're approved to read my books?"

"I'm your biggest fan."

"Oh my God," I say.

"What?" Oliver says.

"The note. The notes under our plates . . . the note I got on Friday . . . That's like what happened at Emma's wedding."

"Why does that matter?" Connor asks.

"Because it's in the book Oliver and I wrote together. *Something Borrowed, Blue or Murdered* . . . We wrote a retelling of the murders on Catalina Island . . ." The book Oliver is supposed to be doing the copyedits for, which I assume we're turning in late now. If Vicki's even alive to turn it in to. Which is a horrible thought.

I haven't been giving Vicki enough thought.

What is *wrong* with me? I hope she's okay. But when is anyone missing in books like this ever okay? Never, right?

"*That* murder started with a threatening note."

"So?" Sandrine asks.

"You think it means that the person behind all of this is someone who read it?" Oliver says. "That's a short list."

I look at Harper. "You didn't give anyone an early copy, did you?"

"No."

"So, who was on the organizing committee that also read the book?"

"Vicki."

"Vicki doesn't want to murder anyone," Harper says. "And there's a good chance that she's also dead... How come they haven't found her yet?"

Her voice cracks, and my throat tightens. I cannot lose Vicki on top of everything.

"But why?" Oliver asks, his voice shaky as well. "Wouldn't that mean she knew something?"

"No way Vicki is behind this," I say. "Just no."

"Connor?" Harper supplies. "He knew about the note because he was on the spot when it happened. He didn't have to read the book."

"We *know* he's involved," I say.

"I was trying to *help*," Connor says. "How many times do I have to tell you?"

"But he arrived with us, after Brian was already dead, so he couldn't have done that," Oliver points out.

"Will you *stop* talking about me like I'm not here?"

I ignore him. "Right, which only leaves . . ." I look around at the faces of the people I've assembled. Who is it? Who is it? It must be one of them.

But wait.

Someone's missing and I've only just realized it. "Where's Elizabeth?"

"In her room, I assume," Sandrine says.

Shit, shit, shit.

"We have to find her."

"Why?" Officer Rolle asks.

"I have a bad feeling." I start toward the door. "Does anyone know where her room is?"

"She's in the other presidential suite. Right behind yours."

I nod and almost run out of the room, the others following behind.

We weave through the paths, our footsteps echoing in the quiet resort.

When we get to her door, I realize we don't have a key. But Officer Rolle has that covered this time. He takes out a master key and presses it against the mechanism.

It beeps in a low sigh, like it's about to give up.

That's how I feel, too.

I open the door as Officer Rolle protests something about finger-prints, but I can already tell it's too late for that now.

She's not in the living room, only one light on low.

The door to her bedroom is ajar, and the drapes are pulled so there's barely any light.

And though it's hard to see, one thing is clear.

There's a rope hanging from the ceiling.

And Elizabeth is dead.

CHAPTER 26

I Thought There Were Only Supposed to Be Three Bodies?[79]

It's an hour later and we're all gathered back in the library, and Elizabeth's body is being removed from the scene by the tech team, who I'm sure are working more overtime than they've ever seen. Officer Rolle has made a preliminary determination that Elizabeth is the latest victim of the definite *serial killer* that's still on the loose. Since there wasn't a chair under her body for her to have hanged herself off of or any note to find, not to mention *all the other dead bodies*, this seems like an obvious conclusion.

Besides, why would Elizabeth Ben kill herself in the middle of a murder investigation?

I have no idea.

It should be painfully obvious right now that I HAVE NO IDEA WHAT'S GOING ON!

"And then there were none," Harper says. "The reality version."

"Not funny. And there's only supposed to be three bodies."

"Who says?"

I do, I want to say, pouting.

Yeah, I'm pouting at a time like this. It's a coping mechanism.

---

[79] This isn't a rhetorical question. What does <u>that</u> mean?

"Maybe Harper's right. Elizabeth was hanged with a rope," I say slowly. "It fits the pattern of the small groups. Gun, poison, rope . . ."

"But there were *two* poisonings," Oliver says. "Guy *and* Inspector Tucci."

"Tucci should've been killed with a heavy object or a knife," I say. "To keep the pattern intact. And there should be *five* bodies . . ."

"Vicki."

"I hope not."

"Marco had a knife," Oliver reminds me. "It was never used."

"But Marco is in custody. Marta, too."

"They must be working with someone else."

"Someone *else* who knew about the details in two unpublished books?"

"Maybe the note is just a coincidence?" Oliver says.

"There are no coincidences," Harper says. "Right, Eleanor?"

"Never." I look at Connor. "Was anyone else here on the organizing committee?"

"No," he says, frowning. "Just me and Vicki."

"So that means . . ." Harper says.

"It must be Vicki," Oliver says at the same time she does.

"No," I say.

"I don't want to believe it either. But the medical examiner said Elizabeth died in the last couple of hours. So it's not anyone who was in the library with us . . ."

I know he's right, but I don't want to believe it.

Maybe it's someone we haven't even considered yet.

No, I'm not doing that to you; that's not fair.

It's Vicki. But Vicki's missing.

Oh, shit. Oh, no. *And Then There Were None*. It's not a joke. It's the solution.

"*And Then There Were None*," I say.

"Didn't I *just* say that?" Harper says.

"I know, I meant . . . maybe *that's* the plot."

"What part of it?"

"The murderer stages his death in that book, right?[80] So people stop looking at him as a suspect? He takes something to slow his breathing so they think he's dead."

"Is that even possible?" Connor asks.

"Oliver?" I say.

He nods slowly. "There are medications that can slow your heart and breathing enough that a cursory examination could lead you to conclude that someone is dead."

"But what does that have to do with this?" Sandrine asks. "Vicki is missing, not dead."

"It's not a literal interpretation," I say. "She's put her own twist on it to keep it from being obvious because Vicki's smart. And it fits the facts. She's read all of my books. She's on the organizing committee. She was here before anyone died. She could be behind everything."

"So she's in hiding?" Harper says. "That's what you mean?"

"She went into hiding so we'd think she was dead."

"When?"

"After she killed Tucci."

"But then who took Tucci's body?" Oliver says. "And why?"

"There must've been some clue she left on it. Something that would give it away that it was her."

Sandrine shakes her head in disbelief. "What did you do to her?"

"Nothing! We're friends."

"She's been having a hard time," Oliver says. "Maybe she snapped."

"And put together a massive plot to kill a bunch of people as a result?" Harper asks. "Why? What would that accomplish?"

"That's a good question."

What's the connective tissue between Brian, Guy, Inspector Tucci, and Elizabeth?

---

[80] Spoiler alert! Oops, I was supposed to say that first. SORRY!

Why are there one too many bodies? Or one too few, if the small group theory is right?

Three bodies or five. Either way, we're one body off.

Three makes sense. Some combination of Guy and the Giuseppes could've killed Brian and Inspector Tucci and Guy. Even if they're denying it. But while Vicki could've killed all four of them theoretically, why would she? Why would she set up this whole thing? She wasn't in danger from the Giuseppes.

There's always one too many things going on in this case, and I can't put my finger on what it is. I only know Vicki can't be the answer. There's just no way. So, if I take Vicki out of the equation, who does that leave?

Oliver.

Connor.

Sandrine.

Stefano.

Harper.

Me.

But Oliver, Connor, Harper, and I arrived *after* Brian died. So unless we were in a conspiracy with someone here, then that doesn't work.

And it's not me, in case you were wondering. I haven't turned to murder.

Not yet.

But here are three things I know:

1. We need to figure this out before anyone else dies.
2. There *is* a solution to everything.
3. I'm not living inside the plot of an Agatha Christie novel—

Then the door bursts open, and Inspector Tucci walks in, very much alive. "I have just heard the awful news."

Scratch that.

☆　☆　☆

Okay, remember back there when I said I wasn't going to trick you with the ending? I stand by that. I didn't trick you.

Inspector Tucci tricked *me*.

And Officer Rolle, who's looking *very* displeased. "There had better be an explanation for this, and I will be cautioning you."

"I am not a suspect, I assure you," Inspector Tucci says, his fedora slightly askew.

"*He* did it?" Harper says. "Why?"

"It makes a certain sense," Oliver says. "The Giuseppes have been eluding him his entire career. And Guy."

"He *did* tell me that Guy was connected to the Mafia," I say.

"Perhaps he didn't see any other way out," Sandrine says.

"No, no, *scuzi*, what are you saying? You think *I* am responsible for all of this? I am one of the *victims*."

"But you aren't," I point out. "You're alive."

"That is only because I did some very quick thinking." He points to the side of his head. "I am very good at, how do you say, seeing patterns."

"Okay."

"Do you want to explain it to us?" Oliver says.

"I would be delighted." He rubs his hands together. "It is Marta and her brother Marco who are responsible for everything!"

"You don't say," Connor says. "I've been saying this the whole time."

"I *do* say. They were working with Mr. Charles. It was their last attempt to kill you"—he points to me—"and *you*"—he points to Connor.

"Only it wasn't," I say.

"You are mistaken. I know this for a *fact*."

"How?"

He cocks his head to the side. "Because I heard them. Conspiring in the corridor in voices that were too loud for the conversation they were having."

"So you didn't figure anything out, you just eavesdropped?"

"You do not need to speak to me in this tone."

"I can use whatever tone I want," I say. "Especially since you *faked your death.*"

"It was a necessary subterfuge. They were planning their escape. Waiting for the weather to turn."

"And the purpose of pretending to be dead was?"

"Avoiding death myself, of course. I was going to be their next victim. And it allowed me to move about the resort unobserved."

"How?"

"I procured a staff uniform. No one ever pays any attention to the staff."

Didn't *I* say that?

I keep getting plagiarized. I don't like it.

"So you've just been wandering around the resort?"

"No, no. I have been on the island."

"The island?"

"The one the property owns. There is a ferry?" He waves his hand dismissively in the direction of the ocean.

Oh. *That* island. The one I meant to visit at some point.

"You didn't search the island?" Oliver says to Officer Rolle.

"We most certainly did."

"Not well enough," Connor says.

"It was Agatha all along," Harper says.

Inspector Tucci's eyes are darting around the room. "I do not follow."

"It's from a famous book by Agatha Christie," I say. "Faking your death."

"Yes, I have seen this book."

"You mean read it," Sandrine says with a smirk.

"It was a play, no?"

"Yes," I say. "But first a book. That's where you got the idea from?"

"I thought of it on my own."

"Sure you did. It was all part of your plot to kill us and blame *them.*"

"I am *not* a killer."

"It's a good cover," Connor says. "Kill Brian, your inside man. Kill Guy as a decoy. Kill yourself to divert suspicion and, as you say, move about the resort unseen, and then you can take your revenge on me and Eleanor."

"Revenge? I am an officer of the law."

"Are you, though?" I say. "How have you not been fired? You were, weren't you?"

Inspector Tucci turns red in the face. "I was not fired. I was sent to a different posting for personal reasons, as I have already explained."

"You were already mad when we came to Italy six months ago. And then several people got killed on your watch, and the Giuseppes were operating right under your nose. You're telling me there were no professional consequences to that? Please." Connor makes a dismissive sound.

"I did not suffer from *your* incompetence a second time."

"It'll only take one phone call to check," Oliver says.

"You can place all the phone calls you like. It will not change the facts."

"You're not telling us everything," I say. "Of that, I'm sure."

Oliver touches my elbow. "Why did you say that, El?"

"He just happened to overhear Marco and Marta conspiring? Didn't we just say there are no coincidences?"

"Good point. Out with it, Tucci. What are you holding back?"

He glances at Officer Rolle, probably trying to calculate just how much trouble he's in.

"If I am going to be subject to accusations, when all I have done since I arrived here was try to solve what has been happening . . ."

I think back to our first conversation on the beach when he scared me out of my skin. He could've killed me then, if that was his purpose in coming. But instead, he was investigating.

"Wait," I say. "Your source . . . You said two days ago that you had one. And you knew things that you shouldn't have known . . . It was Marta, wasn't it?"

His eyes sparkle. "Bravo, Ms. Dash. That is a, how do you say, good catch."

"You were in touch with Marta?" Oliver says. "How?"

"She approached me. After she learned Mr. Charles was coming here . . . she wanted to make, how do you say, a deal."

"What kind of deal?"

"She wanted immunity."

"For turning in Guy?"

He nods.

"Holy shit."

"Is that how you ended up at the conference?" Oliver says. "That's it, isn't it? You came here on purpose. You *knew* we'd be here."

"I knew Mr. Charles would be here, yes. And of course, your presence was announced on the website."

"Why not tell Officer Rolle, then? Why not arrest Guy when you got here?"

"I did not have any evidence of anything. Marta promised she would supply it."

"But something went wrong?" I guess.

He nods again. "Once Mr. Charles was killed, I knew I was not safe."

Oliver cocks his head to the side. "How did you do it? Fake your death?"

"I used a beta-blocker."

"What's that?" Harper asks.

"A medication that is used for many things. It slows down your heart rate."

"You overdosed on purpose?"

"I took a sufficient dose to pass a cursory exam."

"You took an awful risk," I say.

"He didn't do it for *you*, Eleanor," Sandrine says. "My God."

I ignore her. "Did you find anything while you were dead?"

His eyes track back to mine. He looks tired. "I did."

"What is it? And where is Vicki? Did you kill her?"

"No, no, no. I did not kill her. I saved her."

"She's alive?" I say, the relief making my knees weak. I lean against Oliver for support. "Where is she?"

"Somewhere safe."

"Inspector Tucci, I swear to God."

"I had to come be certain before I released her."

"Wait," Oliver says. "Released her? You kidnapped her?"

He shakes his head. "She was about to do something very foolish."

"What?"

"Confront the Giuseppes' accomplice."

"They had an accomplice?" Harper asks.

"Of course they did," I say. "Brian."

Inspector Tucci rights his fedora, brushing his finger along the rim. "He was not the only one."

"Who was it then? Honestly, Tucci, I am so sick of your obfuscation."

He points to the doorway.

"What does that mean?"

"Ms. Ben. That is who I saved Vicki from."

"What?" Harper says. "No *way*."

"It is very much the way."

"But Elizabeth is dead," I say, my mind spinning, then screeching to a halt.

"Yes, a tragedy."

"If she's dead, who killed her?"

Inspector Tucci scratches at his chin. "Ah, yes. I did not know that until I arrived."

"Honestly," Connor says, "I can't believe anyone is listening to this."

But I'm listening. "Why was Vicki going to confront Elizabeth?"

"It was something you said, I believe. When you were talking at the bar. That is what she kept saying."

"When?"

Inspector Tucci tucks his head down. "I was listening to your conversation."

"You were *there?*"

"I was, how do you say, incognito." He makes a motion like he's mopping the floor.

"Why were you listening in?"

"As I have said, I was investigating."

"So you followed Vicki to her room?"

"I did. I already had my suspicions about Ms. Ben. And when I heard Vicki and saw where she was headed, I acted quickly, yes?"

"Wait," Harper says. "Why were you suspicious of Elizabeth?"

"I saw her speaking to Marta earlier in the day."

"How were they speaking?" Oliver asks.

"As if they knew one another. Elizabeth appeared to be giving her orders."

"Maybe she was just asking for fresh towels?" Harper says. "Besides, what motive would Elizabeth have?"

"I did forget to give her a blurb," I say slowly.

"No one kills someone because of something like that."

"It was a joke."

"*Honnêtement?* Still making jokes at a time like this?"

"Really? Still attacking me?"

"El," Oliver warns.

"Sorry. But that's not enough. Them talking. It has to be something more. Elizabeth is dead. She isn't the killer. We need to speak to Vicki."

Inspector Tucci shakes his head. "I am not sure that is safe."

"You will bring us to her immediately," Officer Rolle says. "Or there will be consequences."

A shiver goes down my spine. "You left her alone?"

"Obviously."

"But what if *she's* the villain?" Sandrine says. "You said it, Eleanor. Elizabeth is dead. Vicki is not."

"Maybe they were in on it together," Stefano says with too much relish. "The plot *thickens*."

"No," Inspector Tucci says. "Not Vicki. She could not have fooled me like that."

Officer Rolle flicks his finger at Inspector Tucci. "Let's go."

"Can we come?" Stefano asks.

"No! Return to your rooms. All of you. Lock the doors. Do not answer them. Anyone found outside of their room will be arrested immediately. An officer will escort you shortly."

He leaves us in silence.

But silence abhors a vacuum.

Especially among this bunch.

"You think they'll bring us room service?" Connor says.

And I can't help it. I burst out laughing because why the hell not?

If you can't cry, laugh.

Did I say that?

I've written so many things I can't even tell anymore.

Act 3—Continued

THE EIGHTH SEQUENCE

* Time to reveal what's REALLY going on.

* You've run through all the suspects and come back to the beginning. It's time to bring it all back home.

* What is your <u>actual</u> big reveal/resolution? (Who dies, who survives, and who did it??)

THINGS TO KEEP IN MIND:

* The ending should be <u>fair to the reader</u>. It can't come from nowhere. When the reader goes back and reads the book again, they have to be able to find the clues.

    You cannot reveal a major fact at the last minute or introduce a new character who happens to be the murderer if you haven't at least hinted at it earlier. You have to lay the seeds for all of your suspects throughout the novel so that when everything is finally revealed, the reader is both surprised <u>and</u> satisfied. <u>That's the trick.</u>

CHAPTER 27

Did I Know You Were Trouble When You Walked In?

We're back in our room, and I'm spiraling. I can't think. I can't breathe. I can barely stand erect.

My brain won't stop spinning.

Living with me is exhausting. I need a vacation from myself. Which I'm going to get on *right* after I get off this infernal island.

I can't believe I came to *another* island.

Never again.

"You okay?" Oliver asks.

"Um, no."

"I know." He bends down in front of me. We're in our bedroom. Harper's gone to hers. It's hot in here, the large, heavy fan above the bed spinning lazily and slightly off-kilter, like its position is precarious. "It's going to be okay."

"How can you say that?"

He tries to smile. "Because we can't die right after we get engaged."

"Are we engaged?"

"Think so. You've got the ring, haven't you?"

"How did you . . ." I laugh. "You know me so well."

"Hope so." He holds out his hand.

"What?"

"The ring?"

"Oh, yes." I go to stand, and something tumbles to the floor. The journal I was holding—Harper's journal.

"What's that?" Oliver asks.

"Harper's journal."

"She keeps a journal?"

"That's what I said."

"So many secrets."

"Uh, yeah, that's why we're in this situation."

"Probably." He frowns. "No secrets between us, though."

"Nope. Especially since you can read my mind at all times."

"The ring?"

I reach into the pocket of my skirt, panicking for a minute that I lost it. But it's there, tucked deep. I take it out, placing it in his palm.

"You looked inside, I assume," he says.

"I didn't."

"Come on."

"I was going to, but Harper told me not to."

"Since when do you listen to her?"

"I don't, but I think we got interrupted with a murder."

"That happens."

"Too many times."

"But you want to get married?" Oliver asks.

"So?"

"It implies you believe in a future."

I smile at him. "I do."

"I think that part comes later." He palms the ring box. "So . . ."

"Yes?"

"You're *always* stealing my dialogue."

"I'm sorry, I'll be quiet now."

"Thank you." He pauses, looking a little lost. He's so sweet, this man who's half crouched on the floor in front of me. And he seems at a loss for words, which isn't like him.

"You were saying?"

He smiles. "I had a whole speech planned."

"Summarize?"

"I love you."

"I love you, too."

"Feels like the right time."

"I agree."

He brushes a piece of hair out of my eyes. "Do you remember the first time we met?"

"I . . . It was in Vicki's office, wasn't it?"

"It was. She'd just acquired my novel, and I was having my first in-person meeting with her. It was supposed to be at three, but she was late coming back from lunch with you. And you come in the room, and you've had a few Proseccos . . ."

I smile, remembering. "Naturally."

"And you were telling this story about the worst waiter you'd ever had and you were waving your hands around, and it was——"

"Annoying?"

"Magical."

My face flushes. "Oh."

"Maybe I've never said this, but that's what you are in my life, El. The magic. I'm not that exciting of a guy."

"I don't agree."

"I'm not. I'm okay with that. I write cerebral detective fiction, and I'm not that successful, and I am a little too fussy for my own liking about my sock drawer."

"You like it how you like it."

"You should know that's probably going to get worse as I get older."

"The socks?"

"All of it. They say people mellow with age, but I don't believe that."

"That doesn't bode well for me," I say. "Or you, for that matter, because I'm already pretty nuts."

He smiles. "I'm good with it."

"You're sure?"

"I'm on my knees, aren't I?"

"Asking?"

"You to marry me."

"Truly, really, for real?"

"Truly, really, for real."

"I accept."

He gives me a wide grin. "You haven't seen the ring yet."

"It's exchangeable, right?"

"You're not going to want to exchange it."

"So confident."

"I did my research."

"You got the password to my Pinterest from Harper."

"You have a Pinterest?"

Will I *ever* stop saying the first thing to comes to mind in any situation?

Probably not.

Sigh.

"I use it to storyboard for my books."

"Uh-huh."

"Whatever. Open the box."

He looks down. "I think I'm more nervous about this part than the last part."

"Just open it."

He tips the lid open and my eyes start to water. Tears, good ones. Because it's exactly the ring I wanted without knowing I wanted it. A square-cut solitaire on a platinum band that's classic, timeless.

But also familiar.

"Is this . . . my mom's?"

"It is."

"Where did you get it?"

"Harper said she found it in the box at the bank."

I give myself a little shake. "There was a box at the bank? I didn't know that."

"Do you like it?"

"I love it."

His face is like sunshine as he slips it on. It fits perfectly. I never noticed it before, but my hands look exactly like I remember my mother's looking. And this makes it hard to breathe.

But maybe I'm wrong. She died so long ago that I've forgotten so many things about her.

Her voice.

Her laugh.

I know that's what happens, but I stuffed her down, her and my father, for so long it's almost like they didn't exist. Like this ring. Hidden away in a lockbox in a bank that I didn't know existed.

How much of my life is there that I don't know about yet?[81]

"Thank you for doing this," I say.

"We're getting married."

"We're getting married. Though we already knew that because I did propose first."

He rocks me from side to side. "I'm never hearing the end of that, am I?"

"I'll probably stop mentioning it for a while and then spring it on you when we're in a fight or something."

"Sounds like you." He leans forward and we kiss, a sweet kiss to seal our troth. "I think we should get married at the courthouse."

"Police officers and a security check. That sounds like a good idea."

---

[81] A question for another book!

I smile at him and reach forward, the journal in my lap slipping to the floor. It flies open. Oliver picks it up, glancing at it. Then his eyebrows start to rise.

"Yikes."

"What?"

He reads. "'It was a bright, sunny day, but that didn't change how black she felt inside. It was like tar; it stuck to everything she thought and touched and breathed. She'd tried everything she could think of to get rid of it, but she never managed. It was all she could do to concentrate on other things because the truth of it was, she wanted to kill someone. Not someone. Her.'"

"What the hell." I reach for the book and continue reading. "'We all have someone we'd kill for. Someone who could drive us over the edge if they tried hard enough. If we thought no one was looking . . .'"

"What is this?" Oliver asks.

"It looks like . . . she was doing the exercises from my class."

"Okay."

"What?" I say.

"It's pretty dark."

"It's just a writing exercise."

"I know, but . . .

I look up at him. "Are you suggesting that *Harper* is behind all of this?"

"No."

"You were."

I frown at him. "You were thinking it, too."

"She can't be."

"Let's work it out," he says. "And see. Okay?"

"Okay."

Oliver sits down next to me on the edge of the bed. "She knew everything she'd need to know to plan it—all those hidden details that are only known by someone who was with us in the past or who read the books."

"But she wasn't on the organizing committee."

"She could've figured out what Connor was up to . . . Oh! Connor could've told her. They're in touch, aren't they? Working together even."

I feel sick to my stomach. "On a book, not on a murder."

"That's what we're trying to figure out. Let me see . . . She wasn't here when Brian got killed, but Guy was."

"So now she's working with Guy, too?"

Oliver gives me a grim look. "Maybe Connor tells her about his plan with Guy to snuff them out. Or she figures it out because of things Connor tells her—he's not that smart."

"And then?"

"She decides to put her plan in motion using *their* plan as cover."

"To kill me?"

"No, you're not the target, I don't think."

"But I got the note."

"The note is a red herring. Remember who sent the note in Catalina?"

"Oh!" I say. "The murderer."

"And why did they send it?"

"To divert suspicion. So Harper was diverting suspicion away from me? Because *I* had a motive to kill Guy?"

"Guy wasn't supposed to die, I don't think. He wasn't the target."

"Who was?"

"That's the one thing I can't get to," he says. "Who here does she want to kill?"

"It is *me*."

"Why?"

"Because I fired her."

"But that just happened."

"It's been coming for months. And she's been screwing up. Not having me do Elizabeth's blurb. Other little things. It's like she's wanted me to fire her."

"Why?"

"Maybe she wants to get away from me. Maybe that's why she got with Sandrine . . ."

"She could just quit."

"But if I die, then she inherits. A lot."

Oliver squeezes my hand. "Is she short on money?"

"I have no idea. I pay her well, we co-own the house, but we don't talk about finances . . . It's a weird thing when I have so much more than her."

"I don't feel like Harper is motivated by money."

"No," I say, "you're right, but . . ." I squeeze my hands together. "I think she blames me for everything that's happened in the last six months. I'm always saying that every time I go on vacation, someone dies, but every time I go on vacation, I drag her with me, and she's in danger, too."

"That's not your fault."

"I'm not saying it's logical. But at the same time, I'm the source of the majority of the strife she's faced in her life. Maybe she's sick of it. Maybe she's sick of *me*. And all of it, the loss, it's killed something in her, and so now she wants me dead."

"You think she could've hidden it from you?"

"I don't know. But what she wrote in that journal?" I shudder. "You're right. It's very dark. And it doesn't even sound like her. It's not the way she usually writes or thinks."

"Why would she kill Elizabeth?"

"Maybe Elizabeth saw something? Or it was another misdirection. Because there hasn't been a pattern to any of this, and maybe that's the point."

"Hide the solution in chaos."

"Yes."

"That's smart."

"Harper's smart. I've always said that." I hug myself. "It would be just like her to come up with the perfect murder."

"Only you're still alive. And the list of suspects is getting smaller every time someone dies."

"You're right."

"If she killed you now, it would be too late. There's no one left."

"Only Connor."

"Maybe they *are* in on it together—"

A bitter laugh bursts out from the doorway, and I don't have to turn to know who it is. Harper. Listening.

"Oh my God, you guys, this is the best one yet."

I stand up, feeling sad and desperate. "Harper, I can explain."

"You had to do it, right? Make sure that it wasn't me."

"I didn't want to." Tears spring to my eyes. "I really didn't."

She shakes her head sadly. "If you say so. I'm not the murderer, by the way."

"I'm relieved to hear it. I'm sorry, Harper. I really am."

"You always give me too much credit." Her mouth twists. "I wasn't smart enough to know what Connor was up to with Guy. I should've figured it out, but I didn't."

"He told you?"

"In retrospect . . . he told me enough."

"When? Why?"

She looks at her shoes. Once bright white, now faded. "You were right before. I'm ghosting his books."

"Holy hell," Oliver says.

"Why?"

"Why not? At least I'm getting published."

"Under his name."

"What's in a name? Ego, that's all."

"Why didn't you tell me?"

"Because you would've tried to talk me out of it."

"You're right."

She looks at the book sitting next to me. "I can't believe you read my journal."

"We're trying to figure out who the murderer is. Nothing is off limits."

"*I* should be."

"You're right."

"There's a problem, though."

"What?" I say.

"If I didn't do it, who did?"

Oliver coughs.

"Yes?"

"I think it was Vicki."

"No."

"Who else is left?"

"Stefano? Sandrine? Inspector Tucci? Connor? Cathy?"

"I don't think any of them had all the information necessary. We need to talk to Vicki."

"But we're supposed to stay in our rooms," Harper says. "Arrested on sight, Officer Rolle said. And they'll never let us near her."

"Hmmm." Oliver smiles, and I can see the thought bubble forming over his head. "Maybe they aren't watching the back doors."

"What did you have in mind?" I say.

"There's one place we haven't searched yet. Brian's room."

"Ooh," I say. "Good idea."

We stand up at the same time as the bed gives a weird *creak*.

Then there's a mechanical sound, like a chain being pulled through a cog on a wheel, and then a loud *crash!*

The ceiling fan that was positioned over the bed is now slowly spinning where I've slept the last two nights.

"Holy shit!"

"Are you okay?" Oliver asks me.

"Yeah, I . . . Oh my God."

"What?"

I look at the dark wood fan lying askew on our bed. "It's a blunt object. And it could've killed us."

CHAPTER 28

Is This What They Call a Kill Switch?

It takes us a moment to recover from the crash. But not as long as you'd think, since we're used to attempts on our lives by now.

So, after less time than you might expect, this is what we discover:

1. There's a crude mechanism under the bed that worked to release the *heavy object* that was the ceiling fan.
2. The mechanism is creaky and sticks, which is why it didn't fall until now, we assume.
3. If we'd been under the fan, we'd both be dead or at least seriously injured, since it weighs at least two hundred pounds, by Oliver's estimation.

So, yeah.

That happened.

"This is why our room got changed," I say once we finish our inspection.

"It got changed because of the dead body," Harper says.

"But why was the body *in* our room? It never made sense why they'd kill him there. It was to move us into this room."

"Why, though? Couldn't they set this up in our original room?"

"It probably took a while to set this up," Oliver says. "This room isn't rented that often, I bet, which would give them the time they'd need."

"So someone *was* trying to kill you," Harper says, her eyes round.

"Yeah."

"Yikes."

"Who, though?"

"It must've been Marco and Marta. They had access."

"And it fits with the small group pattern. Gun, poison, rope, heavy object . . ."

"Oh! That double poison. Inspector Tucci . . . it didn't fit the pattern because he faked his death."

"Right," Oliver says. "So, who are they going to use the knife on?

"Who's left?"

"Connor."

"Of course he is. He always slithers away from danger," I say.

"It's over then," Harper says. "The cycle is complete?"

"But we still don't know who did it."

"Weren't we going to Brian's room?" Oliver says.

Harper shakes her head. "You don't think that's dangerous?"

"You just said the cycle's complete. I think we're safe."

"That's a stupid and dangerous assumption. Even if I said it."

"Fair."

"But we're still going, aren't we?"

"Have you met me?"

She pulls a face, then glances at the bed again. "This isn't over."

"I'm sure you're right. But it won't be until we solve it, so . . ."

"Once more unto the breach," Oliver says.

"Once more."

And then never again, I vow to myself.

After this, I'm retired.[82]

---

[82] I mean it, I'm quitting. Solving murders on the page and in real life. You can hold me to that.

* * *

"We should've done this a long time ago," I say as we creep through the hedges toward the staff area with my heart beating too fast. It's just me and Oliver in the jungle. Harper thought the three of us would make too much noise.

Or she didn't want to get arrested.

Same, same.

"We kind of did, didn't we?"

"That was Guy's office."

"True."

"Do we even know which room is Brian's?"

"No, but I assume there's caution tape on it."

"Good point," I say. "Did you bring your lock-picking tools?"

"I have them on me at all times."

"Even when we're sleeping?"

"Nearby."

"So prepared."

He pulls a face. "Don't call me a Boy Scout."

"I wouldn't dream of it."

"I'm not perfect."

"Did I say you were?"

"No," Oliver says, pushing a palm frond aside. "But I know you think about me that way in your head sometimes."

"Is there a way I can turn off this access you seem to have to my brain? Like that locator thing Harper has on my phone?"

"Watch your step." He points down to something slithering near his foot. It's a black garden snake.

I hate snakes. Like Indiana Jones. I hate them a lot.

"Is that poisonous?" I ask.

"I have no idea."

"I bet it is. Which is why I'm making a vow. From now on, I'm living my life in a way that's not getting me involved in more murder plots."

"Sounds like a good plan. Ah, here it is," Oliver says. "The tape is still up."

He points to a white door with yellow caution tape over it. It's part of the same complex that Guy's office was in, but farther away from the main resort. There's a half-dead palm tree above it, its fronds scratching gently against the roof.

"That's not going to stop us," I say about the tape.

"No, but it *is* a crime scene."

"Our room was the crime scene. This is just crime scene adjacent."

"Pretty sure that's not how that works."

"Fine. You picking the lock or chickening out?"

"I'm doing it."

He makes short work of it, and in a minute, we're inside. It's a small white room, one bed, a dresser, a small window, a sink in the corner, and, yes, an entire wall of photos of me made from pieces ripped out of actual newspapers and printouts from the internet.

"Well, that's creepy."

"Seriously," Oliver says. He stands in front of it. "Where did he even get all of this stuff?"

"The internet?"

"Some of it. But some of it's actual paper." He points to a yellowed review. "That's your first *New York Times* review."

"I guess he got it from a library?"

"Or he's been obsessed with you forever. We should ask Harper if he's in the crazy file."[83]

"I haven't had a man in there in a long time. Only women."

He tilts his head at me. "Wonder what that means?"

---

[83] I've gotten a lot of weird mail over the years. If it creeps me out, it goes in the crazy file. If someone ever <u>does</u> kill me, Harper has instructions to turn it over to the police. So don't do anything to get in there, okay? Because the chances of me being killed are <u>not zero</u>.

"No idea."

He steps closer. "There's a lot of stuff in here that's old. But if he's been obsessed with you for this long, how did *he* get here?"

"Maybe he was posting about me in one of those forums. You know the Vacation Mysteries Extended Universe ones?"

"Hmmm. Or someone gave him all of this."

"Why would they do that?"

"To divert suspicion?"

"So the plan all along was to kill Brian?"

"Yes. When he wasn't useful anymore."

I turn my eyes back to the wall and try to trace its history. At first, it seems chaotic, but there *is* a pattern. The articles go back to the very beginning of my career. The press leading up to my first release. The glowing reviews. The profile in the *New York Times*. All the stuff I felt lucky to get then, but now I know how truly lucky I was. So many people don't get the chance I did.

But it also means something. This *isn't* a new obsession. It's someone who's been watching my career the whole time. Who's been angry about it from the beginning.

And I'm about to be convinced that it was Harper all along when I spot something poking out from underneath a review of my fourth novel.

I reach out to touch it.

"That's evidence."

"I need to see something." I lift up the newspaper clipping. It's an old photo of me at the very first conference I went to. The one where I met Shek and Elizabeth and Sandrine.

Elizabeth is ten years younger. She was in her sixties, but she looks much younger.

What a difference a decade makes.

To me, too. Back then, I was so full of hope, and I look like a baby, fresh-faced and starry-eyed. But what *were* those bangs? A terrible decision.

Elizabeth and I are standing next to each other. It's the four of us.

Sandrine and I are on one end, with Elizabeth and Shek to my left. We're all smiling at the camera, me with a silly grin on my face, Sandrine in her serious-author pose, Elizabeth with a small smile, and Shek, looking like the cat that ate the cream.

My eyes track over the photo. It must mean something.

And that's when I see it.

Shek has one arm around my shoulders, but his other hand is by his side, next to Elizabeth's. *No*, intertwined with Elizabeth's.

They're *holding hands*.

Oh, shit!

Elizabeth asked me about how he died. They didn't just know each other from the literary circuit. They *knew each other*.

I close my eyes, trying to think back to that night.

So long ago.

Shek was nice to me. We had a drink at the bar, and he gave me some advice. He was acting like a mentor *then*. Before he trashed my book in the *New York Times*. Before he started to see me as a rival. Before he started to treat me like an object.

Or maybe that's what he was doing even then. I didn't know back then about all of the author hookups that happen at conferences. How certain men troll the bars looking for new members of the clan to lure back to their rooms.

I wasn't in the whisper forums.

I hadn't been warned.

Maybe it was my naivete that saved me or . . . wait . . . no . . . *It was Elizabeth.*

She tapped me on the shoulder, and we started to talk. At the time, I was so flattered I didn't even think twice about it. It was Elizabeth Ben! I was meeting Elizabeth Ben. She was taking an interest in me. But maybe that's not what was happening at all. Maybe she was saving me from Shek.

No. Wait. She wasn't saving me.

She was jealous. Jealous that he was giving me attention. She was stopping *him*. Letting him know that she knew what he was about.

Later, after Sandrine drifted into our orbit, we got a picture together. The picture I'm looking at now.

And he reached down and took her hand to reassure her.

She's smiling in the photo. She was happy. She was safe.

She was *his*.

"What are you looking at?" Oliver asks.

I point to their hands.

"Oh."

"You knew?"

"There were rumors years ago. You know how everyone in the business talks."

"I hadn't heard that."

"Doesn't matter."

"I think it does, though."

"Why?"

"Because she's been angry at me for ten years."

"Who?"

"Elizabeth."

"About? I thought the blurb thing just happened."

"No, that was the icing on the cake. Or maybe it had nothing to do with it. But it all started here." I point to the photo. "And it's because of Shek."

"What? Why?"

"She loved him, I think. But he only cared about himself. She got jealous."

"He made a pass at you?"

"I mean, I guess. I wasn't paying attention. But she was. She paid attention to everything. That's why she was the best."

Oliver shakes his head slowly. "So she *was* behind all this?"

"I think so."

"But she's dead."

"Is she?"

"Come on," Oliver says. "There can't be two people who faked their death on this trip."

"No, you're right. She's dead."

"So, then who killed her?"

"I don't know. But we have to talk to Vicki."

But first:

"My, my, Eleanor, what a glorious tribute."

I sigh and turn. Sandrine and Connor are standing in the doorway. They look like two peas in a pod, and maybe they are. They're the same, in a way. I was extremely close to both of them, and they both betrayed me, but I can't seem to shake them out of my life.

"What are you doing here?"

"We could ask you the same," Connor says.

Sandrine shrugs. "We were waiting for Officer Rolle to give us the all-clear together. Safer in twos."

My God. Sandrine didn't *also* sleep with Connor, did she? No, no. She's diabolical but not stupid. She's never seen the appeal of Connor; she's told me that herself many times. Safety in numbers is smart.

"How did you know we were here?" Oliver asks.

They're silent, and I get a flash of insight. "Harper told you, didn't she?"

Neither of them says anything, and I park my anger. Harper will have some motive for sending them here that makes sense in her mind, because it always does. Maybe she *also* thought there was safety in numbers if there was a killer still on the loose.

Only the list of suspects has dwindled to the people in this room, give or take Crazy Cathy and a wannabe TikTok star.

Are they the ones who've been plotting together this whole time?

Sandrine and Connor?

Does that make any sense? Together, they have the information necessary to do it, and Connor *was* involved in the plot with Guy to get us all here. Has this been a triple bluff? But if so, why? Why would Connor conspire with Sandrine, of all people, to kill me? What does either of them get out of my death besides satisfaction?

"Did you find anything?" Sandrine asks, breaking into my thoughts.

"Yes, actually—" Oliver starts before I cut him off.

"Is it you?" I say, looking at Sandrine. "Are *you* behind all of this?"

She makes eye contact, and for a moment, the creases around her eyes soften. "It isn't me."

And maybe this is crazy, but I believe her. There's no big protest, no pleading. Just a simple statement of fact.

It's enough.

Besides, we have our killer, finally. The spider who's been weaving her web.

It's Elizabeth.

But I don't want it to be her, so I'm falling back into her trap. I'm pointing to a more likely suspect when I should be laser-focused on the person who seems the least likely to have done it.

Because that's how it works in these kinds of books.

There's no escaping your fate when you're the protagonist. Or the reader, too.

"We have to talk to Vicki," I say.

"Why?" Connor asks.

"Because she's the only person left."

CHAPTER 29

Are We Finally Going to Get Some Answers?

Sandrine, Connor and I bicker for a few minutes about how we should get to Vicki and then decide on the easiest course.

Transparency.

I *know*, right? It's not our usual MO.

But there's been too much that's happened in the last forty-eight hours to risk it.

The four of us sneak back to our respective rooms. When Oliver and I get to ours, we fill Harper in on what we found. She's shocked at our conclusions but not at the connection between Elizabeth and Shek. She'd heard the scuttlebutt, too. I don't reproach her for not telling me.[84]

It's not the time for once.

Instead, I step outside and find the officer stationed at the edge of the path, watching our clutch of doors, and tell him I need to speak to Vicki.

There's some resistance, but if you know anything about me by now, you know I don't give up easily. He eventually picks up his radio and calls his superior, and Oliver, Harper, and I are escorted back to the main building. The one where I was interrogated yesterday (was it really just yesterday?).

---

[84] I am a bit mad at her for not talking me out of those bangs, though.

Time has ceased to have any meaning.

Vicki's in the small blank room with Officer Rolle.

She's tired, worn down. Her hair looks like it hasn't been washed or brushed in days. She's wearing the same dress she was when I last saw her. Also yesterday.

Before she ran from me. Before she was hidden away with her secrets and conclusions.

"I didn't know," Vicki says when she sees me, her eyes filled with tears. "I didn't understand."

"What?" Officer Rolle asks, exasperated.

"What Elizabeth was writing," I suggest, taking a leap toward a conclusion I arrived at on the walk here. "Right?"

Vicki nods. "The book I turned down."

"What was it about?" Oliver asks gently.

"A mystery writer who decides to kill off a perceived rival when she learns she's dying. But it was a jumbled mess."

"Is the rival a woman?" I ask.

"Yes."

"And she's jealous of her success?"

"Yes. But also, the man she's in love with had a thing for her. The motivation was muddy in the book—it was one of the issues with it."

"Did he remind you of Shek?"

Vicki's eyes widen. "I didn't think of that."

"But you *did* realize. Something I said when we were drinking at the bar . . ."

"Yes."

"What?"

"You told me about Brian."

"But you knew about him."

"About him yes, but not his name. You said it, and . . . I know him. I knew him." Her voice rises to a frantic pitch. I pat her hand, trying to calm her as she continues. "Something clicked together in my brain, and

I just *knew*. But I'd been drinking. I couldn't just make an accusation like that. I wanted to ask Elizabeth. I wanted to check. But before I got there, Inspector Tucci found me. I told him enough for him to think I was in danger and I guess you know the rest."

"How did you know Brian?" I ask.

Her tired eyes turn to mine. "He's the person I hired to help Elizabeth finish her book. She must've got him involved in all of this somehow . . ."

"You're saying Elizabeth is behind it?" Harper says. "Everything that happened?"

"Yes," Vicki says. "She must be."

"But she's dead."

Vicki shakes her head sadly. "I think she killed herself."

I turn my head sharply to Officer Rolle. "Is this possible?"

He frowns. "I am not sure . . . Of course, given everything that has happened, we assumed she was killed. No note. Nothing obvious to climb up on near where we found her . . . But yes, she could have stood on the bed and swung out . . ." He stops, grimaces. "It is possible."

"But why? It can't be because Shek flirted with me ten years ago. I didn't sleep with him. I didn't steal him from her."

"Oh, no," Harper says, her hand flying up to cover her mouth.

"What?"

"Sandrine."

"Sandrine, what?"

Harper is white. "*She* slept with Shek. She told me. She thought it was funny. You know how she is."

"Oh my God."

"And Shek was into her. He wanted to have a real relationship, not just a fling . . ."

"Did Elizabeth know?"

Harper shrugs. "Maybe not the details . . . Maybe she knew enough, but got the person wrong? She thought it was you the whole time?"

CATHERINE MACK

"Jesus."

We sit in silence for a moment, puzzling it out.

"How did she get everyone here?" Oliver asks. "She wasn't on the organizing committee...."

"I kept her in the loop," Vicki says. "She wanted to know how the planning was going."

"Did she make suggestions about who to invite or where to hold it?"

"Not that I recall."

"How did she do it, then?"

"A useful idiot... Guy," Oliver says. "She must've given Guy the idea. It never made any sense that he thought of all of this himself. Or Connor either. Neither of them is likely to come up with this kind of plan."

"Did she know Guy?"

"I'm sure they met over the years. He's been to lots of conventions, hasn't he? Especially with his book?"

"I introduced them," Vicki says, her voice small. "At ThrillerFest. We all sat at a table together for the awards banquet a couple of years ago."

"So they knew one another," I say after a beat. "And I don't think he ever said how he learned that Marta was here. And he didn't tell us Marco was here, though he must've known."

Oliver snaps his fingers. "If Elizabeth was feeding everything to Guy, it works. She told Brian to come here and get on staff to be a second set of eyes and ears so she didn't have to trust Guy. She didn't tell Guy her whole plan—why would she? Brian could figure out the layout. Install the things she needed installed—microphones, maybe, and that device that almost killed us in our room."

"What are you referring to?" Officer Rolle says.

"Oh," I say. "We didn't tell you." I explain about the heavy object setup to take us out. "That needed someone on the inside."

"Does Brian seem like someone who would go along with murder?" Oliver asks Vicki.

"I wouldn't have thought so."

"But that's why she killed him," I say. "Because he wouldn't. Maybe she didn't tell him the full plan either. Just that she wanted to create some intrigue and scare some people. Or test out her theories for her novel. Whatever she needed to say to get him to go along with it. But he figured out that she was going to do something more than that. I bet he wanted out. He got caught going through Guy's room on purpose so he'd get fired and get out of here before anything went down."

"So, Elizabeth killed him?" Oliver says.

"No, she was on our flight. It must've been Marco. Elizabeth must've been in contact with him, too. Oh! The lights were turned out during Elizabeth's speech. She said she told her concierge to do it, but Marco did it. I saw him. What if that was the plan all along? Did anyone check with the concierge? Either way, Marco could've intervened to make sure it was him because he knew the plan. And then Guy was killed. Marco was there. *He* killed Guy. She must've given him the device . . . She had a copy of my book. She talked about the things you could learn on the dark web yesterday when we were speaking to Officer Rolle . . . She planned all of it."

"Why do any of it, though?" Harper says.

"Because of Shek. When he died . . . that was the final straw. She blamed me, just like Ravi did. She blamed all of us."

"So she formulated a plan," Oliver says. "She tracked down Marco. She enlisted Guy. She told them each what they wanted to hear. Guy enlisted Connor and told him what Elizabeth told him to. That he'd found Marta, and that they needed to turn her over to Inspector Tucci to be safe."

"But Guy's plan was to get free of the Giuseppes. Like Connor thought he was doing when he helped plan the robberies. He'd use us as bait, and when took it, they'd be arrested and take their secrets to prison. Plus, he'd get a book deal out of it. He even had his ghostwriter on the spot to write it all up."

Oliver nods in agreement. "Exactly. Meanwhile, Marco gets his revenge.

And there are enough suspects around that no one's going to suspect him or even know who he is. Maybe they weren't even going to kill Connor, just leave him as the last suspect standing so *he'd* take the fall for all of it."

"I *was* the target. The note. All the people who hated me here . . . All the suspects point to me."

"Yes," Oliver says. "But something went wrong. Brian didn't do what he was supposed to, so he had to go. Marco must've put all those things up in his room at Elizabeth's suggestion to divert suspicion. And they killed him in our room so we'd be moved to the presidential suite where that mechanism over the bed could kill us at the right moment."

"Why not put us in the presidential suite to begin with?" Harper asks.

"*That* would be suspicious. Why give us the royal treatment? No, we got a regular room, only Elizabeth got something special because she's Elizabeth Ben. But Guy was suspicious anyway. He wasn't as dumb as they thought . . ."

"Elizabeth was getting rid of her co-conspirators one by one," Oliver says. "But not Marta?"

"Maybe Marta really *was* out of it. She said she wasn't involved. She could be telling the truth."

"Then Inspector Tucci died, but that *also* wasn't the plan. He pretended to die. That must've thrown her. Made Elizabeth panic a bit. And then Marco got caught, and you went missing, Vicki. Everything was spinning out of control. So she decided to end it. She always planned to be the last victim. That's what you said her book was about. Oh! *Curtain* . . ."

All this time, we thought we were in *And Then There Were None*, but it was *Curtain* all along. *Curtain* plus *The Murder of Roger Ackroyd*, where the narrator did it.

And oh, shit. Elizabeth even talked about *Curtain* to me. She *told me*. She was laughing at me. Watching me spin in circles, trying to figure out what was going on. Leaving me clues so I'd know it was her if the plan didn't work out . . .

But how?

What's the clue I'm missing?

What happened in *Curtain*?

If I'm remembering it right, there was a series of unsolved murders, and Poirot gathered the suspects at Styles to expose the murderer. But when he couldn't, he ended up killing the murderer himself, knowing that *he was going to die anyway.* Four months later, Hastings received a manuscript from Poirot that explained everything.

Elizabeth was sick, Vicki said. Waiting on a diagnosis. But what if that wasn't true? What if she knew all along she was dying?

How would she tell us?

"The last chapter of Elizabeth's book," I say to Vicki. "Do you have it?"

She nods grimly. "Elizabeth sent it to me after I told her the book wasn't going to get picked up. She said I should read it after the weekend was over and see if it changed my mind."

"She wanted us to know," I say. "If it didn't work out . . . she wanted *me* to know it was her."

"Why?"

"We'll have to read it to find out."

When Officer Rolle releases us, we head back to the pool area, where the rest of the conference seems to have gathered to eat, having been released from their rooms now that it's safe.

Even though I slept for a few hours last night, I'm exhausted. My eyes are like sand, and I just want to dive into my bed and never surface again. The light hurts, too, even though it's beautiful and innocent. How many times has this sun risen through this sky and sparkled over this beach? It will go on setting and rising. I won't be here to see it.

But first . . .

Sandrine is sitting at a table with Ravi. Stefano is being talked at by Crazy Cathy. The people in my small group are milling around, showing each other memes on their phones and gossiping about the industry.

"It all looks so normal," Oliver says.

"The calm *after* the storm."

"I guess." He reaches for my hand. "I think we should turn down all further invitations from now until further notice."

"I agree." I squeeze his hand, feeling that unfamiliar weight of the engagement ring on my finger.

I'm filled with lingering fear, but also disappointment in myself.

I need to stop crashing through this world.

I need to stop. Cut the circuit. Remove myself from all of this and settle down with my good man and good life and appreciate it. I've been grinding for ten years. I've had a lot of success. But what has it gotten me? Too many people who want to see me dead, that's what. And I have to take responsibility for that.

I'm the common denominator in these stories. Someone said that to me. Maybe I said it to myself.

No, it was Sandrine, wasn't it?

I can start there.

I let Oliver's hand go and walk toward her. "I'm sorry, Sandrine."

She looks up in surprise. "What?"

"I said I'm sorry. For not being there for you. For being self-absorbed. For not noticing that you were drowning and being a bad friend. I'm sorry for all of it."

Sandrine seems at a loss for words, as is everyone else around us.

Then, finally: "*Ça suffit*, El," she says.

"You forgive me?"

She shrugs. "It can't ever be the same."

"I know that. But I don't want you hating me. I don't hate you."

"I never hated you."

My throat closes because it's hitting me that there isn't anything left to save here anymore. You can't go back to trusting someone after they've betrayed you like we did to each other. There's too much water under the bridge. Too many things have been said that we can't take back.

But it was important to try anyway.

If I'm going to do this—move on—then I have to mean it with my whole chest.

I have to leave nothing behind to regret. So this was a good first step.

I can do this. I can become a different person and move forward with Oliver without my past weighing me down the way it has been for too long.

"Is that an *engagement* ring?" Connor says behind me, a note of jealousy in his voice.

Or maybe not.

THE LAST CHAPTER

If you're reading this, then I'm dead.

Such an odd thing to imagine, though I *am* full of imagination. I always have been. Even as a curious child, I was always making up scenarios in my room while my mother sang downstairs in the kitchen. I don't think she was very happy—she never showed any particular affection for me, one way or the other—but she did love to sing. Maybe in another life, when she wasn't weighed down by two children and a functioning-alcoholic husband, she would've written down those songs and plucked them out on a worn guitar before a darkened audience.

Who can know. All *we* knew was that she didn't want us or what life had dealt to her. So I vowed—as I pretended the dolls I wasn't supposed to play with, because they were porcelain and precious, were a happy family—that I'd be different. I didn't need a no-good man. I didn't need the burden of children. I didn't need to sing my dreams in a dreary kitchen on a sunny afternoon; I could make them come true.

And I did. I studied and I wrote and I wrote some more, and when I was sure I had something worth showing to someone, I did. I went after the career I wanted like it was a mission. I was good at it, everyone told me.

Murder.

I could come up with perfect plot after perfect plot. I was never blocked. I never ran out of ideas. There was always someone else to kill.

How did I do it? That's what I got asked so many times that I'd change my answer just to keep myself from going insane.

It was simple, really. All it took was hours and hours and hours of study and determination. But the thing no one ever knew was that each plot was real. Each murder was something I *wanted* to do in real life. I'd find my victim, plot out their death, and then execute it on the page.

It gave it a certain urgency, you see?

My first victim was my father. I killed him in a vat of beer in a distillery, which I got a certain delight in planning. Then I killed off my sister, cousins, the teacher who told me I wouldn't ever make it, the girls who snubbed me in ballet class. I waited to kill off my mother. I wanted to savor that one, but eventually, I killed her too.

Everyone always remarked on how my victims were so *ordinary*. How they were rarely men. How the talent I had was making the reader understand why so many suspects would want that ordinary person dead as dust. What they never figured out was that the enmity was real.

Humanity is mostly stupid, I've found. It makes it so much easier to get up to no good.

I spent years this way. I was happy, I think. I didn't want for anything or anyone, and the passing slights of life—bad reviews, the occasional disgruntled email from a family member who thought they recognized themselves—I could brush those off and tuck them away. I had other worlds to go to, after all. Other ways to use my time.

Before *him*.

Isn't it so like a man to ruin everything?

When did we first meet?

I remember it like it was yesterday. A hotel basement in New York for a writers' conference. I was being honored, and he was the up-and-coming author my publisher just had to introduce me to! I'd read his first novel and admired it. It had a robust masculinity I found appealing. He was appealing in real life, too.

I knew from the beginning he had a wandering eye. I knew from the beginning he'd be trouble. But I was helpless. I fell so fast it felt *slippery*.

Do you fall harder when the first time you fall in love is in your forties? It would be worth studying. Probably not enough subjects, though. Regardless, he opened something up in me and made me feel wild. Out of control.

I didn't like it. I tried to quit him, but I was helpless. I was helpless, I told myself to explain away my behavior. My jealousy. Of his time. Of his interests. Even of his books because they took him away from me.

For twenty years, we went on like that. Always on for me, on and off again for him. I knew I was a convenience. I doubted that he truly cared about me. How could he when there was always someone new to take his eyes away from me? Or when he'd triage my messages and take days to return them?

I'm ashamed to say, I accepted it. I took what crumbs he threw my way, and I lapped them up like cream. I was a cat purring in his lap.

And when, after so many years, he flirted with that girl *in front of me*, something in me broke. She was new and shiny and so naive, I don't think she even understood what he was thinking.

I swooped in to rescue her. I made it clear to him that he wasn't allowed to touch her. Not on my watch. But I could've murdered *her* right then. For being appealing. For being what I couldn't be—young, trusting, whole.

And then he went ahead and slept with her anyway. That stupid girl.

Somehow, I could forgive him—it was the way he was—but her? No.

No. Especially when he told me he was leaving me for her. And then—*and then*—she spurned him. The love of my life wasn't good enough for her? She thought she could do better?

The arrogance. It was everywhere on her. In her writing. In her careless treatment of those around her. If you're wondering why I've done this, don't look at me. *Look at her.*

That was the end of me and him. Even after she didn't want him, he didn't want me. He said it could never be the same.

I died that day. I knew, then, what drowning felt like. The lack of oxygen, the loss of consciousness. Even my hands hurt, like arthritis has appeared overnight in my joints.

I tried everything I knew how to do to get past it. I killed him in my next novel. But it wasn't enough. This time, it didn't satiate the need. Instead, all I could think was—*more*. I needed more.

It hurt my writing. I found myself rehashing his murder on the page. My books became predictable. Lackluster. My sales, too. I saw it all happen, but I didn't know what to do. I only knew I couldn't write about *her*. That if I set a plan in motion with her at the center, it wouldn't be sufficient. I'd have to go through with it.

And then a curious thing happened.

Life began to imitate art.

He went on a promotional tour with *her* in Italy. And it turned out I wasn't the only person she'd wronged. Someone else wanted her dead, and my love died in her stead. I think the plan began in earnest then. And the book she wrote about it! My darling was made a figure of fun. His murder was laughed off as merely an unfortunate incident!

The gall of that girl.

She had to die. But first, she had to *suffer*. She made it so easy.

She had so many enemies. There were so many potential suspects. It was *simple* to find the conspirators I needed. That stupid oaf with his thick neck and his black T-shirts. The owner of the resort. Our editor, albeit unwittingly. And that gullible young man our editor sent to help me fix my books!

He thought it was all a game. Silly boy.

I considered killing them all, but I didn't want to be too greedy.

I had to be careful. I planned for every contingency, just as I always did.

And then there was the secret that was burning a

hole in my life. Cancer. Six to ten months to live. Another stone in my shoe.

But no matter. It gave me the courage to go ahead. If I was caught—through no error of my own!—I wouldn't spend one minute in jail. I'd be another body that would lie at her feet.

My plan was perfect, every detail accounted for.

There is no accounting for *men*, though. The baby writer chickened out. Another man was arrogant and thought he could blackmail me.

Things were slipping out of my control.

Perhaps I *am* slipping.

It didn't help to have my love's brother in attendance. Every glimpse of him across the room was a reminder. I thought his presence would ensure I'd go through with it. Instead, it distracted me. Made me careless.

And now, I won't even know if my plan worked because as I finish this and tuck it into an email to send, she's still alive. As she might write—of course she is! She was put on this earth to vex me.

But I am stalling. I know what I need to do, and it's a bit gruesome. Finish this. Then loop the rope over the fan in the ceiling, then over my neck, and one, two, three . . .

If you're reading this, just know.

I leapt with joy.

Finis.

EPILOGUE

She's Not Going to Get Involved in Another Murder, Is She?[85]

Two Weeks Later

What do you still want to know?

The police decided Marco was guilty and Marta was innocent. He's been charged with Brian and Guy's murders and is awaiting trial. Marta was charged as an accessory in Italy, though, with Inspector Tucci accompanying her back to face trial with her sister. Immunity was never on the table; it was only the lie Inspector Tucci told her to get access to her information.

The solar storm passed, and we were finally able to leave the island.

We spent a day in New York, but I was too tired/afraid to leave the hotel. Harper made fun of me, and Oliver consoled me, but I felt justified.

Sandrine unblocked me on Instagram.

Harper assured me that things between her and Sandrine were never serious, and she was swearing off women *and* men for at least a year. We'll see. I hope rather than believe that to be true, but people can change. I'm trying to.

Ravi isn't talking to me. I'm not sure if he blames me for Elizabeth's

---

[85] Depends on how this book does!

plan or if it's the lingering issues with his brother's death, but we aren't friends, and I'm okay with that.

Crazy Cathy slithered off to whatever she does between stalking me. I'm sure I haven't seen the last of her. You'll be happy to hear that, I'm sure.

John Hart left prison, and Harper started her podcast. By which I mean she's immersed herself in research on how to podcast, listening to as many as she can, taking copious notes, and drawing up plans. I hope she follows through with it. But even if she doesn't, untangling her life from mine is a good step. She's even moved into the pool house at the back of our property. I told her she didn't have to do that, and she said she did, and oh, by the way, I'm paying to renovate it to her liking, so she's taking her pound of flesh for the firing, and I'm okay with that.

With her moving out, we decided Oliver would move in formally. I let him have two drawers, a third of my closet and Harper's room as his office.

I'm kidding. He got *three* drawers, okay? Satistified?

Every morning and night, I check with him that he still wants to marry me, and he says he does.

I choose to believe him.

Elizabeth's books returned to the bestseller lists, blocking *Amalfi Made Me Do It* from making the list. That seems fitting. She would've been happy with that, I think. I'll never know.

All I *do* know is that being a murderer seems to be great for book sales.

But don't worry. I'm not that desperate for another number one.

In fact, I'm quitting. I meant what I said before. I'm done. At least with murder, real and fictional. You probably think I'm joking, but I'm not. I need to rid my life of darkness and focus on something good. Oliver and me. Our future happiness. *Our future.*

I've managed to escape a bunch of dangerous situations, but I'm not a cat, and even if I were, I must be on my last life. I have to make myself small, less of a target. And I'm okay financially. We'll be okay. Maybe I'll ghostwrite Connor's next novel.

Ha!

I haven't heard from him since we got back. Hopefully, he's reflecting on his life choices, too. Probably not, though. It's hard to change.

Oh, and I'm doing dry-rest-of-January. And February, I think. We'll see after that.

Who am I missing?

Stefano's TikTok series about being trapped at a mediocre resort with a bunch of murderers went mega-viral, and his NetGalley access was restored. He's also doing a new series on writing his first book, crowdsourcing ideas. So he's happy.

Not so sure about Vicki. She's racked with guilt, and I've heard she might get fired. I hope not. She's still deciding about Oliver's next manuscript, for one. And what happened wasn't her fault. We never want to see the bad in those that we love. Even those that we know.

Like the Spanish Inquisition, no one expects a murderer.

I've murdered *that*, haven't I?

I'm definitely repeating myself.

Maybe I'm being influenced by Elizabeth. This story began with a murder that was made to look like a suicide and ended with a suicide that was made to look like a murder.

Even when her plan went awry, there was a certain beauty to it.

Hmmm.

Elizabeth's last book is being published after all. Of course it is. I can't blame our publisher for capitalizing on events, given everything. I'd do the same. A Netflix series is in the works, too, because of course it is. Who's going to play me *this time*, I wonder? Ugh.

Oliver got our copyedits done, and he's turned them in. I haven't told him my decision. He'll notice soon enough that I'm not writing. I'll tell him then.

No, it's not a test. But it's not *not* a test either. Can't change everything about myself in a couple of weeks. But I'm trying.

I'm trying.

Don't expect too much from me, okay?

I'm a work in progress. Like a novel that needs another couple of passes and a serious editorial letter to put it right. I'm good at taking notes; I just don't always manage to incorporate them the first time.

I think that's it.

Vicki will let me know if I'm missing something.

But before I can be *officially* done, I have to get through this bus tour my publisher arranged for their spring slate of titles. Some hop-on, hop off thingy with other writers that's touring the most famous celebrity death sites in Los Angeles. I feel like it's in poor taste, but no one asked me. They just made it clear that I needed to attend with a smile on my face.

So here I am.

Me, Oliver, Harper, Connor.[86] Vicki's here, too, looking worried. My film agent, Rich, is also along for the ride (ha!), along with some new protégé of his who wants to option *Amalfi Made Me Do It* "for the vibes."[87] That's going to be a no, Rich.

The CEO of my publisher is here, too, a man I haven't interacted with much who always seems to be stressed. He's extra stressed today because there's a pack of venture capitalists circling the company, and if they're in, he's probably out.

Easy come, easy go.

He's also babysitting one of the imprint's other stars, Kevin Hollister, who just happens to be *Oliver's* nemesis. What? I *know*. Even Oliver has enemies. You see, he's not perfect. Just almost.

---

[86] Did you ever notice how all of these names rhyme?

[87] Translation: zero dollars.

Anyway, things went sideways between Kevin and Oliver three years ago over a book they were supposed to write together. Kevin mentioned the idea to Rich, and the next thing you know it was optioned for beaucoup bucks *without* Oliver. One *New York Times* bestseller and a (bad) Netflix movie later, he's the toast of the town, and Oliver's shit out of luck.

Personally, I *never* liked the guy.

And after six interminable hours on the bus, I know one thing—I'm not alone in my dislike of him. I know this because of the next thing. Which makes two things I know about him.[88]

When we got off the bus at our last stop, we realized that he's slumped over in his middle seat near the back exit, *dead*.

So I guess there are still going to be murders, after all.[8990]

---

[88] I'm giving up on telling you three things because I'm tired.

[89] That is, if this book and the others in the series do well enough. <u>Your move, readers!</u>

[90] It's called <u>You'll Never Murder in This Town Again</u>.

ACKNOWLEDGMENTS

Would you believe me if I said that the hardest part of writing a book is the acknowledgments? No, right?

Yet . . .

Each book is its own journey, and this one wouldn't be possible without the following:

My editor, Catherine Richards, who has championed this series from the beginning and has signed on for three more books. You and the entire team at Minotaur are a dream to work with—special shout-outs to Kelly Stone, Kelley Ragland, Sarah Melnyk, Allison Zeigler, and Kayla Janas. I couldn't be more excited and thrilled to be working with you until (at least) 2029! Thanks also to Katie Loughnane and the Macmillan UK team for their work on this book!

My agent, Stephanie Rostan. You picked me up when I thought my career was dead, and look how far we've come! Thanks so much for believing in me.

My friends and family, especially Tasha Theophilos, Sara Pedersen, Christie Brown, Candice Modugno, Tanya Bergevin, Sandra Smith, and Darina Groucha.

My writing circles, especially Liz Fenton, Elyssa Friedland, and Heather Webb.

My husband, David, who's still putting up with me after thirty-two (!) years.

Taylor Swift for writing the creative soundtrack for this book and others.

And you, Dear Reader.

See you next . . . book.[91]

---

[91] If you know, you know.

ABOUT THE AUTHOR

Catherine Mack is the pseudonym for the *USA Today* and *Globe & Mail* bestselling author Catherine McKenzie. Her books are approaching two million copies sold worldwide and have been translated into multiple languages. The first two books in the Vacation Mysteries series, *Every Time I Go on Vacation, Someone Dies* and *No One One Was Supposed to Die at this Wedding*, were *USA Today* bestsellers. A dual Canadian and US citizen, she splits her time between Canada and various warmer locations in the United States.